CUPCAKE DIARIES

SIMON SPOTLIGHT

An imprint of Simon & Schuster Children's Publishing Division
1230 Avenue of the Americas, New York, New York 10020
This Simon Spotlight bind-up edition August 2017
Mia's Boiling Point and *Emma, Smile and Say "Cupcake!"* copyright © 2012
by Simon & Schuster, Inc. *Alexis Gets Frosted* copyright © 2013
by Simon & Schuster, Inc. All rights reserved, including the right of
reproduction in whole or in part in any form.
SIMON SPOTLIGHT and colophon are registered trademarks of
Simon & Schuster, Inc. For information about special discounts for bulk
purchases, please contact Simon & Schuster Special Sales
at 1-866-506-1949 or business@simonandschuster.com.
Text by Tracey West and Elizabeth Doyle Carey
Chapter header illustrations by Ciara Gay and Laura Roode
Design by Laura Roode
Manufactured in the United States of America 0717 OFF
2 4 6 8 10 9 7 5 3 1
ISBN 978-1-5344-0965-1
ISBN 978-1-4424-5397-5 (*Mia's Boiling Point* eBook)
ISBN 978-1-4424-5400-2 (*Emma, Smile and Say "Cupcake!"* eBook)
ISBN 978-1-4424-6868-9 (*Alexis Gets Frosted* eBook)
These titles were previously published individually by Simon Spotlight.

CUPCAKE DIARIES

Mia's boiling point

Emma, smile and say "cupcake!"

Alexis gets frosted

by coco simon

Simon Spotlight

New York   London   Toronto   Sydney   New Delhi

Mia's boiling point

CHAPTER 1

A Middle School Miracle?

Oh my gosh, it's a cupcake plunger!" my friend Katie squealed.

I don't think I've ever seen Katie so excited. We were in a shop in the mall called Baker's Hollow. They sell baking supplies, and inside are all these fake trees with built-in shelves and the supplies are displayed on them.

Katie and I were at the cupcake tree, which has pretty, fake pink cupcakes "growing" in its fake branches. The shelves are filled with cupcake baking pans, cupcake decorations, and tons of different kinds of cupcake liners.

Katie was holding up a metal tube with a purple top on it. She pulled on the top, and it moved up and down, like a plunger.

"This is so cool!" she cried. "You stick this in the top of the cupcake and plunge down halfway, and a perfect little tube of cake comes out. Then you fill the hole with stuff and then put the cake back on top and frost it. Just imagine what you could put in here! Whipped cream! Pudding!"

She turned to me, and her brown eyes were shining with excitement. "You could even do ice cream! Can you imagine biting into a cupcake and there's ice cream inside? How awesome would that be?"

"Totally awesome," I agreed. "Plus, it's purple. Your favorite color."

Katie dug into her pocket, took out some crumpled bills, and started to count.

"It's only six dollars. I could get it and still have enough left over for a smoothie," she said, and then she sighed. "I am so glad they opened this store, but I am going to go broke spending all my money on cupcake supplies. I'm obsessed!"

"I know how you feel," I said. "I am totally obsessed with shoes lately. I'm trying to find the perfect pair of neutral heels. I want them dressy, but not too dressy—maybe a shiny patent leather, with a high heel. But not too high. I don't want to fall flat on my face! I can picture them in my mind, but I haven't seen them anywhere for real yet."

Katie looked down at her sneakers, which were decorated with rainbows drawn on with Magic Marker. "I don't think I'll ever wear heels. They're too uncomfortable."

That's the difference between Katie and me— she doesn't care about fashion at all, and I pretty much live for it. Today, for instance, Katie was wearing a purple hoodie, jeans, and sneakers. Which is perfectly adorable on her, but not dressed up enough for me. You never know who you could run into at the mall! So I had on skinny black jeans, my furry black boots, a white lace cami, and a sky-blue cardigan on top. The beads in my hoop earrings matched my cardigan, and the boho style of the earrings worked perfectly with my boots.

But even though Katie doesn't care much about fashion, she's my best friend here in Maple Grove. I moved here a year ago after my parents got divorced. Katie was the first friend I met.

"Okay, I'd better get on line before I buy something else," she told me.

A few minutes later we left the shop, and Katie was happily holding an adorable little paper shopping bag with a picture of a cupcake tree on it.

"That's such a great logo," I said. "I wish I had thought of that for the Cupcake Club."

"I bet you could think of an even better logo if you wanted to," Katie said.

That made me feel pretty good. I love to draw and would love to be a fashion designer or maybe a graphic designer one day. Or maybe one of those designers who does displays in store windows in Manhattan. How cool would that be?

As we walked toward the smoothie shop, the smell of chocolate distracted us. Katie and I didn't even need to discuss it. We walked right into Adele's Chocolates and headed for the counter.

This is a "must-go-to" shop at the mall. Adele makes all the chocolates herself, and the flavors are amazing.

"Mmm, look," I said, pointing to a glistening morsel of chocolate in a gold paper cup. "Salted caramel. That sounds so good."

Katie pointed to a piece of dark chocolate sitting in a pale purple cup. "Dark chocolate infused with lavender. I wonder what that tastes like?"

"That would make a good cupcake," I said, and Katie nodded. We talk about cupcakes a lot because we're in the Cupcake Club with our friends Alexis and Emma. It's a real business. People hire us to bake for their parties and other events.

Katie had a pained look on her face. "Soooo tempting. But I think I really need some smoothie energy right about now. Mom says chocolate makes me loopy."

I grabbed Katie's arm and pretended to drag her out of the store. "Resist! Resist!" I said, and we both started laughing like crazy.

"We should go right to the smoothie place," I said when we calmed down. "No more distractions."

"Right," Katie said. She stood up straight, like a soldier, and saluted. "To the smoothie place!"

It was Saturday, so the mall was pretty crowded as we made our way to Smoothie Paradise. I used to hate the mall when I first moved here, because I was so used to shopping in New York City. But now I like it. It's never too hot or too cold, and when I'm done shopping I just have to carry the bags outside to Mom's car. It's definitely a lot easier than toting things home on the subway.

Even though the mall was full of people, the line at Smoothie Paradise was pretty short. Katie and I each ordered the same thing—a smoothie with mango and passion fruit—and then sat down at a small round table in the corner.

"This is my favorite kind of day," Katie said after taking a long slurp from her straw. "I got all my homework done last night, so I don't have anything to worry about."

I nodded. "Me too."

Katie sat back in her chair. "You know, middle school isn't so bad so far. I mean, it's not perfect, but I think it's easier this year."

"Definitely," I agreed. "It's, like, we know our way around. And besides school, other things are easier too. Like living with Eddie and Dan. That's not so weird anymore."

Eddie is my stepdad, and Dan is my stepbrother. They're both pretty nice.

"Is it getting any easier living in two different apartments?" Katie asked.

I thought about it for a minute. "Yeah, kind of," I admitted. "But mostly when I go to my dad's, I feel like I'm visiting." I basically go out to New York to see my dad every other weekend.

"You must miss him," Katie said.

I wasn't sure how to answer that. Katie's parents are divorced too, and she never sees her dad. He remarried, and I think he even has a whole new family. So as tough as my situation is, I think Katie's is even tougher.

I decided to be honest. "Sometimes I miss him," I said. "But he texts me and Skypes me and stuff during the week. So he's there if I need him."

Katie got a little quiet after I said that, so I changed the subject.

"We should go to Icon after this," I said. Katie knows that's my favorite clothing store. "They sell shoes there, too. Maybe they have my perfect heels."

We left the shop and headed for Icon. It's easy to find because you can hear techno music blasting from it even when the mall is noisy. The decor is really sleek and clean, with white walls and gleaming silver racks. I like it that way because the clothes are really highlighted.

That day I walked right past the clothes and headed straight for the shoes, which were displayed on white blocks sticking out of the back wall. They had chunky heels, wedge heels, and spike heels, but the perfect shoe, the one I could picture in my head, wasn't there.

While I was looking at all the shoes, Katie was giggling and wobbling in a pair of superhigh silver heels. I suddenly heard a familiar voice behind us.

"Hi, Mia. Hi, Katie."

It was Callie Wilson, Katie's former best friend and the leader of the Best Friends Club, which used to be the Popular Girls Club. Things have always been pretty tense between the Cupcake Club and the BFC. A lot of it had to do with Katie and Callie's broken friendship. But recently, they kind of patched things up, and so today Callie was smiling and friendly.

Katie, on the other hand, looked a little startled. She quickly slipped out of the silver heels, embarrassed.

"Oh, hey, Callie," Katie said.

"Hi," I added.

Maggie and Bella, the other two girls in the BFC, walked up behind Callie. Maggie has wild hair and can be pretty funny when she wants to be—and pretty mean, too. Bella is the quietest of the three. She's super into those vampire movies—like, so into them that she changed her name from Brenda to Bella, and she straightens her auburn hair to look just like the girl who loves the vampire.

"Shopping for shoes?" Callie asked, even though it was pretty obvious. I guess she was trying to make conversation.

"I'm trying to find the perfect pair of heels," I said. "But I think they only exist in my head."

"Ooh, I saw this adorable pair online," Maggie said. She whipped out her smartphone and started typing on the keyboard. Then she shoved the screen in front of my face. "See?"

"Those are totally cute, but the ones I'm dreaming of have a pointier toe," I told her. "But thanks!"

"Did you guys see those new wrap dresses they got in?" Callie asked. "Katie, there's a purple one that would look so cute on you."

"We'll definitely check them out," I replied.

"Yeah," Katie added.

Callie gave a little wave and then flipped her long, blond hair over her shoulder. "Okay, we've got to go. Later."

She walked away, and Bella and Maggie followed her. Katie and I stared at each other in shock.

"Did that just actually happen?" Katie asked.

"You mean, did we actually just have a normal conversation with the BFC, with no name-calling or teasing? Yes!" I replied.

Katie grinned. "It's a middle school miracle!"

CHAPTER 2

The Shoes of My Dreams

On Sunday morning when I woke up, the house smelled like bacon. As far as I'm concerned, that is the absolute best way to wake up.

I got dressed and went downstairs to find Mom and Eddie in the kitchen. There was a big plate of bacon on the table, and Eddie was flipping pancakes at the stove.

"She's alive!" Eddie said, teasing me. I looked at the clock, and it was ten thirty.

"Hey, it's still morning," I said. "Besides, I don't see Dan."

Dan is in high school, and he sleeps way more than I do. I was pretty sure Dan must still be asleep.

I was right. "He's still sleeping," Mom said. She had her long, black hair pulled back with a big barrette. People say I look like my mom, but it's mostly my hair; I definitely have my dad's nose, and our faces are both oval. Mom's is more heart shaped.

"Too bad! That means more bacon for us," Eddie said cheerfully.

"Ed, that's not nice. We should save him some," Mom scolded.

Eddie put a platter of pancakes on the table and gave my mom a kiss. (Gross.) "Of course I will, *mi amore*. You know I have a soft heart."

"That's why I married you," Mom said, and I made a loud coughing noise.

"Excuse me! Child present!" I reminded them.

Eddie hugged my mom. "You'll understand one day, Mia, when you're in love."

"Okay, now I am seriously losing my appetite," I said. I like Eddie and everything, but deep down I still wish my mom and dad were together. So I don't need to see Mom and Eddie all lovey-dovey.

Mom gave Eddie a look, and he stopped hugging her and sat down at the table. "Pancakes, anyone?"

"Me, please," I said. "And bacon."

While Eddie piled the food onto my plate, Mom said, "Mia, I know I've been working a lot lately, so I was thinking maybe we could have a girls' day

11

out today. Unless you have other plans with your friends."

I put down my fork. "Can we go to the city? Hang out in SoHo? And get Thai food? And go window shopping? When can we leave?"

Even though I stay with my dad in Manhattan every other weekend, I hardly ever get to go with my mom. I miss the things we used to do there together.

Mom smiled. "I don't see why not. We should leave after breakfast. We can take the ferry."

So less than two hours later we were standing on the top deck of a ferry crossing the Hudson River. It was a pretty chilly out, but I didn't mind because I got to wear a new fall jacket that one of my mom's designer friends had given her. It's cobalt blue, and it has a vintage-style collar that looks like two petals, and three big buttons in the front, and it's fitted around the waist, with a belt and a big buckle.

I wore it with black knit tights and this navy shirtdress I have, which was from another one of my mom's friends. Mom's a fashion stylist, so I am superlucky and can get great clothes for free.

Mom was going for the all-black look, which she does a lot. Black sweater, black knee-length skirt, black tights, black boots, black trench coat. I call it her spy outfit.

"Yes, but I can always accessorize," Mom loves to say, and she can make it look different every time with a bright red scarf or a big silver necklace or a belt or something. She's good at that.

When the ferry docked we took a cab to SoHo, a neighborhood in Manhattan that stands for "south of Houston," which is Houston Street (only people pronounce it "*how*-ston" instead of "*hyoo*-ston," like the city in Texas). There are other places to shop in New York City, like great department stores, but I think SoHo is fun because the streets are narrow and lots of designers have little shops there. New stores are always springing up, so you never know what you'll see.

We were extremely full from the pancakes and bacon, so we went window shopping first. A lot of the clothing boutiques had winter coats on display already. We admired a shop with some pretty cool faux-fur jackets and then moved on to the next store.

I froze. The window was filled with the most amazing shoes I had ever seen. The sign above the door read KARA KAREN.

"She must have just opened up the boutique,"

Mom said. "Everyone's saying great things about her."

I grabbed Mom by the arm. "We are going inside!" I informed her.

Mom didn't argue. A bell jingled as we walked inside the store, a clean, well-lit space with polished wood floors. The shoes were displayed on a round table in the center of the shop with different tiers, like a layer cake. My eyes scanned the display from the bottom, to the middle, to the very top layer, and that's when I saw them—my dream shoes.

The heel was high, but not too high. And it wasn't chunky, but not too spiky, either. The toe was nice and pointy, just like I wanted. The shoe itself was black, but kind of sparkly. Delicate straps crisscrossed the top of the shoe.

Mom must have noticed my wide-eyed look. Or maybe I was drooling.

"Those are great shoes," she said. "Impractical, but gorgeous."

I immediately started to appeal to Mom's fashion sense. "Mom, you know I need heels for special occasions. This is the perfect pair! They'll go with just about anything. And the heel's not too high."

Mom reached up and took the sample shoe off the stand. Then she looked at the price tag.

"How much?" I asked nervously.

"Too much," Mom said. The tag said: $212.

I was so disappointed! "I knew they were too good to be true," I said with a sigh. "I guess when I imagined my dream shoes, I should have imagined a cheaper price."

Mom was turning the shoe over in her hand, examining it with a thoughtful look on her face.

"I'll tell you what, Mia," she said. "If you can raise money for your half of the shoes, I'll pay for the other half." She laughed. "You buy one shoe and I'll buy the other!"

I immediately felt much better. "You mean we can get them now and I'll owe you?"

Mom shook her head. "No, you have to earn the money first. Then you'll appreciate them more."

I did some quick calculations in my head. I had some money saved from the Cupcake business, and I get allowance for helping around the house. I could see if maybe I could do some extra chores, and I knew the Cupcake Club had a big job coming up. It wouldn't take long . . . but just thinking about the wait was unbearable!

I took the shoe from my mom and hugged it dramatically. "I'll miss you! But I will come back for you, I promise!"

Mom laughed again. "Well, before you get carried away, we should at least try them on."

The saleswoman in the shop got the shoes in my size, and I put them on. They looked fabulous! I was a little wobbly when I walked in them, but I got the hang of it pretty quickly.

"It's that extra-pointy toe," Mom said. "But I have to admit, you're pretty good in them."

"It's in my genes," I said. When Mom walks in high heels, she's as graceful as a ballet dancer.

"We should get lunch soon," Mom said.

I looked at myself in the mirror one last time. Then I took off the shoes. I took a gazillion pictures of them with my phone camera. Then I sadly gave them back to the saleswoman.

"Good-bye," I whispered, gazing longingly at the shoes as we left the shop.

Yes, I was definitely in the middle of a shoe obsession!

CHAPTER 3

The New Girl

$\mathcal{I}$ couldn't stop thinking about shoes. The next morning I showed Katie my phone's pictures on the bus.

"They're nice," she said. "But they look hard to walk in."

She quickly got bored with my shoe talk, so I spent the rest of the ride trying to calculate how long it would take me to earn my half of the shoes. I was pretty fixated on this until I got to homeroom, when something happened to distract me.

A girl I had never seen before was standing inside the room by the front door. Her nervous expression was the first thing I noticed about her. The second thing I noticed, of course, was her outfit.

She was about as tall as me, with green eyes and thick brown hair that touched her shoulders and chunky bangs across her forehead. She was wearing skinny jeans, short black boots with heels, a gray ruffled tank top, and this cute, short, long-sleeve blue jacket. Hanging from her neck was a brass necklace with a key dangling from the end.

I walked up to her. "I like your outfit," I said, and she smiled.

"Oh, thanks!"

I would have said more, but the bell rang and our homeroom teacher, Ms. Chandar, entered. She's the science teacher, and she's always dressed very neatly, in a pressed button-down shirt, simple A-line skirt, and sensible shoes. She looks like the kind of person whose house doesn't have a speck of dust in it.

"You must be Olivia," Ms. Chandar said, approaching the new girl. "Please find a seat."

"There's an empty one next to me," I told Olivia, and she smiled gratefully and followed me to the back of the room.

After we said the Pledge of Allegiance and listened to the day's announcements by Principal LaCosta, Ms. Chandar explained that the new girl was Olivia Allen, and she had just moved to Maple

Grove. Right away I felt totally protective of her, because I know how weird it feels to be the new girl. I got lucky, because I met Katie, Emma, and Alexis on my first day of school.

So when the homeroom bell rang, I turned to Olivia.

"I'm Mia," I said. "If you want, you can sit with me and my friends at lunch. I'll wait for you by the cafeteria door."

Olivia smiled. "Thanks, that would be cool."

I didn't think that Katie, Emma, or Alexis would mind one bit. After all, we weren't some exclusive club like the Best Friends Club used to be when Sydney Whitman was the leader and it was called the Popular Girls Club. Anyway, I had a chance to tell them during third period, because it turned out Olivia was in gym with us. Because she was new, Olivia didn't have any gym clothes with her, so she was sitting on the bleachers.

"Who's the new girl?" Alexis asked, nodding toward her as we came out of the locker room.

"She's in my homeroom. Her name's Olivia. I invited her to sit with us at lunch," I said.

"That's cool," Katie said.

"Is she nice?" Emma asked.

I shrugged. "I guess. She just looked kind of sad,

and I remember what it feels like to be new, you know?"

Then Ms. Chen, our gym teacher, blew her whistle and made us do a bunch of jumping jacks and sit-ups. Then she kept us busy playing flag football, so we didn't have much of a chance to talk again until lunch.

Olivia was already waiting by the cafeteria door when I got there. She looked pretty relieved to see me.

"Come on, I'll introduce you to my friends," I said.

"Are those the girls you were hanging out with in gym?" Olivia asked.

"Yes," I replied. "They're totally nice. I guarantee that you will love them."

I led her to our table in the back of the lunchroom, where Katie was unpacking her lunch bag. Emma and Alexis were waiting on the hot-lunch line, like they always do.

"Olivia, this is Katie," I said.

Katie smiled. "Hey. So where are you from?"

Olivia sat down between me and Katie. "Jersey City, right across from Manhattan," she said, sighing. "I used to be able to take a train there whenever I wanted. But now we're, like, in the middle of nowhere. There's nothing to do out here."

"I used to live in Manhattan," I told her. "And I used to feel that way too. But Maple Grove is really nice. And it's not that far from the city. I go there all the time."

Olivia's eyes got wide. "You're from Manhattan? That's totally amazing."

That's when Alexis and Emma walked up, and I introduced them both.

"Hey, so Olivia used to live right by the city," I said.

"I always thought it would be exciting to live in Manhattan," Emma said. "But then I think I'd miss the trees and parks."

"Central Park is eight hundred and forty three acres," Alexis informed her. (She loves facts and figures.) "That's a lot of trees."

"But they're all in one place," Katie pointed out. "In Maple Grove, they're all over."

I noticed that while my friends were talking, Olivia wasn't really listening. She was scanning the cafeteria, checking out everyone at the tables. I didn't really think that was rude or anything. She was probably just taking everything in.

Then we started talking Cupcake business.

"So, Katie, are we meeting at your house on

Wednesday?" Alexis asked and took out her laptop to start checking things off. She's superorganized.

Katie nodded. "Mom says it's okay."

I turned to Olivia. "We formed a Cupcake Club. It's a real business now. We make cupcakes and sell them."

Olivia didn't seem to be interested.

"Every Friday, one of us brings in cupcakes for all of us," I explained. I looked at Alexis. "I'll do the cupcakes this Friday. I'll bring in an extra for Olivia."

Alexis raised an eyebrow like she was surprised I said that, which I thought was a little weird, but then she nodded. "Okay. The four of us can talk more at our meeting on Wednesday."

I didn't see Olivia until seventh period, when we had chorus together. She sat next to me again. When school ended we figured out that she took a different bus than Katie and me.

She took out her phone. "Tell me your number, and I'll text you mine."

We quickly exchanged numbers, and then I ran to catch the bus with Katie.

"So Olivia seems pretty nice," I said as we took our seats.

"Sure," Katie said. "Only, Alexis was talking to

me at the end of lunch when you and Olivia went to the bathroom. She was saying, you know, how the Cupcake Club is a business and everything and how we can't invite anyone to join the business without voting on it or whatever."

I rolled my eyes. "Alexis is such a worrier. I just asked Olivia to sit with us at lunch, that's all. I hope you guys don't have a problem with that."

"Of course not," Katie said. "We're not the PGC or the BFC or whatever. I guess Alexis just wants to keep Olivia separate from the whole Cupcake thing, you know, until we know her."

I suddenly felt suspicious. "Did Alexis ask you to talk to me about it?"

Katie absently twirled a strand of her wavy brown hair around her finger. "Yeah, well, I guess she thought you'd take it better from me."

I shook my head. "She's making a big deal out of nothing. Alexis and Emma made new friends at camp, and it was no big deal, right? We're always going to meet new people. But we're the four Musketeers. Nothing will ever break that up."

Katie grinned. "You mean, *Cupcake*teers. And, anyway, weren't there only three Musketeers?"

"Maybe, but we're Cupcaketeers, and you definitely need four of those," I said.

Katie put her hand over her heart and started to recite dramatically, "Loyal and true, through thick frosting and thin frosting, through runny batter and burned cupcake bottoms! We will stick together!"

And then we laughed, like we always do.

CHAPTER 4

My New "Roommate"

𝓘 have to admit that I was curious to see what Olivia would wear on Tuesday, and I made extra-sure that I wore a cool outfit too. I went with a cute floral-print dress in dark reds and purples, which are perfect for fall. The dress has short sleeves and, like, a puffy skirt. I wore a short black cardigan over it, unbuttoned; my black tights; and my go-to black ankle boots. I checked out my reflection in the mirror. Adorable!

When I spotted Olivia that morning, her outfit didn't disappoint. She went with skinny jeans again, this time in black, and she had a blue cable-knit sweater underneath an unbuttoned short denim jacket. (She seems to like to layer her outfits, which I think always looks stylish.) What I liked best was her red flats with small black bows, because the unexpected color contrast was fun. She also had a red headband in her glossy hair.

"Hey," I said as I slid into my seat. "Love the red shoes and headband."

"Thanks," she said, but she didn't sound happy. In fact, she looked pretty sad again. She made a big sigh, and I could sort of tell that she wanted me to ask what was wrong. So I did.

"Is everything okay?" I asked.

"It's awful!" she replied. "Principal LaCosta says there aren't any open lockers. I'm going to have to carry all my books everywhere! My arms are going to fall off!"

"Why don't you share mine?" I suggested. I definitely felt sorry for her. I couldn't imagine carrying around six classes' worth of books everywhere.

Olivia immediately perked up. "Really?"

I nodded. "Sure."

The bell hadn't rung yet, so I walked up to Ms. Chandar's desk. "Olivia doesn't have a locker, so I'm going to let her share mine," I said. "Would it be okay if we put her stuff in now?"

Ms. Chandar looked up from her planner. "That's very nice of you, Mia. Of course!"

I motioned to Olivia, who quickly got up. She

grabbed her black-and-white leopard print back-pack, which looked totally stuffed, and lugged it out of the room.

My locker was just down the hallway.

"Get out your phone, and I'll give you the combination," I told her. When she was ready, I said the numbers out loud as I opened the lock. "Thirteen, twenty-six, nine."

"Got it!" Olivia said, and then her eyes got wide when I opened the door.

"Oh my gosh, Mia, this is the coolest locker ever!" she cried.

I guess I forgot to mention that as soon as school began I started designing my locker for fun. Over the summer, I sketched out the design I wanted and then shopped for the perfect materials. On the inside of the front door, I put this stick-on wall-paper with a groovy sixties design in purple, orange, and green. Then I went to a carpet store, and they gave me these free carpet scraps—purple shag—that were just perfect. I put the carpet on the floor of the locker and on top of the shelf. Dangling from the shelf is this superadorable mini-chandelier that sparkles when I turn on the little battery-operated light that I stuck under the shelf.

"Thanks," I told Olivia. "Just because it's a school

locker doesn't mean it can't be fabulous, right?"

"It's so nice, I'm afraid to put anything in here," Olivia said.

"Well, I can fit all my books on the top shelf," I said. "I hardly put anything on the bottom anyway. So you can fit all your books there."

Olivia opened up her backpack and gave one of those big sighs I was starting to get used to. "I don't even know where to start!"

"Here, it's easy," I said. I started taking books out of her backpack and piling them in. "Just make sure you have what you need for your next class."

After the books were stacked, Olivia opened up the front pocket of her backpack. "In my old locker I could always have a mirror, so I could check my hair and stuff," she said, pulling out a round mirror. "There are stickers on the back. We could just stick it to the door."

All I could think of was my gorgeous wallpaper being ruined. "Hey, why don't we get one of those hooks that you can put on a wall and it doesn't ruin it," I suggested. "I can bring one in tomorrow."

Olivia shrugged. "Sure, I guess."

Then she pulled out this pink plastic makeup box and stuck it on top of her book pile. The pink didn't exactly go with my design, but I wanted to be nice. So I didn't say anything.

Olivia opened the box, and I saw that it was filled with different shades of lip gloss.

"Hey, is that ETX lip gloss?" I asked. "They have such cool colors."

"I got a whole set for my birthday," she said. "I'll bring you one tomorrow."

"Thanks!" I replied.

Then the homeroom bell rang, so we closed the locker.

"Yay! This is fun. It's like having a roommate," I said.

Olivia gave me a hug. "Thanks, Mia!" she said. "I honestly don't know what I would do without you."

I was feeling pretty good as I headed to my next class, and it wasn't just because I had helped out Olivia. I was sure I had made a new friend.

CHAPTER 5

Sporty but Suave?

$\mathcal{T}$he next morning I went to my locker before homeroom, and I found Olivia putting on lip gloss while looking in her mirror, which was hung on the inside door of my locker.

"Oh cool, I guess you found the special hook," I said. "I brought one too."

Olivia kept her eyes on the mirror. "Oh, I just stuck it on with the sticky pads on the back. It's just easier that way, right?"

For a second my heart sank as I imagined the holes left in my wallpaper once Olivia got her own locker. I figured she didn't understand what I had meant about the special hook that doesn't damage walls. So I didn't say anything.

"Nice color," I complimented her. The lip gloss

she was applying was a shimmery pinkish-tan color. I could tell she was going for a kind of neutral look today, with a tan boyfriend jacket and a white blouse underneath.

"Thanks," she said, smacking her lips one last time. Then she turned to me and smiled. "Come on, let's get to homeroom."

She put the lip gloss back in the plastic box, and for a second I remembered her promise—that she would bring me an ETX lip gloss today. But Olivia didn't mention it as we closed and locked the locker. I didn't think this was a really big deal either. She had probably just forgotten about it.

Then after second period I went to my locker before gym, and I noticed that Olivia had stuffed some of her books on my shelf. I had to put them back down on the bottom so I could fit my stuff.

She's probably just getting used to everything, I thought.

And right now most people would probably be thinking, *Wow, Mia's making a lot of excuses for Olivia.* Which I was. But she was new, and well, none of it seemed like a big deal.

That night, we had a Cupcake Club meeting at Katie's house. Katie doesn't have any brothers or sisters, and she lives with just her mom, who's a dentist. Like Katie, Mrs. Brown also loves to cook and bake things, which seems kind of weird for a dentist to like to do, but once you meet her, it's totally not weird at all. It's just who she is.

At six o'clock, Katie, Alexis, Emma, and I were all sitting around Katie's kitchen table. When we meet together on a school night, we sometimes have dinner, so it doesn't interfere with homework.

Mrs. Brown came to the table carrying a steaming pot of soup. She was wearing a red checkered apron that read #1 CHEF on the front.

"Black bean soup," she said, putting the pot on the table. "And Katie made some quesadillas for us."

"Katie, you are going to turn into a taco if you keep eating all this Mexican food," I teased her. She went to cooking camp over the summer, and she's been on a Mexican food kick ever since.

"Could I turn into a burrito instead?" she asked. "'Cause I like those better."

Katie's mom ladled some soup into our bowls, and we dug in, blowing on the soup to cool it off. I put some sour cream and some chopped green onions on mine.

"Okay, so we've got the big birthday party coming up," Alexis said, sprinkling some shredded cheese on her soup. She always likes to get right down to business. "Emma, what's the deal?"

"So, you guys know it's for Matt's and Sam's birthdays," Emma said. "All their friends are coming, so it's going to be really big."

"I keep forgetting. Why are they having their party together?" Katie asked.

"Even though they're a few years apart, their birthdays are only two days apart," Emma explained. "For a long time we had to have two separate parties, but this year Sam said it would be cool if they did it together, and Matt agreed."

"Sam's so nice," Katie said.

Emma rolled her eyes. "Listen, if you guys start drooling over my brothers, I am going to barf this delicious soup all over your table."

"Ewwww!" Katie, Alexis, and I squealed. But I sort of can't blame Emma. Her little brother, Jake, is six, and he's totally adorable. Sam, the oldest, is in high school, and Katie and I both think he's superdreamy. Plus, he's amazingly nice, too. Then there's Matt, who's one grade above us. He's cute too, and Alexis has a crush on him, even though she swears she's over him.

"Before you barf, could you please tell me exactly how many people are going to be at this party?" Alexis asked.

Emma shrugged. "I'm not sure. Matt's inviting a bunch of guys from the basketball team, and Sam's swim team is coming. Plus our grandparents, I guess."

Alexis did some mental calculations. "So let's say forty people. Three dozen might not be enough, but four dozen might be perfect. Ask your mom, okay?"

"The way my brothers eat cupcakes, she'll probably want five dozen," Emma said.

"Hey, maybe we should do a sports theme," Katie suggested.

"I don't know," I said. "A sports theme seems kind of elementary school, doesn't it? Maybe there's a way to make it older. You know, sporty but suave."

Katie put down her spoon and looked at me. "Did you actually say 'sporty but suave'? What the heck does that mean?"

She started giggling, and Alexis and Emma joined in.

"You know, suave. Like, sophisticated," I said, but I was starting to giggle too. It did sound pretty silly.

"There is nothing suave about my brothers and their friends, trust me," Emma said.

"How about sporty but sweaty?" Katie suggested, and my friends collapsed into giggles again.

"Okay, okay!" I said. "But, seriously, hear me out. We don't want them to look like little kiddie cupcakes."

"Honestly, those boys won't care what they look like," Emma pointed out. "We could do a bunch of Plain Janes and they would be happy."

In the cupcake world, a Plain Jane is a vanilla cupcake with vanilla icing. They're very popular and very delicious, but not terribly exciting, either.

Alexis shook her head. "Every job we have is a business opportunity. We have to make our cupcakes stand out. There will be a lot of kids there, and if they remember our cupcakes, they might go home and tell their parents about them. We need to drum up more business."

"Definitely!" I agreed. "I need to make some extra money if I want that great pair of Kara Karen shoes I saw."

Now it was Katie's turn to roll her eyes. "Oh boy. Here she goes."

I took out my phone and called up my favorite picture of the shoes.

"Aren't they gorgeous?" I gushed, holding the phone out so Emma and Alexis could see.

"Ooh, they're pretty!" Emma agreed.

"Dylan would love those," said Alexis. Her older

sister is totally into fashion. "But they don't look very comfortable."

"That's exactly what I said!" Katie chimed in.

"Sometimes you have to sacrifice comfort for fashion," I told them, which is something my mom says. I sighed and put my phone away. I love my Cupcake Club friends, but they definitely do not care about fashion the way that I do. "Anyway, they're way expensive. I'm trying to save up for them, but it's going to take forever!"

"You know, I have a few more dogs than I can really handle this weekend," Emma said. Besides the Cupcake Club, she has her own dog-walking business. "Why don't you help me? I'll split the fee with you. It isn't much, but it will help."

"That would be great!" I replied, and then I remembered. "But I'm going to be with my dad all weekend."

"Maybe the weekend after that, then," Emma said.

"That would be very awesome," I said. I wished I could earn the money right then, but I guessed I would just have to wait a little longer for my shoes.

"So, we still need a plan for these cupcakes," Alexis prompted, bringing us back on track.

I pushed my empty soup bowl aside and took

out my sketchbook. I always have one on me.

"Give me a second," I said, and I closed my eyes and started envisioning what I thought the cupcakes should look like. In a few seconds my pencil was quickly moving over the paper.

"So, for the basketball team it's kind of obvious to decorate the round cupcakes to look like basketballs," I said. "But we don't have to go with orange icing and piped on laces. Maybe we could have a ball sticking on top of each cupcake."

"Ooh, we could make chocolate basketballs with a mold and use those," Katie suggested.

I picked up a blue pencil and kept sketching. "Then maybe for the swim team we could do blue icing and pipe waves onto it or something."

"I like how there's a different cupcake for each team," Alexis said.

Emma nodded. "My brothers will like that, because there's a special one for each of them."

"So what about flavors?" Alexis asked.

"Let me ask Matt and Sam what they want," Emma said.

Alexis looked satisfied. "Sounds like we have a plan."

"And it might not be suave, but I definitely think this is sporty chic," I said.

Katie shook her head. "Again, what does that even mean?"

I grinned. "It means that these cupcakes will be fabulous!"

"As always," Alexis added.

"So we're not doing sweaty cupcakes?" Katie asked, and we all started laughing again.

I love my Cupcake friends!

CHAPTER 6

I'm Not Sure What to Think

On Thursday morning I went to my locker before homeroom as usual to put in the books I didn't need and make sure I had the ones I did. And, as usual, Olivia was already there, looking in the mirror.

"Hi, Mia!" she said. "I just can't get this headband right. What do you think?"

She had on a blue headband, and as always, her hair looked perfect. There wasn't a strand out of place.

"Perfect!" I told her. Then I made a move to put my books in my locker.

But Olivia just turned back to the mirror. "How can you say that? I look terrible!" And then she started messing with her hair again.

"Well, the bell's going to ring soon," I told her.

"I know! It's so unfair. I can't go to class looking like this!" she wailed.

She had not taken my hint at all. I stood right next to her as she fussed some more. Then, finally, the bell rang.

I sighed. Now I'd have to rush to get to my locker between homeroom and first period. I hated doing that. But I guess I could understand. I know what it's like to have a bad hair day. Like, sometimes I swear I look like a monster, and Mom tells me I look beautiful.

Anyway, I couldn't wait until lunch because I had done some new, improved sketches of the basketball and swim-team cupcakes, and I was eager to show my friends. The morning crawled by and then, finally, it was lunchtime. I waited until we were done eating so the drawings wouldn't get messed up, and then I took out my sketchbook.

"Hey, so last night I—" I began, but Olivia interrupted me.

"Oh my gosh, the funniest thing happened in math class!" she said. "I totally forgot to tell you guys. You know Pat Delaney, right? So, Mr. Rodriguez called her to the board and she took like, two steps and then she totally tripped on her shoelaces! And then she tried to stop herself from falling and she was, like, waving her arms all over the place. It was hilarious!"

"That doesn't sound hilarious to me," Katie said. "I like Pat. She's really cool."

"Was she hurt?" Emma asked.

Olivia shrugged. "I guess not. Anyway, it was just funny. She's, like, a total spaz."

"If you ever saw her play softball, you wouldn't say that," Alexis pointed out.

"Yeah," I joined in. "Pat is awesome. It's not cool to make fun of her like that."

Olivia held up both hands in protest. "Whoa, chill out! It's, like, classic comedy, right? You're *supposed* to laugh when someone falls down."

I saw Alexis shoot a look to Katie and Emma, a kind of raised-eyebrow look. At that moment, I started feeling bad for Olivia all over again. Maybe in her old school that kind of thing was funny.

I also noticed that when Katie and I took the bus, we never talked about Olivia, not since that first day. A couple of times I tried to bring Olivia up, but Katie would always change the subject. So after a while, I just stopped mentioning her.

"I can't believe you have to go to your dad's this

weekend," Katie said. "That movie about the polar bears is opening."

"I know," I answered. "But I promise I won't see it without you. Maybe we can go next week."

"Then I promise not to see it either," Katie said. "It'll be more fun if we go together."

That night, after soccer practice, homework, and dinner, I remembered I had volunteered to bring in the Friday cupcakes.

"Mom, what should I do? I totally forgot," I told her.

"I can help you," she said. "Anyway, you can make cupcakes in your sleep by now, can't you?"

I wanted to make something special for Olivia's first cupcake, but my best thing is decorating, so we went with chocolate cupcakes and chocolate frosting. Then I rolled out some light blue fondant, which is this creamy sugar paste that you can sculpt, or roll out and cut shapes from it. When you see flowers on fancy wedding cakes, they're usually made of fondant.

Anyway, I've been trying to perfect my fondant flowers, and this was a good chance to practice. I cut the flattened fondant into circles and then rolled them up, so they looked like little roses. Then I cut out some tiny green leaves.

The finished cupcakes looked beautiful—shiny chocolate icing topped with perfect blue roses.

"Mia, they're beautiful!" Mom said when we were done. "You are becoming such a professional!"

I hugged her. "I couldn't have done them without you. Thanks!"

When I got to school the next morning, Olivia was happy with her hair and her lip gloss, so I had plenty of time to get into my locker before homeroom. I had the cupcakes with me in a small plastic cupcake box, and I carefully placed it on top of my books.

After first period I realized that I had forgotten to take out my English notebook for second period, so I quickly ran to my locker. When I opened it up, I saw some of Olivia's books piled on my shelf again, on top of the cupcake box.

I shook my head. It's a good thing I hadn't used a cardboard box, or the cupcakes would have been ruined. I moved Olivia's books to the bottom shelf and then went to grab my English notebook—only it wasn't there.

"Oh, come on!" I said, frustrated. I *know* my notebook was in there. I had a feeling I knew what had happened—Olivia must have taken it by mistake.

43

I was about to be late for class, so there was nothing I could do but go to class without my notebook. Friday is the day that our teacher, Ms. Harmeyer, checks to make sure we've written journal entries.

When I got to class, Ms. Harmeyer told us to read chapter twelve in the novels we were working on and to pass up our notebooks. I hated not having something to pass up. After a few minutes, I heard her call out, "Ms. Vélaz-Cruz. No notebook today?"

"Well, I'm sharing my locker with Olivia Allen, and I think she took it by mistake," I said.

The teacher shook her head. "You girls simply have to get more organized," she said in a frustrated voice, and I could feel myself blush. It wasn't fair! After all, I was just trying to help out one of my fellow classmates.

I didn't mention anything to Olivia during gym, but I did bring it up at lunch, as soon as we sat down. Katie was the only other person at the table.

"Olivia, did you take my English notebook by mistake?" I asked. "It's a red composition book."

"Oh, that? Yeah, it looks just like my science book," she said. "Oops!"

"Well, maybe that's why we should keep our

44

books on separate shelves," I said, trying to be as tactful as possible. "Then this kind of thing wouldn't happen."

"Mmm hmm," Olivia said, but she wasn't even really listening to me. She was gazing over at the BFC table. "Wow, that is a great jacket Callie is wearing, isn't it?"

I am so easily distracted by fashion! I looked over and saw that Callie was wearing a really cool black jacket with no buttons and sort of puffy shoulders.

"Very cute," I agreed.

Emma and Alexis came to the table with trays of burgers and carrot sticks. Emma eyed the plastic cupcake box.

"Ooh, what did you make, Mia? I bet they're beautiful!" she said.

I opened the box and gently took out a cupcake.

"I'm practicing my fondant flowers. What do you think?" I asked.

Olivia answered right away. "Oh my gosh, Mia, that is gorgeous!" she squealed. "You are, like, soooo talented! I bet you could go on one of those cup-cake competition shows and win, like, a million dollars."

"Well, I couldn't go on without the Cupcake Club," I said. "We're a team."

"But I bet nobody but you can do flowers like these," Olivia gushed. "They're fabulous! You are probably the best cupcake maker in America—no, change that—the best cupcake maker in the entire world!" I blushed at the praise. I was pleased but also a little embarrassed.

"Do we want to talk about flavors?" Emma asked. "I got some suggestions from my brothers about the kind of cupcakes they like. Maybe we could go over them after we eat."

Alexis gave Emma a look again, and I saw Katie give kind of a nod.

"Actually, we all have a lot of studying to do right now," Alexis said. "We can do it at our next meeting."

Emma nodded without a word, and I was left feeling weird. I didn't know what to make of the secret looks my friends were giving one another. I felt kind of excluded. On the other hand, I wasn't really sure what to make of Olivia either. All this locker stuff was starting to get on my nerves.

Believe me, when your new friend *and* your old friends are starting to bug you, it doesn't feel good!

CHAPTER 7

Katie Vents

𝒦atie and I tell each other everything, so on the bus ride home, I told her about Olivia and the locker.

"And then I didn't have my English notebook for class, and you should have seen the look that Ms. Harmeyer gave me," I told Katie. "And the worst thing is, Olivia didn't even apologize to me."

"Mia, I'm so glad you said that!" Katie said. "I didn't want to say anything before, because I didn't know how you felt, but I just don't like Olivia. I really wish we didn't have to eat lunch with her."

I was surprised. Katie was always polite to Olivia, and I guess I'd always assumed that my friends liked Olivia, just like I did.

"Katie, I'm just a little annoyed with the locker

situation," I said. "But I really like Olivia."

Now it was Katie's turn to be surprised. "Oh, I thought you were just being nice to her because she's new. You mean you really like her? But she can be so mean!"

"What do you mean?" I asked.

"Like how she thought it was funny when Pat Delaney tripped," Katie said. "And Alexis has English with her, and she says Olivia makes rude comments about how everyone looks during most of the class. Well, except for Alexis. I think Olivia knows you won't be friends with her anymore if she does that."

I shook my head. "Honestly, Katie, I've never heard her do that. And as for Pat, I don't think that's such a big deal."

"So you seriously *like* her?" Katie asked. "I can't believe it!"

I started to get mad. "We have things in common. Besides, you've only known her for, like, a week. We need to give her a chance. When I first came here, it took a while before anybody even talked to me besides you and Alexis and Emma. What am I supposed to say? 'Sorry, but you can't eat with us anymore'? What's she supposed to do then? Sit all by herself?"

Katie held up both hands in protest. "Okay, okay, I get it. I don't want to hurt her feelings or anything," she said. "She can still sit with us if she wants to."

"Of course she wants to," I said.

"But I don't think she can be in the Cupcake Club," Katie said. "At least not now, anyway."

That sounded fair. "Fine," I said.

Secretly, I thought Katie was a little jealous. It really hurt her when Callie ditched her to join the Popular Girls Club. So I think she's worried that I'm going to do the same thing. Sometimes, when I go to the mall with Sophie and Lucy, these two girls I met last year who are pretty cool, Katie does this whole thing where she acts like it doesn't bother her, but I can tell it really does.

"You know, just because I'm friends with Olivia doesn't mean I'll stop being friends with you," I told her.

"I know," Katie said, but she sounded a little sad.

Then I started to sing this song I learned at summer camp. "Make new friends, but keep the old. One is silver and the other gold!"

Katie burst out laughing. "You are crazy," she told me, and then I knew that everything was okay between us.

Then the bus pulled up at the stop at the end of her block.

"Have a good weekend," I said.

Katie waved. "Yeah, have fun with your dad!"

A few stops later, I got off the bus, walked down the block, and found Eddie waiting for me by the front door.

"Your mom's at a meeting, so I'm on train station duty," he informed me. "She said you packed last night."

I nodded. "My bag is upstairs. I just have to pick it up and get my toothbrush."

Since my parents divorced, I have become an expert in packing. If I bring too much stuff, my bag is too heavy to drag through the train station. But I also have to make sure I'm prepared for anything I do over the weekend, from hanging out outside to going to dinner in a nice restaurant. Once, my dad took me shopping, and I got a jacket and some clothes that I keep in my old bedroom, so that helps a lot.

Oh, and I also have to bring my school backpack, which can be extremely heavy. So my clothes suitcase is the kind that's on wheels, so I can pull it around. The hardest part is going up and down stairs with everything.

Eddie's really nice, and he helped me carry my stuff to the car and put it in the trunk. I climbed into the passenger seat and then put on my seat belt, and we headed to the train station.

"So what's new and exciting?" Eddie asked.

"Not much," I said, but then I found myself launching into the whole Olivia story. "There's this new girl, Olivia, and we're sharing a locker because there isn't one for her. I like her, but the locker thing is getting kind of annoying. She takes forever looking in the mirror when I'm trying to get my stuff. And she's supposed to keep her stuff on the bottom shelf, but she puts it on the top shelf with mine, and it gets mixed up."

Eddie nodded. "You've got yourself a Carlos."

I was puzzled. "A Carlos?"

"Carlos Sanchez, my college roommate," Eddie explained. "He was a great guy, and we had a lot of fun together. But he was the worst roommate in the world. He would borrow my clothes, spill stuff on them, and then stuff them back into my drawer. And he always ate my bologna and never replaced it."

"That is just rude," I agreed.

"It used to make me furious," Eddie said. "But the thing is, I still wanted to be his friend. So I just

51

pretended that Carlos the roommate was a different guy. And then I could hang out with Carlos the friend and enjoy myself."

Eddie's story was a little unusual, but I had to agree that it made sense. "So I guess I could do the same with Olivia," I said.

"Exactly," Eddie said. "Some people are just not meant to be in close quarters together. But that doesn't mean you can't be friends. In fact, why don't you invite her over for dinner one night next week? Your mom and I would like to meet her."

"Okay," I replied. I took out my phone and texted Olivia.

Off 2 my dad's. Do u want 2 have dinner at my house next week?

☺Yes!!!!!!!!!!!!! Monday? Olivia texted back.

"Is Monday okay?" I asked Eddie.

"Sure," he replied. "I'm pretty sure your mom and I don't have anything scheduled."

Monday, I texted back. Ask ur mom if u can ride the bus home with me.

☺☺☺ Tx !!!!!!!! Olivia replied.

It made me feel good that she was so happy. In fact, I realized, I had made both Katie and Olivia happy in less than an hour. That's pretty good, don't you think?

CHAPTER 8

Sushi ... and a Surprise

The train ride from Maple Grove to New York City takes more than an hour because of all the stops. It is extremely boring, so I always make sure I have music to listen to and a sketchbook. I know Katie feels sick if she reads or draws in a moving vehicle, but I am very lucky I don't have that problem. Otherwise, I would probably go insane. Insane on the train. I made a note to tell Katie about that one; she'd probably make up a funny song about it on the spot.

Dad was waiting for me when I got off the train at Penn Station. He always takes my luggage for me, so I don't have to lug it up the stairs. But first he gives me a superbig hug.

"*Mija*, you're getting taller every time I see

you!" he said. (Dad likes to call me "*mija*," which means "my daughter" in Spanish. It's pronounced "mee-ha," so it sounds a lot like my name.)

"Dad, I don't think I grew in two weeks," I protested.

"I think you did," Dad replied. "You are growing so fast!"

Then, like always, we piled into a cab and headed down to Tokyo 16, our favorite sushi restaurant. Besides having the most delicious sushi in the world, the place is beautiful on the inside: dark and calm, with a waterfall along the back wall. It's like you've been transported into another place.

We stuffed my bags against the wall and sat in our usual table by the waterfall. Our server, Yuki, brought us two steaming hot towels, so we could clean our hands. The towels smelled like flowers.

"Good to see you, Yuki," my dad said.

Yuki is in her twenties and wears her hair in a cute short haircut. She's very friendly.

"Will you and Mia be having the miso soup today?" she asked.

Dad looked at me, and I nodded. "*Mmm*, miso."

A few minutes later we were slurping on

steaming bowls of salty soup with green seaweed and tiny cubes of tofu floating in the broth.

"So, what's on our schedule this weekend, *mija*?" Dad asked.

"Well, I have to leave early Sunday, because of my soccer game," I said. "I hope that's okay."

"Of course," Dad said. "Your mom told me. I was thinking I could take the train out with you and see you play."

"Really?" I asked, and I felt really happy. Dad didn't used to like coming out to Maple Grove because he felt awkward being around Mom and Eddie. To be honest, it was a little awkward for me, too, to see my mom and dad in the same place, even though they're not together anymore. But I guess things were less awkward for them because he's been coming out more often for school events and stuff like that.

Dad misunderstood my response. "Only if you want me to."

"Definitely! Absolutely!" I told him. "I scored two goals last week."

Dad smiled. "That's my girl! I can't wait to see you play."

Then Yuki came and took our sushi order (spicy tuna roll and mango roll for me, and a sashimi plate, which has thin slices of raw fish, for Dad). When Yuki left the table, my dad had a serious look on his face.

"*Mija*, I want to talk to you about something," he said.

Uh-oh, I thought. My dad hardly ever begins sentences like that. I flashed back to a year before, at this very table, when he told me he had a girl-friend named Alina. And she was just . . . well, awful!

So I must be psychic, because the next words out of his mouth were, "I have a new girlfriend."

"I knew it!" I cried, and I was probably pretty loud, because I noticed that people were looking at us. "Sorry," I whispered.

"It's okay," Dad said. "I know it didn't go so well last time. But Lynne isn't anything like Alina, I promise."

"I hope not," I said.

"And I think I made a big mistake the way I handled it last time," Dad admitted. "I didn't take your feelings into account. So this time, I'm going to ask you instead of telling you. Would you like to meet her sometime?"

I had to think it over. Sure, I like my stepdad, Eddie, but it took a long time to get used to him. I don't know if I could handle a stepmom, too.

But I knew Dad was going to date this Lynne person whether I wanted him to or not. And he was asking pretty nicely.

"Okay," I said hesitantly. "But maybe next visit? I need some time to get used to the idea."

Dad smiled. "Of course, *mija*. I have a feeling you will like her."

Yuki put our plates of food in front of us. I picked up a piece of spicy tuna roll with my chopsticks (I've been using them since I was three, so I'm pretty good) and dunked it in soy sauce.

"Mmm, umami," I said.

"Umami?" Dad asked.

"You know, like in the commercial," I said. "It's the way soy sauce tastes. It's like that extra-special flavor that makes everything taste better."

"Then you are my umami, Mia," Dad said. "You will always be my special girl, no matter who else I meet. That's how life is. We will both always be making new friends. But we'll always be important to each other. What's that saying? Make new friends, but keep the old. . . ."

"One is silver and the other gold," I finished for him, and I felt all shivery. That's just what I said to Katie on the bus! Freaky, right? I wondered if this was a sign of some kind about Dad's girlfriend.

"So, what have we got planned for tomorrow?" Dad asked.

I grinned. "I'm meeting Ava, and we're going window shopping . . . *shoe* window shopping," I told him.

After dinner we just headed home for the night. We watched a little television, and then I went to sleep thinking about my wonderful shoes.

The next afternoon, me and my dad and my friend Ava were standing in front of the Kara Karen store. The shop had moved the heels—*my* heels—to the window.

"Your mom warned me about these," Dad said. "She said that under no circumstances am I to buy them for you. You're supposed to be earning half the money yourself."

I sighed. "I know, Dad," I said. "I just want to look at them, that's all."

Dad glanced across the street. "I'm going to grab a coffee. You girls have fun, okay?"

Ava and I stepped into the store. Ava Monroe is my first best friend, and she's gorgeous. She has shiny black hair and these beautiful brown eyes, and she's very petite, which helps make her graceful. We grew up together and played soccer on the same team for years.

"Wow, Mia, they're even more beautiful in person," Ava said (because, of course, I had already sent her the photo).

"They're the shoes of my dreams," I said with a sigh. "I knew you would understand."

As I lay in bed that night, my mind was jumbled with thoughts of silver and gold friends. Ava was my oldest friend, so she was gold. Then Katie was my next best friend, so that would make her silver (along with Alexis and Emma, of course). So what was Olivia? Bronze? That didn't seem right. Bronze didn't seem so nice; plus, I already told Katie that *she* was gold.

Maybe Ava was platinum, and Katie and Alexis and Emma were gold, and Olivia was silver. That felt better. Then I thought about what would happen when I made new friends *after* Olivia, and my thoughts got jumbled up again.

Maybe, I thought, as I drifted off to sleep, *it is just nice to have so many friends. Because all of them, in their own way, are supersparkly.*

CHAPTER 9

Olivia's Not-So-Sweet Side

When Katie and I got off the bus on Monday, Olivia was standing on the school steps waiting for me. She had a big grin on her face and looked superexcited.

"Mia, I can't wait to go to your house today!" she said, and she looked really excited. "It was soooo sweet of you to invite me."

I was glad that Olivia was so excited, but I was cringing inside, because Katie was right beside me. I probably should have mentioned my plans while Katie and I were on the bus, but I guess there was a part of me that was hoping she didn't have to know. I didn't want to hurt her feelings.

I glanced at Katie, and she looked okay, so I relaxed a little.

"Well, it was Eddie's idea," I said, partly for Katie to hear too. "He and my mom want to meet you."

"That is soooo sweet," Olivia repeated, and we all walked inside the school. Katie stopped at her locker, and Olivia and I headed farther down the hall to ours. When I opened the door, a bunch of crumpled papers fell out. I looked at Olivia.

She shrugged. "Oh, I dumped those in there on Friday. That's what lockers are for, right?"

No, that's what garbage cans are for, I thought. But I didn't say it out loud. Olivia was just being a Carlos, and I was going to do what Eddie said and separate locker Olivia from everyday Olivia.

"Well, if you don't need them, maybe we could throw them out," I said cheerfully.

"I guess. There's a garbage right over there," Olivia said, motioning with her head.

So I picked up the papers and threw them out while Olivia applied her lip gloss in the mirror. As I was walking back, my friends Sophie and Lucy walked by. One of the reasons I like them both is because they have their own unique senses of style. Sophie tends to dress sort of like a hippie, with big hoop earrings, peasant blouses, and long skirts. Today, she was wearing a blue sweater over a tan billowy skirt, and flats.

Sophie and Lucy said hi and kept going. When I got to my locker, I saw that Olivia was staring at them.

"What is up with that skirt?" she asked. "It looks like a tent. She could go camping in it!"

"Hey, Sophie is a friend of mine," I said. "And I like her look. I think she really pulls it off with her long curly hair and everything. Besides, I think her skirt is pretty."

Olivia shook her head. "Oh, come on, you wouldn't be caught dead in that!" she said and then started laughing.

"Well, just because I wouldn't wear it doesn't mean it doesn't look good on Sophie," I responded, hoping Olivia would understand. But she didn't.

"Well, if it rains today, we can all take shelter under her skirt," she said, cracking herself up again.

I was kind of upset with Olivia for saying that about Sophie, but I get that not everyone's idea about fashion is the same. Also, have you seen those TV shows where people talk about the fashions that celebrities wear? They say nasty things all the time, and everyone thinks it's funny.

At lunch that day, Olivia kept talking about how excited she was to go to my house. She was full of questions.

"What does your stepbrother look like? Is he cute? How many dogs do you have again? I can't wait to meet them!"

Katie got superquiet, and I could tell she was mad about the whole thing. But instead of feeling sorry for Katie, I felt kind of angry. I mean, I already told her I was going to be her friend, no matter what. Why couldn't she just trust me?

Katie and I always walk to social studies together after lunch, but not today. Olivia was distracting me with her questions, and when I looked up, Katie had already left without me.

"See you on the bus!" Olivia said happily, and then she ran off to class. As I walked out of the cafeteria, Alexis stopped me. I think she had been waiting for me by the door.

"Mia, are you cool with what Olivia was doing during lunch?" Alexis asked.

I was puzzled. "What do you mean?"

"The way she was bragging about going to your house, just to make Katie feel bad," Alexis said.

I shook my head. "She's just excited. She wasn't trying to hurt anybody."

Alexis made a face. "Did you not see her shooting looks at Katie the whole time?"

"She's not like that, honest," I said, although a

tiny part of me was beginning to wonder about that. "Just give her a chance."

Alexis glanced at her watch. "We'd better talk later, or we'll be late for class."

I was pretty distracted during social studies, thinking about what Alexis had said. I really didn't believe Olivia would hurt Katie on purpose like that. But then I remembered her mean comment about Sophie. Maybe locker Olivia wasn't the only one with problems.

I guess I'll find out later, I thought.

The bus ride home was a little awkward, because Olivia was riding the bus with me and Katie. But I wasn't about to make Katie angry by leaving our usual seat, so when Olivia came on, I just kind of shrugged, and Olivia found a seat in the back. I turned to Katie and said, "I know you don't like Olivia, but I really think the more you get to know her, you'll change your mind. She can be really fun."

Katie sighed and then said, "I don't think so, but I hope I change my mind, I really do—I don't like disagreeing with you about anything, and especially about friends. So let's talk about something else—I'd rather talk about *anything* instead of Olivia—even shoes!" We both laughed, and

I changed the subject. Katie and I chatted away until she got off the bus, and then Olivia joined me. Soon we got to my stop.

"Ooh, your house is so pretty!" Olivia said as we walked up to it.

I have to admit the house is one of the nicest things about living in the suburbs. It was Eddie and Dan's house before my mom and I moved in. It's a white two-story house with a porch in the front and a big lawn that Dan hates to mow.

"Thanks," I said.

When I opened the door, my two little white Maltese, Tiki and Milkshake, came to greet us. Tiki always pats his little paws on my ankles, and Milkshake does a happy dance and wags her tail.

"Awww, they're soooo cute!" Olivia said, and she knelt down to pet them. "I have a Chihuahua at home. Maybe they could be friends."

Then my mom came out of the kitchen. "You must be Olivia," she said. "Nice to meet you."

"Nice to meet you too, Mrs. Vélaz-Cruz," Olivia said.

Mom smiled. "Actually, it's Mrs. Valdes now. Confusing, isn't it? It's been nearly a year, but I'm still getting used to it myself."

Then she nodded toward the dining room. "I've

set up a snack in there for you, so you can do your homework before dinner."

"Thanks, Mom," I said, and I motioned for Olivia to follow me. She was frowning.

"Homework?" she asked. "I thought we could, you know, see your room and stuff."

"Yeah, well, my mom's pretty strict about that," I said. "Homework first, fun later."

Mom had put out some yogurt cups, fruit, and a pitcher of iced tea for us. I grabbed a mango yogurt and sat back. "We can eat first," I told Olivia.

Olivia took a strawberry yogurt. "So, I was wondering about those girls in the BFC," she said. It was the first time she had mentioned them to me. "You know, Callie, Maggie, and Bella. So what's their deal?"

"Well, last year they were led by this girl, Sydney, but she moved to California," I said. "They used to be called the Popular Girls Club. Sydney was kind of mean and didn't let anybody join except for Callie. Now I guess Callie's kind of in charge. They let girls sit with them sometimes, but I don't think they have any new members yet. They're kind of exclusive."

"What about you?" Olivia asked.

"What do you mean?" I replied.

"Well, you're like the most stylish girl in the whole school," Olivia said. "So why aren't you one of them?"

"Actually, Sydney asked me to join," I admitted. "But I didn't want to. I'd rather stay with my real friends in the Cupcake Club."

Olivia looked impressed. "You know, I don't understand why the BFC are so high-and-mighty. Maggie's hair looks like she stuck her finger in a socket. Doesn't she know she can buy products to fix it?"

"Hey, I thought you were friendly with her!" I said. "Don't say mean things about her. And, anyway, Maggie's not so bad."

"I wasn't being mean," Olivia protested. "I just said her hair is horrible. That's constructive criticism. If you're trying to be popular, you should have good hair, right?"

I was starting to feel uncomfortable. This was the second time today I had heard Olivia's "constructive criticism," but it sounded just plain mean to me.

"It's just the way you said it," I told her.

Then Olivia's eyes got teary. "Oh, Mia, come on. Don't be like that. I have no one but you to really talk to at school. Don't be mad."

"I'm not mad," I said slowly. And I wasn't, exactly. But I was starting to think that everyday Olivia was just as bad as locker Olivia, and I wasn't sure what to do about that.

"You must know how it feels, because you were new," Olivia said. "Half of the girls won't even talk to me. If it wasn't for you, I'd be a total loser."

And with that, she got me. I felt like I owed it to her to be her friend.

"Hey, I can't believe I haven't showed you these yet," I said, changing the subject as I reached for my phone. I held up the screen so she could see. "My dream shoes. I found them in the Kara Karen boutique in SoHo. What do you think?"

"Oh my gosh, they're fabulous!" she said, practically screaming. "They're the greatest shoes I've ever seen in my entire life!"

"I know!" I replied.

Then we heard my mom's voice coming from the kitchen.

"Girls? Are you doing homework in there?"

"Of course, Mom!" I replied, and then Olivia and I burst into giggles.

CHAPTER 10

Trying to Find the Right Mix

*T*he rest of my day with Olivia was really fun. We did our homework, and Mom made Caesar salad, fish, and rice for dinner, and Olivia had funny stories to tell about her Chihuahua, and everyone seemed to like her.

Then, while Olivia and I were waiting for her dad to pick her up, Olivia asked me something.

"So, you know, I was wondering," she said. "You were saying how exclusive the BFC is. Is the Cupcake Club exclusive too?"

It was an awkward question. We always got down on the BFC for not inviting new members, but we had never invited anybody to join the Cupcake Club either.

I replied with Alexis's standard answer.

"Well, it's more than a club, it's a business," I said. "So we keep it small, you know? So we can actually make a profit."

"Oh, well, I was just wondering, that's all," Olivia said. "I mean, it sounds like fun."

She wasn't asking outright to join the club, but it was a pretty big hint. And I kind of felt like she had a point. If we were a club, we should be open to everybody. Maybe there was a way to separate the club part from the business part somehow.

I knew I was going to have to talk to the Cupcake Club about this, and I kind of dreaded it. I had already promised Katie that Olivia wouldn't be in the club. And now I was kind of going back on it.

I had my chance to bring it up the next night at our Cupcake Club meeting. After school we all walked to Alexis's house. She and Emma live on the same block, and it's close to the school, so we don't have to take the bus. We gathered around Alexis's spotless kitchen table, and she took out her laptop.

"So, everyone agrees on Mia's designs for the cupcakes?" Alexis asked, and we all nodded. "Before I can make up a shopping list, we need to decide on flavors. Emma, what did your brothers say?"

"Well, Matt loves peanut butter and jelly more

than anything, so he was wondering if we could do a P–B–and–J cupcake," Emma said. "Katie, I remembered that your mom made you one for the first day of middle school."

Katie nodded. "They're pretty easy. You make a vanilla cupcake, and then you put grape jelly into an injector thingie and squirt some into each cupcake. Then you top it off with peanut-butter-and–cinnamon frosting."

"The little basketball will look cute sticking out of the peanut butter frosting," I said. "The colors will work together."

Alexis started typing. "So besides our usual ingredients, we will need grape jelly, peanut butter, and . . ."

"Cream cheese," Katie said. "I'm pretty sure the peanut-butter frosting is made with cream cheese. Oh, and we already have the cupcake injector, so we don't need that."

"Cream cheese," Alexis said aloud as she typed, and then she looked at Emma. "Okay, what about Sam?"

"Sam said that everything we make is delicious, so he doesn't care," Emma said.

"That is so sweet!" Katie said.

"He is the best," I added.

Emma made a face. "You should smell his sneakers after he goes running," she said. "Anyway, we still need to pick a flavor."

"I am dying to try out my new cupcake plunger," Katie said. "Maybe we could do, like, pudding-filled cupcakes or something."

"Mmm, pudding cupcake," Alexis said. "So, like, a vanilla cupcake with chocolate pudding?"

"Vanilla pudding would go better with the blue icing," I pointed out.

"But the pudding will be *inside* the cupcake," Alexis argued.

"Yes, but when you bite into it, you'll see the pudding," I said.

Alexis nodded. "Good point. Okay, then. We need some boxes of vanilla pudding. I like this. A cupcake with a surprise inside will get people talking. It's good for business."

"It's kind of a lot of work, though," Emma said. "I mean, we're doing six dozen cupcakes, and both of them have extra stuff inside them."

I figured this was my chance to jump in.

"Maybe we just need some extra help," I said casually.

Alexis narrowed her eyes suspiciously. "What do you mean?"

"Like, maybe, once in a while, we could invite people to help us," I said. "People who are interested in being part of the Cupcake Club. We wouldn't have to split the profits with them or anything."

"You mean people like Olivia," Alexis said flatly.

"Well, yes," I said. "I mean, she pointed out that the Cupcake Club seems kind of exclusive, and we don't want to be like the BFC, do we?"

"Of course not," Emma spoke up. "It's just . . ."

"Olivia likes *you*, but she hardly ever talks to us or tries to be nice to us," Katie blurted out.

"Katie's right," Alexis agreed. "When we're in lunch, she's always looking around the room, like she's scoping out someone better to talk to. It's like we're not good enough for her or something."

"And she is such a flirt!" Emma jumped in. "Anytime a guy comes near her, she turns into a whole different person."

"What does that have to do with making cupcakes?" I asked.

There was an awkward pause for a moment. Alexis and Emma and Katie looked at one another. Finally, Katie spoke up.

"I think Mia has a good point," she said. "We don't want to be exclusive, like the BFC. But, remember, we're not just a club. We're a business, too."

"So, maybe we can keep the business separate," I said. "Businesses hire people, don't they? Maybe we could hire Olivia to help us with the cupcakes."

"But then we'd each make less money," Emma said. "Oh, and that reminds me. I have an extra dog-walking client on Saturday. Can you come help me after practice? Like I said, I'll split my fee with you!"

"I should be done by eleven," I said. "Is that okay? I would love to help. I still don't have enough money for my shoes."

"Which is another reason why we shouldn't hire Olivia to help with the cupcakes," Alexis said.

"Okay, you win!" I said. "But maybe there's something else we could let her do where we don't have to pay her. Let's just think about it, okay?"

Alexis shrugged. "Sure. Now let's get back to our shopping list."

And just like that, we were back to business again, which was okay with me. Even though Olivia wasn't part of the club, at least my friends weren't mad at me. I could never stay mad at my Cupcake girls!

CHAPTER 11

How Could You Forget a Whole Kid?

On Wednesday night I Skyped with my dad. He gave me a laptop with a webcam, just so we could see each other on the days he doesn't have me. I have to admit that it's kind of nice to see his face instead of just talking on the phone.

"*Hola, mija.* How's it going?" Dad asked after his face popped up on the screen.

"Good," I replied. Sometimes I don't really know what to say with him. "I got an A on my Spanish quiz."

"Good job, *mija*!" Dad congratulated me. "I'm so proud of you."

"Thanks," I said.

"So, I wanted to talk with you about the next weekend I have with you," Dad said.

"You mean the weekend after this one," I said.

"Right," Dad said. "I checked your schedule, and I know you have a soccer game that morning. But I was still hoping you'll come out on Saturday afternoon. Because I was wondering if you'd want to go to the American Museum of Natural History with me and Lynne and Ethan on Sunday."

I was puzzled. "Ethan? Who's Ethan?"

"Remember, I told you," Dad replied. "Ethan is Lynne's son. He's five years old."

"Um, no, you definitely did *not* tell me," I said.

"I'm sure I did," Dad protested.

"Well, I think I would have remembered that," I said. "Seriously, how could you forget to tell me about a kid?"

I could see that Dad was getting a little frustrated with me. "Well, I'm telling you now. He's a sweet little boy. So how about the American Museum of Natural History?"

Now, my favorite museum in New York is the Metropolitan Museum of Art, because there are these awesome costume exhibits. I had a feeling that five-year-old Ethan probably didn't want to look at costumes and that's why we were going to the natural history museum. I haven't been there since I was about five.

I could have complained, but Dad seemed so happy about it all, and at least he was asking me, right? So I decided to be mature about it.

"Sure, Dad," I said. "We can go to the museum."

Dad was practically beaming with happiness. "We will have fun, I promise. I can't wait, *mija*."

"Okay, Dad. Love you," I said.

"Love you, too!" And then we signed off.

Mom walked by my bedroom door. "Talking to your dad?" she asked.

"He was asking about next weekend, if I can come after my soccer game," I said. "I told him okay." I left out the part about going to the museum with his new girlfriend and her son, because I didn't want her to feel weird.

Mom nodded.

"Oh, and I forgot to tell you, I'm going to help Emma walk dogs this Saturday after my game," I said. "For the shoes, of course."

"Good for you," Mom said. "And Eddie and I were talking. If you want to rake some leaves this weekend, we'll pay you."

Inside, I groaned. I hate raking leaves. But I love shoes more, so I answered her happily.

"I'll do it!" I replied. "I will be the best leaf raker in all of Maple Grove."

❖

So Saturday, after my early soccer game, I began Operation Save for Shoes. Mom dropped me off at Emma's house, so that I could help her with the dogs.

Emma was outside waiting for me.

"I'm so glad you can help," she said. "I have this new client, Mrs. Oliver, who has two dogs, and she's watching her sister's dogs while her sister is away, and it's hard for me to walk four at the same time."

"It'll be fun," I said. "I walk Tiki and Milkshake all the time."

Then Emma handed me some brown plastic bags. "For . . . you know, clean up."

I nodded. I was pretty used to cleaning up after my Maltese.

"We can walk there," Emma said. "She lives over on Thompson Street."

As we were about to leave, Emma's little brother, Jake, ran up. His blond hair was all messy and he looked adorable, as always.

"Emma, I want to come! I can help!" Jake said.

"Jake, I already told you, Mrs. Oliver's dogs are too big for you," Emma said. "Go back inside. Dad's watching you this morning."

Jake's blue eyes got wide. "Emma, pleeeeease?"

He looked cuter than any kitten video you've ever seen on the Internet. I don't know how Emma resisted him, but she was pretty firm.

"Inside, Jake."

Jake frowned, but he listened to Emma and ran right inside.

"Thank goodness," Emma said. "He can be so annoying!"

Listening to Emma made me think of that kid Ethan. If my dad and Lynne got serious, that would make Ethan my little brother.

"Seriously, Emma," I said as we walked. "I know you said that Jake is annoying, but we all think Jake is so cute. Is it really that bad having a little brother?"

Emma looked thoughtful. "Well, most of the time it's okay. But he can be annoying a lot. Like, I never have any privacy because he's always bugging me. But then sometimes I look at his face and just want to hug him, you know?"

I nodded. "It's just . . . my dad wants me to meet his new girlfriend, and she has this five-year-old kid, and it's freaking me out a little bit," I admitted. "I was an only child for a long time. Then I had to get used to having an older brother. I'm not sure I could handle having a little brother, too."

"I think about being an only child sometimes,"

Emma confessed. "But then I think I would miss my brothers sometimes. Even Matt."

"Well, maybe Ethan will be as adorable as Jake," I said. "That wouldn't be so bad."

"Besides, your dad just started dating this woman, right? So it's not like it's serious," Emma said.

I thought about the way my dad's face lit up when he talked about Lynne, and I wasn't so sure.

We stopped in front of a small gray house, and Emma used a key to open up the back door.

"Stand behind me," Emma warned.

I did as I was told, and just in time, because four huge, slobbering yellow dogs bounded to the door and pounced on Emma. She's shorter than I am, so I was surprised they didn't knock her down. With her blond hair and blue eyes and pretty dresses, Emma doesn't exactly look tough, but she's one of the toughest people I know.

"Sit!" Emma commanded, and all four dogs sat at once, gazing at her expectantly. Emma took four leashes off a hook on the wall.

"I'll leash them up, then you can take Goldie and Tigger," she told me.

"Which ones are those?" I asked, because all the dogs looked pretty much the same.

"I'll give them to you," Emma said, and soon I was holding on to leashes with a giant dog at each end. I was pretty sure they both weighed a lot more than I did.

Emma is a real pro, because she led the way as we walked the dogs down the street, and all four dogs followed her, like furry soldiers. Goldie and Tigger didn't even pull or strain, and I was glad, because walking two tiny Maltese had not prepared me for this.

When the walk was over, we brought the dogs back to Mrs. Oliver's house and Emma took an envelope from the kitchen table before we left and locked up. She handed me fifteen dollars.

"Here's your half," she said. "Any time you want to help out, just let me know."

"Thanks!" I said.

When I got home, my arms were already aching, but Eddie greeted me with a big smile—and a rake.

"Can I please eat lunch first?" I moaned before he even said a word.

"Why not? The leaves aren't going anywhere," Eddie joked.

So after I ate a cheese sandwich I raked . . . and raked . . . and raked for hours. I mean, literally, hours. I'm not exaggerating. My body hurt all over and I was exhausted, but I didn't care, because Eddie gave me twenty bucks. I didn't need much more to get the shoes. In fact, I'd probably have enough money after we got paid for Matt and Sam's party.

That night, I stretched out on my bed and gazed at the sketch of the shoes I had drawn.

"Soon, soon, you will be mine," I whispered, and then I laughed because I realized I sounded like a creepy movie villain or something. But I couldn't help it. I couldn't wait to get those shoes!

CHAPTER 12

My First Design Client

The next morning I woke up to the sound of my phone beeping. My CC friends know to never text me before nine a.m. on a weekend. Maybe it was Dad? He knew better than that too.

Groaning, I reached for the phone and looked at the screen through blurry eyes. It was from Olivia.

Want 2 hang out this afternoon?

I had to think for a minute. I still had an essay to write for English class, but that wouldn't take long. Mom hadn't said anything about plans for today. And I definitely didn't feel like raking more leaves.

Sure. What do u want 2 do? I typed.
Let's hang at ur house, Olivia replied.

That sounded okay with me.

C u at 1, I typed.
TTYL!!!! ☺☺, she responded immediately.

Then I rolled over and went back to sleep. When I went downstairs later, Dan was sitting at the kitchen table eating a plate of eggs, bacon, and toast.

"You must have been tired, Mia," Mom told me as she walked into the kitchen. "You even slept later than Dan."

"Hey, I don't sleep late," Dan protested.

"Do you want some eggs?" Mom asked me.

"I'll just eat some cereal," I said, reaching for the cabinet. "Oh yeah, and is it okay if Olivia comes over for a while? Like, at one?"

"Just as long as it's okay with her parents," Mom replied.

I got a bowl, a box of cereal, and some milk from the fridge and started to get my cereal ready, still yawning. Then I heard my phone beep in my pocket. Another text.

I took out my phone and saw that this text was from Katie.

Want 2 see the polar bear movie today?

"Oh no," I said out loud, and Dan looked at me quizzically.

I remembered talking to Katie about seeing the movie, but I don't think we had set a date. I really wanted to go, but it would be rude to cancel on Olivia.

I also thought about making some excuse to Katie, but then I realized Olivia would probably talk about it at lunch tomorrow. There was no easy way out of this.

Can't. Olivia coming over. Maybe 2 nite? I cringed as I typed those words.

Can't go 2 nite. Mom and I are going 2 her friend's for dinner, Katie wrote back.

I wasn't sure what to say, so I went with a frowny face.

☹

I might go see the movie anyway, Katie texted me. Hope that's ok.

What could I say? I really wanted to see it with her, but I couldn't tell her to wait. That wouldn't be fair.

K! I typed. Txt me a review when it's over.

K, Katie typed back, and that was the end of our conversation.

I couldn't tell if she was mad or not.

But there was no point in worrying about it, right? I wasn't going to have a miserable afternoon just because I might have upset Katie. And when Olivia came over, we had a great time.

"We need to spend some time in your closet," Olivia said when she arrived. "Last time was too much homework, not enough clothes!"

"What are we waiting for?" I asked, and we headed upstairs.

I used to kind of hate my bedroom. When I first moved in, it had old-lady wallpaper and old furniture that didn't match, but Eddie helped me totally redo it. He took down the wallpaper (which was the really hard part), and after changing my mind, like, a thousand times, we painted the walls in this pale turquoise color, and then we painted the furniture gleaming white, with black around the trim and stuff, and it looks totally cool. Plus, I have a really big closet, which is almost as big as my whole bedroom in my dad's apartment in Manhattan.

"Oh my gosh, Mia, this closet is ah-may-zing!"

Olivia cried as she opened up the door. "You have the most fabulous clothes!"

."I get a lot of them for free," I explained. "From my mom's clients."

"It is sooo cool that your mom has a fashion career," Olivia said. "My mom sells mattresses. Boooring!"

She pulled out a white sleeveless dress with black polka dots that I got this spring.

"Ooh, this is adorable! Can I try it on?"

"Of course," I said. When I'm in Manhattan, Ava and I are always trying on each other's clothes. I miss having someone to do that with here.

The afternoon went by pretty quickly. Since winter is coming up, I've been trying to figure out how to style my winter outfits, and Olivia's mad layering skills came to the rescue. We came up with seven new outfits just based on what was in my closet. And Olivia didn't say anything mean about anybody—not once.

Right after Olivia left at four o'clock I got a few texts from Katie.

Baby bear cute.
Baby bear gets lost.
Baby bear finds mom.
The end. ☺

So it looked like everything was okay with Katie after all, and I was really relieved.

I got more good news the next morning at school. I was walking to my and Olivia's locker when Olivia came out of the principal's office and headed toward me.

"Hey, so this kid Michael Hanna moved or something and I can have his locker," she told me. "It's right around the corner from yours."

She held up a note. "Principal LaCosta gave us a note so we can skip homeroom and move the stuff to my new locker."

"That's great!" I said, but Olivia didn't look exactly happy.

"It's fun sharing a locker with you," she said. "I'll miss you."

"I'll miss you, too," I said, but I was kind of lying. Because inside I was thinking, *Hooray! No more locker Olivia!*

We went to my locker and each grabbed a handful of Olivia's stuff and brought it to her new locker. Olivia opened it up and turned to me.

"Would you mind bringing the rest? I'll start getting it organized," she said.

"Um, sure," I said. I made a couple more trips

with Olivia's books and makeup, and on the last trip, I took the mirror off the door, cringing as it tore my wallpaper. I'd have to find something to put there to cover it up.

When I handed Olivia the mirror, she gave a big sigh.

"My locker is sooo boring!" she complained. "I wish I could make it look cool like yours."

"Of course you can," I said. "You have an awesome sense of style."

"Not like *yours*," Olivia said. "I could never be as good as you, Mia. You're practically a professional!"

"Maybe I should go into business," I joked. "Mia's Locker Makeovers."

But Olivia took me seriously. "You could make over my locker! I would love that. I could be, like, your first client."

I thought about it. Designing my locker was a lot of fun. It would be fun to decorate Olivia's, too.

"Okay," I said. "Let's talk more at lunch."

So at lunchtime, Katie was telling me about the polar bear movie when Olivia interrupted us.

"So, Mia," she said, "I was thinking of how we can decorate my locker. Maybe turquoise and black, like your room. Or maybe animal prints. Or both! What do you think?"

I took out my sketchbook.

"Animal-print wallpaper could be cute," I said, sketching it out as I talked. "And you need a cool mirror, of course. Maybe that could be the focal point. Oh, and extra shelves for your makeup!"

I could see Alexis roll her eyes across the table, but I didn't care. I was having fun.

"That all looks ah-may-zing!" Olivia said. "How soon can we do it?"

I thought about how my mom handled her clients. "Let me come up with some sketches for you, and a budget. Maybe by Friday, okay?"

Olivia pouted. "Friday? That's forever!"

But I wanted to do the job right. I kind of liked the idea that Olivia was my first client. I wasn't going to charge her, of course, but I still wanted to do things professionally.

"I'll definitely have it by Friday, I promise," I assured her.

So when I wasn't doing homework or having soccer practice, I worked on sketches for Olivia's locker. I found samples of wallpaper and mirrors and shelves online and printed them out. By Friday, I had a whole presentation for Olivia. We looked at it while we ate the lemon cupcakes Alexis had made.

"Ooh, this mirror is perfect!" Olivia said, pointing to one I had printed out. "And I love the wallpaper and the shelves and the makeup light. Soooo cool!"

I did some quick adding. "The stuff all comes to about forty dollars. You can get all of it at the stores in the mall. You can keep the proposal, so you know what to look for."

"Wow, that's all so complicated," Olivia said. "I probably wouldn't even get the right stuff. Would you mind doing it, and I'll pay you back?"

Once again, I saw Alexis roll her eyes, but Olivia wasn't asking anything outrageous. Mom did this kind of thing for her clients all the time. She did the shopping, and then she sent them a bill, and they paid her.

"No problem," I said. I could use my shoe savings to get the stuff over the weekend, and then I'd have the money back on Monday. "This is going to be so fabulous. Even more fabulous than my locker!"

"I hope so," Olivia said.

For a second, I wondered, did she just mean that she hoped her locker was fabulous? Or did she hope that hers looked better than mine? But then I felt silly thinking that. Mostly, I was superexcited to be doing the locker design. And I really liked knowing that Olivia admired my sense of style. She was turning out to be a really nice friend.

CHAPTER 13

The Monster at the Museum

Saturday was a pretty hectic day, because after my soccer game, I had to shower and change so I could make the one thirty train to Manhattan. It's always weird when I have to go in on Saturday because Dad and I don't have our usual sushi routine. But this time I had a plan: Dad was bringing Ava with him, and we were going to go shopping for Olivia's locker stuff in midtown, which is crowded and filled with all kinds of stores.

Ava ran up to me and gave me a big hug as soon as I got off the train.

"Mom says I can have dinner with you guys," she told me. "Yay!"

"I'm kind of in the mood for Italian," I said. "When it starts to get chilly out, I crave pasta."

"How about the Ravioli Hut?" Ava suggested. "They have forty-six different kinds of ravioli!"

I looked at Dad, and he shrugged. "Whatever you girls want. But you need to do some shopping first, right?"

The stores I needed were close to the train station, so we walked. Because it was Saturday afternoon, the streets were crowded with tourists. Dad walked right behind me and Ava, so he wouldn't lose us.

After about ten blocks we reached Dazzle, an accessories shop. They had the mirror I wanted, along with racks and racks of other amazing stuff, like jewelry, scarves, and hats. Dad went to get coffee, like he always does when he takes us shopping, and Ava and I walked around the shop.

Ava picked up two long, dangly earrings with keys hanging from them. They reminded me of Olivia's necklace. She held them up to her ears.

"What do you think?" she asked.

"Adorable!" I replied. "I think keys must be a big thing this year. Olivia has a necklace that would match those perfectly."

"So what are we getting for Olivia again?" Ava asked.

"I'm designing her locker." I reached into my

bag and took out the proposal I had created for Olivia. "I did a bunch of sketches and printed out samples of stuff, and she picked what she wanted. I'm going to buy it for her, and she'll pay me back."

"I thought you were saving for those shoes?" Ava asked.

"I know, but I don't have exactly enough yet, and anyway, Olivia will pay me on Monday," I replied.

"Wow, you're being totally professional," Ava told me, and the compliment meant a lot. That's what I was trying to do.

I bought the perfect mirror, just the right size and with this really pretty border with lots of bling on it. Then we headed to the Organizer Store two blocks down to get a special light that we could stick above the mirror so Olivia could see better when she put on her lip gloss. We got some small shelves there too.

"This is going to be an awesome locker," Ava said. "Olivia is lucky. Hey, I forgot to ask you. Did you see that polar bear movie yet?"

I shook my head. "I was supposed to go with Katie, but . . . well, Olivia came over."

"Wow, you're spending a lot of time with

Olivia," Ava remarked. "How does Katie feel about that?"

"I think she's a little bit hurt," I admitted. "But it's not fair. I'm still her friend. She's just sensitive, that's all."

"I'm just saying, you've been talking about Olivia a lot lately," Ava said.

I didn't get mad when Ava said that, because she's outside the situation, if you know what I mean. Since I moved to Maple Grove, she's always given me good advice about what happens there. So it got me thinking—maybe I was ignoring Katie a little bit. And that wasn't cool.

So that night, after we finished shopping, stuffed ourselves with spinach and cheese ravioli, and took Ava home, I stretched out on my bed and texted Katie.

Miss u. Want 2 hang out Monday?

Science report due Tuesday. ☹, Katie texted back right away.

Me too! Let's do it together! My house? I wrote.

K! ☺, Katie wrote back.

I have to admit I was feeling pretty good about things. Katie was happy, Olivia was happy, and I was

97

close to getting my dream shoes. I went to sleep with a smile on my face.

And then on Sunday, my good mood was totally destroyed.

Dad arranged for us to meet Lynne and Ethan at the museum. It's a huge, beautiful building with big stone steps and it's right across from Central Park. The steps were pretty crowded, so I looked around to see if I could guess who Lynne and Ethan might be. Then Dad pointed to a woman at the top step.

"Hello!" he called out, waving, and Lynne waved back.

She was wearing a plaid peacoat, a denim skirt, and knee-high black boots. Her hair kind of reminded me of Katie's—light brown and wavy. I didn't see what Ethan looked like right away because he was hiding behind his mom.

Lynne smiled as we walked up. "Mia, I'm so glad to meet you! Your dad has told me so much about you," she said.

"Thanks," I said. "It's nice to meet you too."

"And this is Ethan," Lynne said, reaching for his arm. But Ethan just grabbed on to her leg and held on.

I sort of knelt down and said in my friendliest voice, "Hi, Ethan. I'm Mia."

Ethan stuck his head out, and I saw a head of messy brown hair, blue eyes, and a runny nose.

"Go away!" he yelled, and then he ducked behind his mom again.

"I'm sorry," Lynne said. "Ethan is getting over a cold, and he didn't sleep well last night."

Dad looked behind Lynne. "Sorry you're feeling bad, little guy," he said, but Ethan didn't respond. Then Dad looked at Lynne and me and gave us a big smile. "What do you say we explore this museum?"

We followed Dad inside, and he paid for our admission.

"Can we look at the blue whale first?" I asked.

The blue whale is probably the most famous thing in the whole museum. It's a life-size model of a blue whale, the largest animal on Earth. It hangs from the ceiling and you can walk underneath it. It's totally incredible. Besides, I know Katie loves it, and I wanted to take a picture to send her.

"I want to see the dinosaurs!" Ethan yelled.

"We'll see the dinosaurs," Lynne said patiently. "But first we're going to see the whale."

"But I don't *like* the whale!" he said, stomping his foot.

"That's okay," I said. "We don't have to see the whale."

"No, it's all right," Lynne insisted. "Ethan has to learn to be patient."

So we walked to the big room where the whale is, and before we could even walk through the door, Ethan ran away like a rocket.

"Ethan!" Lynne cried, panicked.

"I'll get him," my dad volunteered.

Let me tell you, this kid was fast. Dad goes to the gym almost every day, but he had a hard time catching up with him. Then when he did catch up to him, you could hear Ethan screaming.

Lynne and I looked at each other.

"We'd better find them," Lynne said apologetically.

We followed the sound of the screaming to the dinosaur wing. Dad was holding Ethan's hand, but the kid was just yelling and yelling and people were staring. He ran to Lynne as soon as he saw us.

"Mommy! Mommy! I want to see the dinosaurs!" he wailed.

"It's fine," I insisted. "Let's see the dinosaurs."

Lynne and my dad gave in because we all stayed to see the dinosaurs. Ethan raced around and asked a million questions about each one. Finally, Ethan said he was hungry, and we went to the snack shop in the museum. It was packed, but we managed to find a table. My dad asked what we wanted, and then he got on line to get the food for us.

"I'll help," I offered.

"Don't worry, sit and relax," Dad said. "I want you guys to get to know one another."

I reluctantly sat down and Lynne smiled at me. "So, Mia, how do you like school this year?"

"Well, a lot better than I did before," I said, but before I could explain why, Ethan started whining and complaining about how hungry he was and asking if he could go back to see the dinosaurs. So Lynne and I couldn't have much of a conversation.

Finally, Dad came back with a tray of food. He put an order of chicken fingers in front of Ethan, along with a carton of apple juice.

Ethan picked up the juice and frowned.

"I wanted orange juice!" he yelled, and he slammed down the carton so hard that the cardboard container split and juice spilled all over the table.

"I'll get it!" Dad cried, and he jumped up and ran to get some napkins.

I was totally appalled. This kid was a monster! I imagined having to be his big sister and shuddered.

CHAPTER 14

Thank Goodness for Katie

$\mathcal{D}$ad didn't have much to say after the museum disaster, and I could tell that he was embarrassed and disappointed. I couldn't think of anything comforting to say to him, because all I could think about was how terrible it would be to live with Ethan.

The next morning, I told Katie the whole story on the bus, and she was very sympathetic. Then we said good-bye and headed to homeroom, where I handed Olivia a bag with all of her locker supplies.

"Oh my gosh, Mia, thank you, these are soooo awesome!" she squealed as she looked through the bag.

I handed her the receipts. "It came to forty-one dollars and thirty-six cents," I said.

Olivia absently took them from me. "Mmm

hmm," she said, and she tucked them into her notebook. She didn't say anything about paying me back.

"So you would not believe what happened to me yesterday," I said. "Remember I told you my dad wanted me to meet his girlfriend and her kid? Well, we went to the museum and—"

"So when are you going to put all the stuff up?" Olivia asked, interrupting me.

"Well, I thought we could do it together," I said. "Maybe tomorrow after school?"

"Can't we do it today?" Olivia asked.

"I'm working on my science report with Katie," I explained, and Olivia pouted.

"Okay," she said, with a long, drawn-out sigh. "I guess I'll have to wait."

If Olivia was trying to make me feel guilty, it didn't work. There was no way I was going to back out on Katie.

So that afternoon I was happy when Katie got out at the bus stop with me. Eddie was home, and he had cookies and milk on the dining room table for us. (My mom is the healthy snack person in the house, but Eddie is happier with a cookie than a carrot.) I got out my laptop, so Katie and I could work on our reports.

"I was thinking about what you said on the bus this morning," Katie said. "About Ethan. I feel so bad for you!"

"Thanks," I said. "He was totally awful!"

"But then I was thinking about Jake," Katie said. "He's better now, but he used to be really bratty sometimes, remember? Like that one time we were baking and he had, like, this tantrum because he wanted a cupcake and they weren't ready yet?"

I shuddered, remembering. "I didn't know a kid could be so loud."

"We should probably ask Emma, but I'm thinking that maybe little kids get better when they get older," Katie said. "And besides, your dad is just dating her, right?"

"I guess, but he really seems to like Lynne," I confided. "You should have seen him running around, doing everything. 'I'll get that!' 'I'll do that!' Like he's totally in love with her."

"Or maybe he's just being extra polite," Katie suggested.

I sighed. "I hope so," I said. "If not, I'll just buy a pair of earplugs."

Then I switched on my computer. "So, we need to find pictures of the endocrine system, right?"

"No, I want to do a report on dinosaurs!" Katie said, using a little kid's voice.

I started to laugh. "No, Katie, today we need to do a report on the endocrine system," I said, using my best dad impression.

"No!" Katie yelled. "Dinosaurs! Dinosaurs! Dinosaurs!"

Eddie stepped into the dining room. "Wow, you girls are really excited about your homework, aren't you?" he asked, and Katie and I started cracking up.

Katie totally made me feel better about everything, just like she always does. Which is just one more reason why I will always, always, always be her friend.

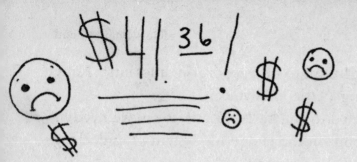

CHAPTER 15

Losing My Patience

The next day I kept my promise to Olivia, and we stayed after school to decorate her locker. I brought all the supplies we needed, like scissors and double-stick tape for the wallpaper, and a special hook for the mirror that wouldn't ruin the wallpaper (like mine was).

There were still kids in the hallway, people who don't take the bus or people who stay for after-school activities, and a lot of them were curious about what we were doing.

"Okay, so first we need to take everything out," I said, which wasn't going to be easy because even after only a few days, Olivia's locker was a total mess. I started taking out crumpled-up papers, but Olivia just stood there with her back against the locker next to hers, watching people go by.

"Those girls look totally cool," she said, nodding to two girls who walked past.

"Oh, I guess," I said. "They're a grade above us. I don't really know them."

Then this girl Hanna from our grade walked up.

"Hi, Olivia," she said. "What are you doing?"

"Mia and I are totally redecorating my locker," she said. "We, like, designed it from scratch. It's going to be soooo cool."

I noticed that Olivia said "we," which was pretty annoying. It was also kind of annoying that she wasn't actually doing any work. So I dumped a bunch of garbage in her arms.

"Here, throw this out," I said.

Olivia stuck her tongue out at me in a sort of funny way and went to throw out her trash. I piled her books and makeup boxes onto the floor and then got to work measuring and cutting the wallpaper. While I worked, Olivia just kept talking and talking.

"I mean, those BFC girls don't seem so bad," she was saying. "Maybe one day we could sit with them, you know?"

"Count me out," I told her. "I've been there before, and it didn't work out, remember?"

Olivia acted like she hadn't heard me, and she just kept talking about this cool outfit that Callie wore yesterday and wondering what Callie's closet looked like. Then she started talking about Emma's brothers.

"Matt Taylor is sooo cute," she said. "You guys must see him all the time when you make cupcakes, right?"

"Sometimes," I replied.

"And I heard Emma's oldest brother, Sam, is totally gorgeous," Olivia went on.

"Definitely," I agreed. I was too busy to feel chatty. Every time I tried to get Olivia to help, she found a way to get out of it. Like, when I asked her to put the double-sided tape on the back of the wallpaper, she kept saying, "Oh no, I can't get it to go on straight! You'd better do it, Mia. I'd ruin it."

Basically, I ended up doing the whole thing myself. When it was done, it looked pretty great. The light looked cool shining on the mirror, and the wallpaper was totally hot. Plus, I had found these strands of plastic jewels, and I strung them from the top shelf so that they dangled down. The whole effect was very cool.

"Mia, this is ah-may-zing!" Olivia cried when it was all done. She started snapping pictures with her phone. "My old friends are not going to believe this. Thank you sooooo much!"

So far, I had been shy about asking Olivia for the money for the locker stuff. But she seemed so happy that I figured this was a good time to bring it up.

"So, the forty-one dollars . . . ," I said. "I kind of used my shoe savings to get your stuff, so if you could get it back to me soon . . . like tomorrow, maybe? It's actually forty-one dollars and thirty-six cents. But I don't care about the change."

"Oh, of course!" Olivia promised. "I'll bring it in tomorrow, I swear!"

But Olivia didn't. When I got off the bus and walked up to her, I said, "So, Olivia, did you remember the money?"

"Oh my gosh, Mia, I'm soooo sorry!" she said. "I totally woke up late this morning because my mom didn't wake me up, and I, like, rushed out. Tomorrow, I promise."

"Oh, okay," I said, trying to hide my disappointment. After all, she had an excuse.

Then when we were in homeroom, Olivia did that thing where she made me feel sorry for her. She turned to look at me with big, sad eyes.

"So, you know, Mia, I keep hearing you and

Emma and Alexis and Katie talk about that party," Olivia said.

"Yeah, well, we're baking a lot of cupcakes for it," I explained.

"Well . . . it's just . . ." She did that pouty lip thing again. "I haven't been to a single party since I moved out here. It's soooo depressing. I feel like such a loser, you know? So I was wondering if maybe you could ask Emma if I could come."

"Well, we're not really hanging out at the party," I said hesitantly. "We're sort of working."

"I know you guys don't want me in the business, so don't worry about that," Olivia said. "But I'll come and help and do whatever. Come on, we'll have fun."

"Well . . ." I wasn't sure how my friends were going to feel about this.

"Oh, please, Mia?" Olivia asked, making a supersad face, the kind Jake uses on us when he wants an extra cupcake. "I really need to make some new friends in this town."

"Okay, I'll ask," I promised, even though I regretted the words as soon as they came out of my mouth. But it wasn't a terrible idea, really. It could be like a test, to see if Olivia fit in, in a Cupcake situation.

So homeroom went like it always does, and I went to my locker to get my math book, which I had forgotten to take out before. I turned the corner and saw Callie, Maggie, and Bella gathered in front of Olivia's locker.

"You will not believe what I did yesterday!" Olivia said, opening the door.

I wasn't sure if I heard right. What "I" did? Olivia hadn't done a thing!

"Ooh, Olivia, this is fabulous!" Maggie squealed. "Look at that wallpaper!"

"I love the mirror," Callie added.

"Yes, and I even put in a light so I can do my makeup," Olivia bragged. She didn't even mention my name! Can you believe that?

"Olivia, you totally have to decorate my locker for me," Maggie said.

"Me too," Bella added.

"That would be fun," Olivia said. "I'll start coming up with some ideas."

How is she going to do that? I wondered. But I guess that's her problem!

Anyway, I had to go to class, so I walked past Olivia's locker and waved.

"Hi, Olivia. Showing off your new locker?" I asked.

A guilty look crossed Olivia's face, and I knew she was wondering how much I had heard.

"Um, yeah," she said.

"See you later," I said, and walked away. I was starting to wish that I hadn't promised her I'd ask about Matt and Sam's party.

CHAPTER 16

From Good to Bad Again

That afternoon we went to Katie's house after school for a Cupcake meeting. Katie was kind of in a bad mood because Ms. Chen had announced today that we were going to play volleyball for a few weeks.

Katie is a fast runner, but she's a terrible volleyball player. Whenever a ball comes to her and she hits it, it goes all over the place. For a while, she had a horrible time playing volleyball, but it's been a little better because Emma, Alexis, and I are all in gym with her. So when we were playing, we made sure to run up and help her whenever the ball came her way.

Of course, we couldn't help her when she served the ball. I don't think she ever gets it over the net or on the right side. George Martinez (who I am sure likes her) teases her and calls her Silly Arms, but in a nice way, which cheers her up. But mostly she just hates volleyball.

"If I could go back in time, I would find the inventor of volleyball and convince him to keep his game to himself, so it wouldn't torture kids like me," Katie said as we were sitting around her kitchen table. She had her head in her hands and looked superbummed.

"I'm not sure if anyone actually invented volley-ball," Alexis said thoughtfully. "I mean, it's basically just hitting a ball back and forth. I bet cavemen did that."

"With what? Rocks?" Emma asked. "I don't think cavemen had volleyballs."

"You know what I mean," Alexis protested.

"Don't worry, Katie. It's only for a few weeks," I assured her. "Plus, we're in your class now, so we can make it fun."

Katie sighed. "I will never use the words 'volley-ball' and 'fun' in the same sentence."

Alexis brought us back to business, as usual. "So, we need to make up a schedule for the party on Saturday. We're baking on Friday night, right?"

"Right," Emma said. "Mom was wondering if

we could do it at one of your houses, because she needs to get our house ready for the party."

"We can probably do it here," Katie said.

"And what about the shopping?" Alexis asked.

"Mom and I are going to get everything tomorrow night," Emma replied. "We have to go shopping for the party, anyway. I'll bring it all with me on Friday."

Alexis gave us each a sheet of paper. "I printed out a copy of the final shopping list. I need everyone to check it and make sure we're not forgetting anything."

We all studied the list for a minute. Katie spoke up first.

"Looks good to me. But maybe we should put down that we specifically need creamy peanut butter. Chunky won't work so well."

Emma nodded and wrote on her list.

"I think it's fine," I added.

"All right," Alexis said. "So we bake, decorate, and pack on Friday night. The party starts at three, so we should probably get to Emma's by one or two to set up."

"We should probably put on the chocolate basketballs on Saturday," I said. "They might get soggy if we stick them in the icing the night before."

"Okay, so then we'll get there at one thirty?" Alexis asked, looking at Emma.

"That's fine," Emma replied. "I'll double-check with my mom."

It looked like we had a plan, which meant our meeting was about to end, and I still had something to bring up. I was definitely nervous about it.

"So, I need to ask you guys something," I said. "I know we don't want Olivia in the business, and I get that. But she feels really left out, and she asked if she could help with the party. She doesn't want money or anything, she just wants to come and hang out. She's lonely."

Katie started chewing on her finger and didn't say anything. Emma looked at Alexis, and then Alexis spoke up.

"I don't know, Mia," she said. "I mean, does she really want to hang out with *us* or just you? She doesn't seem very interested in the rest of us."

"I know, you said that before," I said. "But maybe it's because she doesn't feel welcome because we have this club and she doesn't belong to it. Listen, I know she's not perfect, but she doesn't have anyone else at the school to hang with."

"Well, if she wants to help . . . ," Emma said hesitantly. "I guess I could check with my brothers to make sure it's okay . . . since it's their party."

"Do we really have to?" Katie whined. "I mean, we sit with her every day at lunch. Isn't that good enough?"

Suddenly I felt a little angry and fed up.

"Why is hanging out with Olivia such a big deal for everybody?" I asked. I looked right at Katie. "It's, like, every time I want to make a new friend, you try to sabotage it. I'm not Callie, Katie. I'm not going to dump you."

Katie looked really stunned. Alexis and Emma exchanged a look, but didn't say anything.

"I'm going text Eddie to pick me up," I said, and I walked outside. I didn't like feeling this way. Mostly, I felt confused. Why couldn't everybody just be friends? Why did it have to be so complicated?

It also bugged me that I was sticking my neck out for Olivia while I was kind of mad at her too. It definitely was not cool of her to tell people that she had decorated the locker herself. And she still owed me that forty-one dollars!

I texted Olivia that night.

Sorry 2b a pest, but I no how hard it is 2 remember things in the am. Can you bring in the money 2mrw?

She replied right away.

I.M. So Sorry. Keep forgetting! 2mrw for sur.

Tx! I typed.

I hoped she would remember this time. Because I really didn't like how things were going.

I was kind of mad at Olivia. I was kind of mad at Katie. Emma and Alexis were annoyed with *me*. Unless I could figure out how to work things out, I wasn't going to have any friends left in Maple Grove at all!

CHAPTER 17

Did She Really Do That?

I got another text that night, from Emma.

Matt & Sam say Olivia can come.

Tx! I typed back. She will be excited.

I thought about texting Olivia, but I figured I could just tell her in person at homeroom. I knew how happy she would be. So maybe things were working out after all. I mean, Emma could have lied and said her brothers didn't want Olivia to come. So maybe my Cupcake friends were finally coming around about Olivia. (Or Emma and Alexis were, at least.)

So the next morning I decided to face the day

with a positive attitude. I was worried that the bus ride with Katie would be awkward, and at first she was a little quiet, but luckily, the new season for this cooking competition show we both like had just started, so we talked about that for the whole ride. It was obvious we both wanted to put the argument we had the night before behind us.

Then when I got to homeroom, I talked to Olivia.

"So, you can help at the party on Saturday," I said. "Can you get to Emma's house by one thirty?"

"Ooh, Mia, thank you!" Olivia said, practically knocking over her desk to hug me. "Just text me her address, and I'll be there. Oh my gosh, I'm not sure what to wear. Can I come over to your house today to see if you have anything I can borrow?"

I mentally went through my schedule in my head. "Um, sure," I said. "Meet me by my bus, okay? We're just going to wear team shirts and jeans to go with the sports theme. But maybe we can think of some cool ways to accessorize."

Olivia nodded, but I could tell she wasn't really listening, and instead she was mentally going through my closet.

"Maybe I can borrow that cute skirt you have

with the ruffles," she said, mostly to herself. "I have a shirt that would go great with that."

I noticed Olivia didn't say anything about paying me back the money, and I felt weird asking her again. So I let it slide. If she brought it with her, I could always get it from her after school at my house.

In gym third period, Ms. Chen made me and George team captains. I made sure to pick Katie, Emma, and Alexis for my team. George picked Olivia for his team before I had a chance. When Ms. Chen wasn't watching, one of us Cupcakers switched places with Katie, so that she would never have to serve. I could tell that she was grateful, and it made me feel good.

When the game was over and we all walked to the locker room, Olivia walked up to me.

"Oh my gosh, now I know why George calls Katie Silly Arms," she said. "She looks totally ridiculous out there! I'm surprised she didn't whack you in the face."

I stopped walking. "Olivia, Katie's really sensitive about that. George can tease her because they've been friends for a long time."

Olivia shrugged. "I'm just saying. It's sooo obvious because she's such a klutz!"

We have lunch right after gym, and I thought Olivia would spend the whole time talking about Matt and Sam's party and what she was going to wear. But when I walked into the cafeteria, I was surprised to see Olivia sitting at the BFC table!

Maybe she's just talking to them about something, I thought. I bet she'll move over to our table in a minute.

But I unpacked my hummus and crackers and carrot sticks, and Katie unpacked her P-B-and-J, and then Emma and Alexis came to the table with trays of spaghetti and meatballs. Olivia stayed at the BFC table. I glanced over and saw that her lunch bag was open and she was eating sushi.

Alexis noticed too and raised an eyebrow.

"Well, that's interesting," she said. She looked at me. "Did she tell you she was changing tables?"

"No," I admitted. "But I guess she's free to sit wherever she wants, right? I mean, it's good that she has other friends, right?"

I believed what I said, but at the same time I was kind of hurt. I mean, I thought I was Olivia's best friend at the school. So why wouldn't she at least tell me she was sitting with the BFC? And was it permanent?

It's just lunch, I told myself. *No big deal.* And in a

way, it was nice that she wasn't sitting with us. Katie was a lot more relaxed and Alexis wasn't rolling her eyes or shooting looks at Emma when she thought I couldn't see her.

After school, I waited outside the bus for Olivia, so we could go to my house like we planned. I waited until every single person got on the bus, but there was no sign of Olivia anywhere. Then when the bus driver said, "Time to go, Mia," I had no choice but to get on the bus.

Katie gave me a quizzical look.

"Olivia was supposed to take the bus with us," I explained. "But I don't see her."

"Maybe because she's with them," she said, pointing out the window, and I looked over her shoulder to see Olivia walking down the street with Callie, Maggie, and Bella.

"Oh," was all I said, because I wasn't sure what to say. I felt even more hurt than I did at lunch.

Then I waited to hear what Katie would say, because she could have said something like, "Wow, she dumped you" or something like that. But Katie is too nice to say something like that. So she said, "Maybe she just forgot."

"Yeah," I said, thinking of the forty-one dollars. "She forgets a lot of things."

I was starting to think Olivia might not be a silver friend or even a bronze friend. And then I got even madder at her later, when I was doing my homework and Mom came home from a meeting in the city.

"Mia, you're not going to believe this," Mom said after she bent down to give me a kiss on the head. "I was walking past the Kara Karen store, and they're having a forty-percent off sale this weekend! I think you have enough to pay for your half now, don't you? I'll take you on Sunday."

I quickly did the math in my head. I definitely had enough . . . except for the fact that I had laid out that money for Olivia's locker.

"Well, kind of," I said. "I used part of my money to buy stuff when I redecorated Olivia's locker. She said she would pay me back, but she keeps forgetting."

Mom shook her head. "Mia, that's not right," she said. "It was very nice of you to help out your new friend, but she needs to pay you back."

"I asked her yesterday," I said.

"Then ask her again," Mom said firmly.

I cringed at the thought, but I knew Mom was right.

"You know, Mia, I have some concerns about

Olivia," Mom said, sitting down next to me. "This business of forgetting to pay you back, when she knows how much you want those shoes. She doesn't seem as . . . well, as nice as your other friends."

For once, I didn't have the heart to defend Olivia. Mom was right.

"I know," I said. "It's just . . . She was new, and I didn't want her to feel weird or alone or anything."

"And that's one thing I love about you, Mia," Mom said. "You have such a good heart. Helping out Olivia was the right thing to do. But if she's not being a good friend to you, then you don't have to remain friends with her."

I thought about Olivia ditching me for the BFC today. "She might have already found some other friends, anyway," I told her.

I didn't know what felt worse—realizing I might have lost a new friend or knowing that the Kara Karen shoes were in my grasp, but I couldn't get them. I decided to text Olivia again that night.

What happened after school?

Oh no! Totally spaced. Callie asked me to walk home with BFC, she replied.

I noticed that the word "sorry" was completely absent from her text.

So those shoes I want are on sale, I typed. Can u pls bring in the $ 2mrw?

K, Olivia texted back, and she didn't say anything else.

The next morning I just asked Olivia outright, "So, do you have the money?"

She immediately got defensive. "Come on, Mia, chill out! I've got a lot on my mind, you know? I'll bring it on Saturday."

"That would be good," I said. "Because I need the money on Sunday."

"Okay, okay," Olivia said, acting really dramatic about it. "It's not like I borrowed a million dollars or anything."

I couldn't wait for the day to be over, so I could go to Katie's and make cupcakes. But instead of going quietly, the day dragged on. And then gym was a nightmare.

We have, like, more than thirty kids in our gym class, and Ms. Chen divides us into two groups to play volleyball at the two nets set up in the gym. Then she picks two people from each group to pick team members (four teams, two nets), so there's eight people on a team.

Anyway, on Friday I was in a group with all of my Cupcake Club friends, as well as Olivia and Maggie and Bella. Ms. Chen picked Olivia and Wes Kinney to be captains.

Olivia got to pick first, and she picked me. Then she picked Maggie and Bella next, and then some boys. Emma and Alexis got picked for Wes's team. And then it came down to two people: Katie and Jacob Lobel, who's the shortest kid in our whole class.

It was Olivia's turn, and I was sure she was going to pick Katie. But instead she pointed to Jacob.

"I'll take Jacob," she said.

I couldn't believe it. Then Wes made it worse, because he groaned and said, "Oh, great, we're stuck with Katie!" On our team, Maggie and Bella started to crack up.

I was really angry this time.

"Why did you do that?" I asked, pulling Olivia aside. "Katie's our friend. You should have picked her!"

Olivia shrugged. "I'm the captain. I'm supposed to pick the best players. We want to win, don't we?"

It was another perfectly reasonable-sounding Olivia excuse. Except this time I wasn't buying it.

"Some things are more important than winning," I said, and then I walked away.

CHAPTER 18

The Real Olivia

I was so relieved when school was over on Friday and we all headed over to Katie's for some cupcake baking. Her mom ordered pizzas, we cranked up the oven and the music on my iPod, and then we got down to the business of cupcake baking.

The whole process was kind of complicated because both kinds of cupcakes were filled with different things. First, we baked seven dozen vanilla cupcakes. Even though the basketball and swim-team cupcakes were different, they both started with plain vanilla cupcakes. At first we were going to make six dozen, but we agreed it's always good to make a few extra. While they cooled, we ate our pizza and talked.

I didn't want things to be tense between me and

Katie anymore, so I just jumped right in.

"So, that wasn't nice what Olivia did in gym today," I said.

Katie shrugged. "That's all right. I'm used to being picked last."

"Well, I thought it was wrong, and I told her so," I said, because I wanted Katie to know. She smiled.

"Thanks, Mia."

"Anyway, it didn't matter because we beat you guys, anyway," Alexis pointed out. "So maybe Olivia's team-picking strategies aren't so great."

"Yeah, you kicked our butts," I admitted, because it was true.

"Do you think she'll still come to the party tomorrow?" Emma wondered.

"I don't know," I answered honestly. "I'll try texting her later. I know she's been hanging with the BFC, but she really wanted to come."

When we finished our pizza, it was time to fill the cupcakes. Katie and Emma made some instant vanilla pudding from a box to fill the swim-team cupcakes. Alexis and I got to work on filling three dozen of the cupcakes with jelly. We used Katie's cupcake injector, which is kind of like the cupcake plunger she bought, but instead of removing the cake, you fill the injector with jelly or whatever, and then you stick it into the cupcake and squirt the jelly right into the middle.

It's kind of messy, and pretty soon, Alexis and I were laughing and getting jelly all over the place.

"Hey, you're supposed to fill cupcakes with it, not paint with it!" Katie teased.

"Oh yeah, well, let's see how well you guys do with the pudding," I teased back.

Katie held up the bowl to show me the vanilla pudding inside. "So far, no spills," she said.

Looking at the pudding gave me an idea. "Oh my gosh, we should totally dye the pudding blue!" I cried. "Then when you bite into it, the pudding will kind of look like water."

"Nice! Plus, it will be a real surprise," Emma agreed.

Katie picked up a tube of gel coloring. "Blue it is," she said, and she added some drops and stirred until the pudding was a perfect shade of swimming-pool blue.

After both kinds of cupcakes were filled, we put peanut-butter frosting on the jelly ones and piped blue frosting on the pudding ones to look like waves.

"Those peanut-butter cupcakes will look even better with the basketballs," I said.

Alexis slapped her forehead. "Oh my gosh, the basketballs!" she said. "We still need to make them."

I looked up at the clock, and it was already eight. "We can do them in an hour, I promise."

Emma had picked up some plastic chocolate molds with small circles. We melted orange-colored chocolate pieces in the microwave, poured them into the molds, and then put the molds in the freezer until the chocolate got firm. Then we popped them out and used a toothpick dipped in dark chocolate to draw dark lines on each piece to look like a basketball.

"We can only do one side at a time," I realized as we carefully placed the chocolate pieces on a cookie sheet. "Otherwise, the lines on the other half will get smooshed."

Katie yawned. "Maybe we should do the other sides tomorrow."

We all agreed. "Definitely," I said. "That way the lines can set overnight."

The next day, Mom drove me to Katie's, so I could help her pack up the car with all our cupcakes, plus the chocolate basketballs. When we got to the Taylors' house, Alexis was already there, and Emma's mom and dad were running around, getting everything ready. As soon as Katie and I placed the cupcake carriers onto the kitchen table, Matt walked up and lifted the lid.

"Dibs on the first cupcake!" he said, reaching for one.

Emma slapped his hand. "Not yet, Matt. Wait until the party starts."

"But it's my birthday," Matt argued. "I get special tasting rights."

Then Sam came into the kitchen. He looks kind of like Matt, except taller, and he was wearing his swim-team T-shirt.

"Matt's right," Sam said. "Come on, birthday rights."

It's easy to argue with Matt, but Katie and I both have a little crush on Sam. We looked at each other, and then at Emma.

She sighed. "Okay. One each."

I handed Matt a P-B-and-J cupcake. "It's not really done yet. It's going to have a basketball on top."

Matt took a big bite. "Awesome! Jelly explosion."

"I've got pudding in mine," Sam said. "I bet that was your idea, right, Katie? You're cupcake geniuses."

Katie turned bright red. "It was Mia's idea to make the pudding blue."

"All right, enough!" Emma yelled. "Out of the kitchen! We've got work to do."

We got busy finishing the chocolate basketballs, and we were almost finished when Mrs. Taylor ran into the kitchen. A few strands of hair had come loose from her ponytail, and she looked frazzled.

"Girls, I'm setting out all the food on the dining room table, and it's getting pretty crowded," she said. "So maybe you could just put out one tray of each kind of cupcake to start and keep them filled during the party."

Alexis nodded. "No problem, Mrs. Taylor. We've got it under control."

Emma's mom gave us a grateful smile and then raced out of the kitchen.

We had the cupcakes set up in about an hour, and then we pitched in and helped Emma's mom and dad set up the folding chairs in the backyard. It was a slightly chilly day, but still sunny and warm enough to be outside.

"So, it looks like Olivia's not coming after all," Alexis remarked as we positioned the chairs around a large table.

"I guess not," I said. "She never answered the text I sent last night."

Then a football came sailing out of the sky and knocked over one of the chairs. We looked up to see a small army of teenage boys walking up the Taylors' driveway and into the backyard.

"Yo! Where's the party?" one of them yelled.

"Quick! Let's retreat to the kitchen!" Emma suggested, and we followed her without question. Mrs. Taylor whizzed by us.

"What was I thinking? Two parties at once?" she asked no one in particular.

Then we heard a knock on Emma's back door.

"Hello? Emma?"

It was Olivia! Emma went to answer the door, and Olivia walked in.

"Your dad said you girls were in here," she said. "I hope I'm not too late."

None of us said anything right away, because we were all sort of stunned by Olivia's outfit. We were all dressed in jeans and T-shirts or sporty shirts, to go with the sports team theme. But Olivia had completely ignored my advice and was dressed up like she was going to a dance or something. She had on a black bubble skirt with pink polka dots, a black top with lace down the front, tights, and heels.

Then I noticed—they weren't just any heels. They were *my* heels! Olivia was wearing the Kara Karen shoes!

"The shoes!" I blurted out, pointing.

"Aren't they fabulous?" Olivia asked, lifting up a foot so we could all see.

"Yes, I know they're fabulous, because I'm the one who told you about them," I said. "When did you get them?"

"Well, my dad took me into the city last night, and wouldn't you believe it, they were on sale! I couldn't resist," Olivia said.

I didn't know whether to scream or cry. I was sure Olivia had used the forty-one dollars she owed me to get those shoes. Alexis must have noticed the look on my face, and she quickly handed Olivia a tray of P–B–and–J cupcakes.

"Olivia, since you're here to help, would you mind seeing if the cupcake tray in the dining room needs to be refilled?" she asked.

Olivia made a face and stepped back. "I don't want to get icing all over my new shirt!" she said. "You guys are better dressed for that than I am. Besides, these shoes are really hard to walk in. The toes are so pointy!"

It was all I could do to keep from screaming.

Katie took the tray from Alexis. "I'll do it. The dining room is full of boys. I bet they've emptied both trays by now."

"Boys?" Olivia asked. She walked (or wobbled, is more like it) over to the doorway and peeked inside the dining room. Then she turned around and took the plate from Katie.

"That's okay, I'll do it," she said. "I'll just be extra careful."

She put one hand on her hip and walked into the dining room. We headed in after her to watch the scene unfold. Olivia strolled right up to Matt and Sam. They were talking with their friends and didn't notice her. Olivia began to twirl her hair.

"I heard you boys needed some more cupcakes," she said.

"Oh my goodness!" Alexis cried, turning to us. "Do you know what we're seeing? The rise of Sydney the Second!"

Katie, Emma, and I gasped. I couldn't believe I hadn't seen it before.

"Well, she's not *exactly* like Sydney," Katie said. "But they do have some things in common."

"They're both mean," Alexis said.

"And boy crazy," Emma added.

"And underhanded," I said, thinking of how

Olivia bought the shoes. "And self-absorbed."

It was like I was seeing Olivia clearly for the first time. Every time she tried to make me feel sorry for her, she was just manipulating me. Olivia wasn't a silver friend or even a bronze friend. She was a totally fake, plastic friend.

Olivia pranced over with an empty tray. "Emma, your brothers are so adorable! They need more cupcakes. Can you get me a plate so I can bring them some more?"

"You can get them yourself, Olivia," Emma said. "They're on the kitchen table."

Olivia rolled her eyes. "Well, I didn't know I'd be, like, part of the waitstaff!" she huffed, and marched into the kitchen.

"What does she thinking 'helping' means?" Alexis muttered.

Olivia stomped back out with an annoyed look on her face. She still had one hand on her hip and was holding the tray on the other hand. She started wandering around and she must have been looking for Sam, but I had seen him take his plate of food outside.

Then all of a sudden . . . *Blam!* Olivia lost her balance in the shoes and fell forward. Matt was nearby, and he sprinted forward and grabbed her arm, keeping her from hitting the floor. But the cupcakes went flying everywhere, and a bunch of them hit Olivia. She had a blob of blue icing on her forehead, and her new shirt was streaked with peanut-butter frosting.

CHAPTER 19

The Cupcaketeers: Together Again

"Oh nooooo!" Olivia wailed.

There was a big commotion as the boys scraped cupcakes off their jeans and picked up the fallen cupcakes from the floor. Then Matt yelled out, "Hey, it's not a party until somebody smashes a cupcake!"

Everybody started laughing, and Olivia's face turned red. She spun around and pointed at Katie.

"Hey, Silly Arms, you really need to control yourself!" she yelled.

The room got quiet, and Katie turned pale. I quickly stepped in.

"Olivia, Katie wasn't anywhere near you," I said. "You tripped over your pointy shoes. And calling Katie names is not cool."

Olivia looked furious. She wiped icing off her

shirt. "I don't get this club, Mia. I mean, you're just waitresses. This is not cool. Or fun. I'd rather hang out at the mall with the BFCs."

"No one is stopping you," I said evenly, and Olivia started to storm out with her head held high.

"Say, Olivia, when you have a chance, I'd really like that money you owe me," I called after her.

Olivia stopped and then turned around.

"You know, for all the stuff I bought when I decorated your locker. So I could buy the shoes," I said, pointing to her feet. "Those shoes I showed you. I think it's so great that we both have the same taste in decorating and fashion, don't you?"

"Um, whatever, I'll bring it next week," she said, and then she marched out the back door.

We were all quiet for a minute.

"Something tells me I won't ever get that money back," I said. "But honestly? Those shoes don't seem so fabulous anymore."

Then we all started to giggle.

"I'm sorry, but that was kind of funny!" Emma said.

"She had icing from head to toe!" Alexis said, shaking her head.

"Thanks for sticking up for me," Katie added.

"That's what friends do," I told her. "Listen,

guys, I'm really sorry about everything. I was just trying to be nice."

Katie hugged me. "You don't have to try. You *are* nice!"

"All right, let's end this love fest," Alexis said. "We have some cupcakes to clean up."

"I'll do it," I offered. "It's kind of my fault that Olivia was here."

"No way," Emma said. "We're a club. We do things together."

It didn't take long to clean up the mess, and pretty soon we were able to enjoy the party. There were two giant hero sandwiches and potato salad to eat, but while our cupcakes looked gorgeous, we waited until the party was over to have one. Luckily, we always make extra cupcakes, just in case something happens . . . like if someone drops a bunch on the floor! There were six cupcakes left over, so we each took one and retreated to the kitchen.

Alexis held out her cupcake. "A toast! To another successful Cupcake Club project!" she said.

"Hear, hear!" we all cried, and then we clinked our cupcakes together.

"And," Alexis said with a mischievous look in her eyes, "to getting rid of Sydney the Second at our lunch table!"

"I'll second that!" I cried. "To the four best Cupcaketeers—and the four best friends—ever!"

We clinked cupcakes again, and then we each took a bite. Mine was delicious—but the sweetest thing of all was that everything was good with my friends again.

Emma,
smile and say
"cupcake!"

CHAPTER 1

On Pins and Needles

I woke up extra early this Saturday morning to frost the mini cupcakes I was delivering to our number-one client, Mona, at The Special Day bridal salon. Well, the truth was, frosting wouldn't take long, but I wanted to wash and set my hair in my mom's big rollers before I went to the bridal salon. I would be modeling today for Mona's clients, and I wanted to try a new hairstyle and see what everyone at the shop thought.

It's kind of crazy how I started modeling for Mona. One Saturday morning I was making a regular cupcake delivery to the store (my friends and I in the Cupcake Club have a cupcake business, and Mona buys cupcakes from us for her Saturday brides each week), and an important mystery client was there for an early showing of dresses. It turned out to be Romaine Ford, our only hometown celebrity, and I ended up modeling junior bridesmaid dresses for her because there was no one else available. Meeting Romaine Ford and everything that came after that was the most exciting part of my life yet.

Since then, I've been modeling for Mona about once or twice a month for trunk shows, which is when specialty designers bring in their line for the day. It's fun. I get to dress up and sometimes have my hair styled (no makeup, though! It could ruin the dresses!) and hang out in a totally girlie environment for the morning, away from my three smelly brothers. Best of all, Mona pays me.

So this morning I showered, then put on my fancy jeans and a pretty turtleneck sweater, some tiny pearl stud earrings, and a belt. Then I rolled my hair and forgot all about it for a while as I finished up the cupcakes. Well, until my brother Matt walked into the kitchen and fell down on the floor laughing. I guess I looked pretty funny with my hair all in rollers, but there are times like these when I really wish I had a sister. Anyway, it only took about half an hour to frost and pack the cupcakes since they're minis, which are not much wider than a quarter. Mona loves them. Brides are always on diets, so they're hungry, which makes them cranky. These cupcakes are so tiny, no one can resist, and she says they make cranky brides friendlier. Isn't that funny?

Afterward, I ran the blow-dryer over my curlers to really set my hair, then I unpinned the rollers and swung my head from side to side. My hair is a very yellow blond on top, from the sun, but underneath it's a much darker shade. The curls made the colors all swirly and mixed together, and the style gave me a lot of height. I looked two inches taller! I laughed at the sight of it. It might be too much, but who cared? It was just an experiment, anyway. Well, my mom might care. She's always concerned about being "age appropriate."

My mom called up from the kitchen that we had to go or I'd be late, so I flipped off the bathroom light and took the stairs down, two at a time. As I swung around the banister and into the kitchen, my mom turned around and then did a double take.

"Oh, Emma! Your hair looks gorgeous!" she said with a gasp.

I grinned. "Thanks! You don't think it's too much?"

My mom laughed. "Well, maybe for soccer

practice or something, but under the circumstances, I think it will be a huge success!" She smoothed her own perky blond ponytail and laughed again, looking down at her Nike sweatpants and Under Armor top. "I am feeling very underdressed!"

"You look great, Mama," I said, calling her by my private baby name for her. "You're the prettiest mom in school." I grabbed my jacket off the hook in my locker in the mudroom, stepped over about five piles of sweaty boys' sporting goods, and headed out to the car.

"Thank you, lovebug, you do say the sweetest things, even if they're not always true!"

At The Special Day, Mona and her assistants were bustling around getting things set up for the day's trunk show.

The Special Day is just what you would imagine if you were trying to picture the most awesome, over-the-top, bridal store. It's like a magical castle, and someday that's where I want to buy my wedding dress. First of all, outside the store they have beautiful green trees, and topiaries in white wooden flower boxes, and a pretty white awning with white lanterns hanging on either side of the door. It looks like something from movies I've seen of Paris. Then, inside is white, white, white everywhere. A boy couldn't last one minute in there without ruining something, I tell you. There are thick white pile carpets, which make it really quiet; superplush white sofas and chairs that you sink into; low white marble coffee tables where tea is served in fine white china; and everywhere are white boxes of white Kleenex, because everyone cries when women try on wedding dresses. Once, I even saw Mona tear up when a young woman with cancer came in to try on her dress. She was bald from her treatment, but very brave and getting healthier, and Mona cried when she saw her in her beautiful dress.

Today, Mona's main assistant, Patricia, came striding over to help me with my cupcake carriers. "Oh, Emma! Your hair! You look incredible!" said Patricia.

I smiled. "Thanks. It was just an experiment."

"Well, it looks wonderful. Mona! Come see Emma's new hairstyle!"

Mona looked up from the rack of dresses she was arranging, and I saw her tilt her head and squint at me. "Emma!" she cried. (Mona is really dramatic, by the way. Did I mention that?) She raced across the store toward me, her arms outstretched. "Darling! You look divine! Simply divine!" She had her

151

hands on my arms, and now she pulled me in for a European-style two-cheek kiss. I laughed.

Mona said, "Oh, Patricia, isn't she divine?"

Smiling, Patricia nodded and added, "Divine!"

(Did I mention that "divine" is Mona's favorite word?) But now Mona stopped gushing over me and patted her severe black bun. "Patricia!" she snapped, all business now. "I have an idea!"

"Yes, Mona? What is it?" asked Patricia. Patricia is very patient, but I guess I don't need to mention that either.

Mona circled me, looking at my new hair with her arms folded, tapping her chin, slightly bent at the waist. "Mm-hmm. Mm-hmm. Yes. Yes!" After what felt like an eternity, she looked up at Patricia with a gleam in her eye. "Call Emma's mother and ask if we can photograph her today, and if so, could we use it in the paper. Then if she says yes, call Joachim and get him over here on the double. I'd like to run another ad!"

I raised my eyebrows at Patricia and she raised hers back at me, and we smiled like coconspirators. An ad?! Holy smokes! *Wait until I tell my friends,* was all I could think! I prayed my mom said yes. Sometimes my parents can be funny about stuff like that—they always are nice when people tell them

I'm pretty, like if we're out to dinner or something, but they always tell me after that looks don't last and that schoolwork and teamwork are more important than appearances. I know what they mean, but I still like it when people say I'm pretty. Especially because I don't think I'm pretty all the time; only when I try a little and, like, wear something fancy or do my hair. Otherwise I think I just look normal.

I went with Patricia to sort through the dresses I'd wear today while she dialed my mom's cell on the cordless phone. Today's dresses were by Jaden Sacks, a famous designer from New York City. The line is superchic and exclusive. She usually only sells in her boutique on Madison Avenue. I know this because Mona told me the week before. She was very excited to be able to carry the dresses in the store. The junior bridesmaid dresses were gorgeous, made of incredible materials—thick, slippery satin that pooled in my hand and slid through my fingers like quicksilver; pleated sheer silk so light and thin, it was like cotton candy on my skin; and lace that was somehow detailed and fancy on one side but cotton soft on the underside so it buffered me from the scratchiness of the stitching. The designs were simple—fashion forward but not tacky or overdone. Jaden Sacks is famous for using the finest supplies and craftspeople. Mona also told me that, but I looked it up on the Internet, too. Her dresses for brides are not traditional puffy "wedding cakes" with lots of layers, but rather columns or sheaths or mermaids with trains. Very glamorous and understated. Her dresses for junior bridesmaids don't really look like bridesmaids dresses. They aren't too poufy or lacy or anything, and they don't look like mini brides, but they still look what my mom would call "age appropriate." Which is good, because when it comes to modeling, my mom is all over being age appropriate. Mona has to show Mom all the dresses I'll wear beforehand, so she can okay them. It's kind of crazy. I mean, how can a bridesmaid dress be too sexy? But Mona says you'd be surprised.

Patricia whispered to me as she waited for my mom to pick up the phone, telling me that Mona was hoping Jaden Sacks might consider letting her carry the dresses for good, selling the line as a regular attraction at the store. Mona had already run a number of ads in the local paper about today's trunk show, and she was expecting a big crowd—not just brides but local fashionistas who were curious to see the exclusive line on their home turf. (I already knew that one of my best friends, Mia, and her mom, Mrs. Valdes, who were major fashionistas and were clients of Mona's, were coming today to inspect the line and cheer on Mona. I couldn't wait to tell Mia about the potential ad!)

I could hear Patricia speaking to my mom.

"Oh, Mrs. Taylor! Hi! It's Patricia at The Special Day! No, everything's fine. She's here. Everything is wonderful." There was a pause. "No! The hair is divine! That's actually why I'm calling you. Mona loved it so much that she had an idea to shoot photos of Emma today to run in an ad in the paper, and she wanted to know if that would be okay with you. We'd pay her extra, of course." There was another pause. "Yes, I totally understand. No, it's not a problem at all. Okay, talk soon. Bye!" Patricia clicked the off button on the phone and set the receiver on the bench in the large fitting room. I waited for Patricia to give me the scoop. When she didn't immediately say anything, I had to ask.

"What did she say?!" I couldn't contain my excitement any longer.

"She said it sounded like fun, but she wanted to talk it over with your father before she gave her permission."

"What? That is such a bummer!" I complained. I knew it was babyish, but I didn't care. How could my mom even think of saying no to an opportunity like this? My mom was protective, but oh boy, my dad was even more protective of me. There's no way he'd say yes.

"Hey, modeling is a big deal," Patricia reminded me gently. "You're talking about putting your photo out there for all the world to see. It might seem like fun for you, but maybe your parents are worried it will give you an image that's not consistent with what they want for you. I completely respect your mother's response. Trust me"—Patricia rolled her eyes—"in the fashion business you get plenty of mothers who are just the opposite—pushing their very young daughters at you, willing to sell their souls to the devil just to make some money off their child's looks before they change or get braces or whatever. It's a tough business."

"One ad doesn't mean I'm in the modeling business!" I protested.

Patricia smiled a wry smile. "It might," she said. "I'm calling Joachim, just in case, and telling him to stand by." She grabbed my hand and squeezed, then handed me my first dress and motioned that she was leaving.

I beamed at Patricia and held up my crossed fingers as she left. Then I began to get ready. I hate changing in front of other people, so Mona got me a slip to wear under the dresses—it's kind of like a long stretchy nude-colored camisole, and it makes me feel more comfortable, in case someone accidentally barges in. But Patricia always leaves me alone to get the slip on and get started, and she calls in to make sure I'm ready before she comes back. We have a good routine now, and we totally get each other. It's kind of weird to think that one of my friends could be forty years older than me and working full-time in a bridal salon, but I'd have to say that's the case with me and Patricia.

The first Jaden Sacks dress was just so gorgeous. It had a high square neckline and what Patricia called "tulip" sleeves, which were capped kind of midway down my upper arm with overlapping petals of fabric. Then a high plain waist with a pale blue ribbon to define it, and a floor-length skirt of satin that swished heavily as I walked. The best part was it had a very light tulle underskirt in a pale blue that matched the ribbon and peeked out only when I moved. I loved it.

I called Patricia, and she came back in, the phone pressed to hear ear, nodding. Whoever she was talking to wouldn't let her get a word in edgewise. I hoped it wasn't my mom!

I watched her face in the mirror as she bent her knees and clutched the receiver between her shoulder and chin so she could tie my ribbon with both hands. Then she leaned to the side to look at me in the mirror and gave me two thumbs-up and a wink. That meant I looked great. But who was on the phone?

"Uh-huh. Yes. Yes. Okay. Right." Patricia was nodding again.

I knitted my eyebrows together and mouthed, *My mom?* I was on pins and needles waiting to hear. But Patricia shook her head and covered the receiver with her hand. *Joachim,* she mouthed, and she rolled her eyes for the second time today. "Right. Well, listen, Joachim, that's all great. I think your vision sounds wonderful, and we will have all the snacks on hand that you requested, as well as a space roped off for your shoot, and total privacy. Yes. I understand it will be a Sunday rate because it is so last-minute. I will confirm as soon as I hear back from the model. Thank you."

Patricia sighed a deep sigh and sat down heavily on the bench. "This is going to be a really long day," she said.

designed by JAYDEN SACKS!

CHAPTER 2

American Beauty

$\mathcal{M}$y parents were killing me! It was midmorning, and they still hadn't called Patricia back yet. Meanwhile, the store was packed, and Mona had made one of the assistants hide the cupcakes in the back because all the people who came to just look at the dresses were eating them, and there weren't going to be any left for the scheduled brides who might actually buy dresses. I knew that my best friend Alexis, who was the business brains of our Cupcake Club, would die if she thought we were missing a business opportunity, so I borrowed Patricia's phone and called her house to see if she could rush over a few dozen more minis and some business cards to lay around. She said she would and that she'd call Katie and Mia, the other Cupcakers, to come and help if they could, just to speed things along. She hoped to be there by midafternoon. Feeling proud of that accomplishment, I raced off to change again.

Mona wanted me to rotate looks every half hour, working my way through the six junior bridesmaid dresses and then taking a lunch break and starting over. By eleven thirty I was starting to fade. I put on the final dress before lunch. It was an Asian-influenced dress Patricia called a "cheongsam." It was made of white satin, with white dragons embroidered all over it, and it had short sleeves and a high Mandarin collar all piped in white. The dress was very fitted, with a diagonal flap across the front that closed with small Chinese rope catches called "frogs." I loved the look of it. It would be really cool to have a Chinese wedding, Patricia and I decided, with Chinese food and a tea ceremony and fireworks! As Patricia fastened the final frog, the store's phone rang and Patricia answered it. "Hello! It's The Special Day!"

I was adjusting my dress, looking in the mirror, when she said, "Hi, Mrs. Taylor. Of course, she's right here." And she handed me the phone. "It's your mom. I'll be at the front desk when you're finished." She left, closing the door discreetly behind her.

I wished I could sit, but the tight dress made it impossible. Mentally, I scratched the idea of the Chinese wedding. The clothes were too snug! I leaned against the wall instead. "Hi, Mom. Can I do it?!" I asked impatiently.

"Hi, honey. Your dad and I have had a long talk, and we think there are pros and cons to being in the ad—"

"But, Mom!" I interrupted, ready to unleash the torrent of reasons I'd been stewing about all morning.

"No interrupting, Emma. Let me say my piece," said my mother in the stern voice she mostly uses on the boys. When I hear it, I know she means business.

"Fine," I muttered, feeling more in control for saying it, but also hoping she wouldn't hear me or I'd get in trouble for being fresh.

"Your father and I are nervous about the idea of you being in an ad. We are not sure this is a route you should be taking in life. As you know, we think your looks are a wonderful gift, but they are just one of many gifts you have that you need to develop. Your father and I also aren't crazy about the whole beauty culture in this country; we see eating disorders and masses of makeup and insecurity and competition among young girls, and it is just not healthy. You need to keep a level head. In addition, we don't love the idea of your photo being out there for all the world to see. Some weirdo might clip it out and hang it on his wall, and that gives us the creeps."

"Mom!" I protested. But that *was* kind of creepy, now that she mentioned it.

She continued. "We also want you to know that being photographed by professionals is hard work. If you agree to do this for Mona, there is to be no eye rolling or sulking or slouching or all the many things you pull when we try to take a family photo at home."

"But that's totally different!" I cried.

"I know, but it's something to bear in mind. Modeling is hard work," she repeated.

"I know." I sighed in exasperation, looking down at my seat-preventing dress.

There was a pause on the other end of the phone.

"Mom?" I asked.

"Yes. So, if you understand all those things, and more, and are still interested, Dad and I consent to having you photographed for an ad—just this once. Okay?"

I couldn't believe it!

"Yay! Thanks, Mom! Thank you so much! It will be great. Don't worry!"

"And Dad will be there to supervise."

"Wait, *what?*"

"Just have Patricia call him with the timing. Good-bye!" And she hung up.

I stared at the receiver in shock. My *dad* was coming to The Special Day? To supervise me?

OMG!

At twelve I took off the Chinese dress with relief and went to a Mexican fast-food restaurant in the food court to grab a quick bite of lunch. After I ate my burrito, I still had twenty minutes of my hour break time left, so I strolled to the bookstore and went to the beauty section. They had books on modeling there, and I wanted to flip through one or two before I got back to the store.

I had to think about the whole modeling thing in a new way now.

Before, it had been the one lucky occasion when I'd modeled for Romaine. Then, when Mona had asked me back, it had seemed like a fun way to earn money. Since my family is perpetually short on cash (especially me), I always like the opportunity to make a little more. I'm not a future CEO or anything like Alexis, but I do have a little neighborhood dog-walking business, and the Cupcake Club, of course, and lately, the trunk-show modeling. It's a nice, small, steady stream of income, but it's not life-changing money. It just means I can eat at the food court at the mall instead of bringing a P-B-and-J sandwich from home, for example.

But I knew that being in ads could actually earn you some real money. Not just eight or ten dollars an hour.

I selected a book called *World Models*, and I flipped through it. It showed models in their home towns (and cities and villages), dressed in wild fashion couture that made them look really out of place, like freaks. I guess that was the point. I sighed and replaced it and then selected another.

This one was called *American Beauties*. It was organized by state, and I flipped through Alaska (a surprising number of models come from there, as it turns out) and on to Arizona, California, and Connecticut before I realized most of these models were just a little bit older than me (sixteen, seventeen, and eighteen years old) or had started out in the business as kids, like me (or even younger, I guess). In the interviews alongside the big photos, the models talked about how they were discovered. You can't believe how many of them were discovered at their local mall!

Intrigued, I looked around to see if there were any modeling scouts nearby, but everyone seemed pretty engrossed in their books. I rifled through the pages one last time and was about to shut the book when a highlighted quote in bright orange type from a Native American model (from Arizona) jumped out at me. It said, "Just don't let them steal your soul."

Okaaay! I thought. Now that's another creepy thing to think about! I shut the book and reshelved it, then stood up to head back to work. My friends would be there soon, and I was looking forward to seeing them. My dad would be there after that, and I was *not* looking forward to seeing him. As I walked back to the shop, I played out different scenarios in my mind of my dad at The Special Day. In one, he was like a bull in a china shop, knocking into things and spilling tea on the sofa and generally embarrassing me. In another, he was his usual fun self, chatting everyone up and asking his or her life stories and generally embarrassing me. In yet another, he was falling asleep on the sofa and snoring, like he does in front of college football games on TV, and generally embarrassing me. Are you getting the idea here? I knew embarrassment was in store for me no matter what. Back at the store I ran to the ladies' room to wash my hands (clean hands are a must at a bridal salon—most of the employees wear white gloves) and to make sure my face didn't have random flecks of salsa still on it.

Then I found Patricia and confirmed the lineup of my next round of dresses, and I went to change.

"Yoo-hoo!" I heard as I pulled the tulip-sleeved gown back over my head. It was Alexis!

"In here! Let me just get this dress on and you can come in. Was Mona surprised about the cupcakes?" I asked through the closed door.

"Yeah. I told her they were on the house if she'd let us put out our cards, and she said great. Hey, it's packed out there, by the way. If we don't get at least one job out of this, I'll be shocked," Alexis said happily.

I smiled. Alexis is happiest when growing a business.

"Okay, ready! Come in! And you can tie me," I called. Patricia was so busy, Alexis could easily do the styling work for me.

"Wow! Your hair really looks amazing!" said

Alexis as she entered the changing room.

After looking at myself in the mirror all day, I had forgotten about the curls. "Thanks!" I said, patting my hair. "Will you tie me, please?"

Alexis kept staring at me in the mirror as she deftly tied the bow. "Really, I can't get over it. It's like you're a different person," she said. "You look like a model!"

"I am!" I laughed. "And guess what?" I said, spinning around to face Alexis. "Mona asked me if she could put me in an ad in the paper, and my parents said yes! We're having a photo shoot later today with a professional photographer, who sounds cuckoo, by the way!"

Alexis's jaw dropped. "OMG. Do you know how much money you can make doing that?"

I laughed again. "Leave it to you, Miss CEO, to think of the money."

Alexis furrowed her brow. "Well, what else would you think of? It's not like it's fun."

"I think it will be. I think the photo shoot will be really glamorous, and I think it will be unbelievable to have a few people see my photo in the paper."

"I don't know. . . . But, anyway, it's great news and I'm so happy for you!" said Alexis, and she grabbed me in a big hug. "I know a supermodel!"

"The dress!"

"Oops. Sorry. I guess this dress wasn't made to withstand BFFs," she said with a giggle.

"I guess not. . . ." I giggled too. "Hey, are the others here?"

"Yeah, come on. They won't believe your hair when they see it. I can't wait!" Alexis grabbed my hand and pulled me out of the dressing room, through the throngs of women in the store, searching for our friends.

Along the way, a couple of ladies noticed my dress, "Ooh, isn't that exquisite?" said one.

And "That is a gorgeous dress!" said another.

"Alexis!" I protested. They were the people I was meant to be talking to right now. They were the potential clients, and I was there to sell. But Alexis was whisking me right past them. "Alexis! Stop!" I cried, finally yanking back my hand.

She turned around, and her smile faded. "What?" she asked, seeing my worried face.

"I'm working. And you just dragged me past two women who were interested in my dress. You can't do that. I have to go back there and tell them about it."

Alexis looked perplexed. "Oh. Right. Okay."

"I'm sorry. It's not that I don't want to see the others; it's just that Mona is paying me to do this. Can you just find Mia and Katie and bring them to me instead?" I felt bossy and horrible, killing Alexis's enthusiasm like that. Guilt settled heavily in the pit of my stomach.

"Okay," said Alexis again. Then she smiled. "You go back, and I'll come find you when I get the others." If anyone got the fact that I was working and making money, it was Alexis.

I turned back to find the interested women. Pasting a gracious smile on my face, I walked back very slowly, making eye contact with everyone, just as Patricia and Mona had taught me at my first trunk show. That's one of the ways people know you're an employee, and then they feel you're approachable and they can ask you questions about your dress. Part of my job is to know the designer's name, the dress's style name, and the price of each and every dress I wear. Just enough info so that the clients can follow up with Mona for more specifics, like sizing and lead time (that's how long it takes to have the dress made).

I found the first woman standing with her friend, and I began chatting with them, telling them all about the dress. They loved it and were pretty impressed by all the information I had. (I couldn't resist throwing in the term "tulip sleeve." What can I say?) Then I moved on to the other interested woman and let her look at the seams and feel the fabric and generally judge the quality of the dress, which she found "impeccable." Not that I was surprised. All the Jaden Sacks dresses are impeccable, which made it fun to wear them and have clients be impressed.

When she'd finished, I turned and went looking for someone else to show the dress to. But suddenly the crowd parted, and Katie and Mia and Alexis appeared. I was happy to see them, even if I was self-conscious about socializing on the job. Katie and Mia squealed about my hair and the news about the photo shoot, and Katie said, "Oh, Emma, I'm so jealous! I can't believe you're a model and you're going to be in the paper. You're famous! You're like Maple Grove's next Romaine Ford!"

I had to really laugh at that one. "Romaine Ford is a talented dancer, singer, and actress, Katie. I am just a clothes hanger!"

"It's a big deal!" said Mia, whose mom is a fashion stylist. "I've been to modeling shoots in the city with my mom lots of times, and let me tell you, it is no picnic. Those hot lights, the cranky photographers, the uncomfortable clothes with pins poking you, the competitive models who all want your spot. . . . It is a J-O-B, for real!"

"Yeah," I agreed, but I could feel my brow furrowing as it always does when I'm nervous. Well, how bad could one photo shoot be, anyway?

Mia's mom appeared then. "Oh, Emma, you look lovely, *mi amor*!"

I smiled. "Thanks, Mrs. Valdes."

"I love that dress, and I simply adore your hair like that!"

"Mom, Emma's going to be in a print ad for the store. Isn't that great?" said Mia.

"Wow, that's spectacular! I can't wait to see it! I hope they're paying you well. It's hard work," she said, leaning in so no one else could hear.

I grinned. "That's what I hear."

She rolled her eyes. Then she said, "All right, chicas, Emma is working, so we'd better be running along now. Good-bye, darling. Have a great time. I can't wait to see your ad!" Mrs. Valdes blew me a kiss, and they left.

I watched them walk away until the crowd swallowed them, and I couldn't help but wonder where they were all going and what they were going to do. It would be fun to just put on jeans and hang out with them. Maybe they'd shop around the mall for a while; Mrs. Valdes is the best mom to go to the mall with, because she loves clothing and loves to shop (unlike my mom). She has an eye for the inexpensive item that can really tie everything together. Or maybe they'd head to the movies and then the new milkshake place, and there would be cute boys there to flirt with. I felt lonely and left out and suddenly wished I was going with them. And yet I had two more hours of modeling and then the shoot.

"Emma!" Patricia was calling me, and I snapped to. "Time to put on the next look, please!"

"Right," I said, and I hurried back to the changing room alone.

CHAPTER 3

Makeup Session

At least my father looked good when he showed up. He is a good-looking guy—tall, burly, and athletic, with bright blue eyes, dark hair, and a smile that makes the corners of his eyes crinkle up in a cute way. Today he had changed out of his customary Saturday T-shirt–and–shorts sports attire (he plays soccer in an adult rec league and coaches at least one of my brothers' sports teams each season), and he was wearing what I think of as his out-to-Sunday-dinner attire: brown cords, loafers, and a striped button-down shirt under a navy blue zip-neck sweater. He had the Sunday paper under his arm (we get most of it delivered with the Saturday paper; don't ask!), and he looked ready to settle in for the rest of the day.

Mona was impressed, I could tell, and this made me relax a little. Maybe he wouldn't embarrass me in some awful unpredictable way. She fussed over him and brought him a cup of coffee and a plate of mini cupcakes and then told him she and her staff were at his beck and call and not to hesitate if he needed anything.

"I can see why you like coming here!" he said to me with a laugh. "I'm thinking of spending every Saturday here from now on!"

"Dad, please!"

"Just kidding, angel. How was your morning?"

He had been surprised when he arrived and saw my hair, because he hadn't seen it earlier. When he recovered from the surprise, he told me how pretty it looked, even if it was a little done up for the jeans and turtleneck I had changed back into by then.

As we waited, a tiny, skinny man in a black leather jacket and black leather jeans came to the door. He had a faux hawk of jet-black hair, and big black combat boots on. I could see my dad's radar go up, and he sat up a little straighter, alert. The guy looked like trouble, and suddenly, I was really glad my dad was there.

But then Mona said, "Oh, here's Joachim! Late as usual!"

I know my jaw dropped, and I turned to my dad in shock. "That's the photographer," I whispered breathlessly.

"That scary-looking little dude?" My dad shook his head like he couldn't believe what he was hearing and what he was seeing. "But where is his ..."

Suddenly, three other people struggled into view, carrying all sorts of metal strongboxes and lights and cables. My dad and I looked at each other again, and we smiled. "I guess that answers your question, right?" I said.

To see the next half hour unfold was mesmerizing. Mona was bossing Joachim and his team around, cautioning them not to touch anything, not to stain anything, to be careful of their equipment marking anything. And Joachim was pushing back, asking where things would go otherwise and how could he work like this, and at the same time barking orders at his staff. It was like a standoff. I wondered who would win and at the same time, I fervently hoped I wouldn't be the biggest loser of the day. If they treated one another like this under these circumstances, I could only imagine where I'd fall in the pecking order!

My dad settled in with his newspaper (Mona had an assistant drape a white sheet over the sofa, so the newsprint didn't stain it; how that could happen, I don't know) and he seemed happy as a clam, but I was growing more and more nervous by the minute. All this lighting? All this equipment? Computers? Backdrops on rolls? All for one photo of me, a girl who had never posed professionally before? I kept gulping as each new component was put into place.

Finally, Patricia and one of Joachim's assistants, a goth-looking girl who was also all in black, came to get me ready. Patricia introduced me to Serena and said Serena'd spruce up my hair and do my makeup.

My dad, who had been totally checked out, suddenly came alive from behind his paper.

"No makeup," he said.

Patricia and Serena paused and looked at each other. "Excuse me?" Patricia asked politely.

My dad lowered his paper and looked at them from over his reading glasses. "No makeup. I don't want you to glam her up and have her looking like an adult. She's still a child."

Patricia smiled. "Mr. Taylor, I promise you that the kind of makeup we are considering will be very sparingly applied and only used to enhance Emma's natural beauty. She will be totally recognizable as your daughter."

Serena spoke up, much more polite than I would have expected a goth to be. "It's just that with the lighting and with the transition from a computer image to the printed page, certain features tend to wash out; we need to prevent that from happening. We can do it on the front end with some inexpensive makeup or on the back end with expensive retouching in the studio. You'll see her before we shoot. And we'll let you see the pictures, and then you'll understand."

My father mulled this over. "I promised her mother no makeup. Let's see how she looks when she comes back out, and we'll make any adjustments if we need to, okay?"

I rolled my eyes, mortified by how clueless my father was, and followed Serena and Patricia to the changing room. Well, at least he didn't say no.

Inside, an entire makeup bench had been set up, with two high stools facing each other and very bright lighting. There was a makeup box—one of the black strongboxes I'd seen the team carrying in—opened on the table and a whole miniflight of "stairs" was expanded out of it, each with a dozen makeup colors on it. There were makeup brushes and hairspray bottles, cotton balls, a hairdryer, nail polish—everything you could think of.

"Now, dress first, do you think, or makeup?" asked Patricia.

"Makeup," said Serena definitively.

She gestured to the chair, and I clambered aboard. It was high, and my legs dangled frantically until I found a perch to settle them on.

Serena looked at me very closely, tilting her head this way and that, adjusting the light, then touching my chin and tipping it here and there. It was kind of weird, like I wasn't even a person but just a face with nothing behind it.

She pulled away and squinted at me, then she said, "Eyes." And with that, she got to work.

I glanced at Patricia, who was standing a little behind Serena, watching with a very serious look on her face. She smiled encouragingly at me, but her face instantly resumed its serious look, which wasn't exactly comforting. I felt like I was being operated on.

"Close," commanded Serena, and I closed my eyes. This part was easy, so far, if a little scary.

I felt Serena wiping something wet on my eyelids, and my eyes started to flutter. Serena sighed and stopped. I opened my eyes and found her staring at me with a kind of an annoyed look on her face.

"Aren't you a pro?" she asked.

"I . . . What?" I wasn't sure what to say.

Patricia leaned in and said, "This is her first photo shoot. She does in-store modeling for us, no makeup. Why don't you just talk to Emma as you work, and tell her what you're doing before you do it. That way she won't be nervous and she'll also have the chance to learn something."

Serena let out an aggravated sigh that sounded like she had something stuck in the back of her throat. "Fine," she said, sounding like me when I was being bratty on the phone with my mom earlier. I could feel a blush rising up my neck and into my cheeks.

"Emma," said Patricia. I glanced at her and found her smiling encouragingly once again. "Don't worry! You're going to do great! Just relax." She winked at me, and I felt better. "It's just makeup," she said, then she made a funny face at Serena's back, and I giggled.

"Right now I'm priming your eyelids," said Serena. "Close. It's a sponge with . . . uh . . . primer on it."

"And that's for . . . ," prompted Patricia.

"That's to make sure all my hard work doesn't slide off under the lights," said Serena.

I could feel the sponge dabbing at my eyelids, and now that I knew what it was, it was actually kind of relaxing. There was a pause, and I opened my eyes again, but Serena quickly said, "Stay closed. Let it dry."

Next I felt a brush along my eyebrows. I raised them, and she said, "Hold still. I'm just darkening your brows a little. Brows are the first things to go in the lights. They just disappear."

I have pretty dark eyebrows, despite my blond hair, so it was hard to imagine them disappearing at all (my mom won't let me tweeze them because, she says, they never grow back right).

Serena blew on my eyelids and it surprised me, but I did not open my eyes this time! I was learning!

"Okay, now I'm going to do a little base color," she said. I felt a fluffy brush pouffing all over my eyelid. It felt nice. *I could get into this,* I thought. Once I knew not to be scared, it felt like I was being pampered.

"Now something darker in the crease," Serena continued, and there was more pouffing, but with what felt like a smaller brush.

"Open," she commanded. I did, and found her staring very hard at me, looking critically back and forth between my eyes. "A little more for the left," she said. "Close." And I closed, then there was pouffing, then, "Open."

Okay, maybe I couldn't get used to it. I was starting to feel a little bored.

"Liner," she said. "Or, actually, let me use a wet liner." She selected a long black tube from the box and unscrewed the cap, revealing a long wand with a tiny pointed paintbrush on the end. "You are going to need to hold very, very, *very* still. Because if you blink, and I mess up, we have to wipe all the eye makeup off and start over. Do you understand?" I nodded, nervous again.

Serena approached my eye with the wand, and I began to blink really fast. She stopped and looked at me carefully. "Can you hold still?" she asked, like she was trying really hard to be patient.

"Yes," I said. But as she started to approach my eye, I began to blink rapidly again.

"Okay." She put her hand down. "What am I supposed to do here?" she asked Patricia.

Patricia bit her lip, then she said, "Emma, honey, Serena is going to line your upper lid, from the inner corner to the outer corner, with some wet liner. It will not end up in your eye, but it might be a little cold and may be a tiny bit ticklish. You can stand it, though. Serena, why don't you stretch the lid out first, then approach it with your other hand. Emma, maybe just close your eyes."

I felt better now, knowing what to expect, and I closed my eyes and let Serena pull my eyelid one way, then the other way, out to the side. The liner *was* wet and tickly, but it wasn't too bad.

"Don't open. Not till I say so," ordered Serena.

She busied herself with her kit, and then after a minute or so (a long time to sit with your eyes closed in a room with other people, by the way), she said, "Open." And I did. I glanced in the mirror, and I couldn't believe what I saw. I looked like an adult! Or practically one. Like an old teenager.

"Wow!" I said, gaping at my reflection.

"I know," said Serena proudly.

"Hmm," said Patricia. "I think Mona is hoping for something a little more . . . wholesome. The dress she's thinking of is certainly more . . . innocent looking, maybe."

Serena looked at her, then back at me. "Just wait till you see it on the computer, okay? No changes till then." She rolled her eyes and muttered to herself; it sounded like, "Amateurs." Or maybe I just thought that was what she said because I had a guilty conscience about being inexperienced.

She withdrew a kind of scary-looking clamp from the kit and said, "Now we'll curl your eyelashes."

"Umm . . . okaaay . . . ," I said. Curly eyelashes? Who knew such a thing was desirable?

Serena had me close my eyes again, and then she clamped my lashes, each eye in turn, and she counted to thirty while she had them clamped.

When I opened my eyes and looked in the mirror again, my eyelashes didn't look curly, exactly, but their angle was definitely different. It made me look more awake or something, too. "Cool!" I said, turning my head from side to side to try to see my lashes at different angles.

"I think I'll skip the mascara," said Serena to herself. She selected a bottle of skin-colored liquid and began to dab some around my face. "Just evening out your skin tone now," she said.

"Is it uneven?" I asked, my voice muffled as the sponge passed over my lips. Yuck!

"Everyone's is," said Serena, looking at me. "Shows up more in pictures. That's why we need to correct it first. Now some powder." There was lots of pouffing with the biggest brush yet. It felt great. "And some blush . . ."

Serena took another brush and dabbed from a

pink pot and onto my cheeks, nose, chin, and fore-head.

"Hey! Blush is for your cheeks! I know that much!" I said.

Serena narrowed her eyes at me. "Not exclu-sively," she said.

Oh.

"It brightens up everything," offered Patricia, who'd been quietly watching.

"Some nude lip liner . . . ," said Serena, outlining at my mouth with a kind of dry stick. That did *not* feel good.

I glanced in the mirror. Wow, did I look older!

Serena put her fingers under my chin and turned me back to face her again. She looked at me criti-cally, leaning back, then leaning in. Squinting again.

"Oh, what the heck," she said, and she selected a dark tube of lipstick and dabbed it on my lips with a makeup brush. "There."

I looked in the mirror and couldn't believe it! I actually looked like a model! "Wow!" I said. If I hadn't known, I would have put my age at eighteen, at least. It was an incredible transformation.

Serena smiled like she was proud of herself. "I know. It's really an art."

I looked at Patricia. She didn't seem thrilled.

Her mouth was set in a kind of a line. "Let's see how Mona likes it," she said. "Come, Emma. Before we get the dress on, okay?"

"You might as well do the dress and give them the full effect. . . . ," said Serena. "It's kind of out of context like this, with the . . . jeans and whatnot." She gestured at my outfit in a dismissive way.

But Patricia ignored her. "Come," she said again.

We left the dressing room and went out into the main salon. Joachim and his team had finished setting up, and Mona and my dad were chatting in the seating area where I'd left him.

"Mona?" said Patricia, pushing me a little ahead of her into the room.

Mona and my dad turned and looked at me blankly. It was like they had no idea who I was for a minute. Then their faces changed.

My father came to his senses first. "No way!" he shouted as he jumped to his feet.

Mona stood quickly. "All wrong," she said emphatically.

And I burst into tears.

CHAPTER 4

Emma Taylor's a Hottie

*W*ell, that was mortifying.

I had figured all along that my dad would embarrass me. I just didn't expect it would be in the form of a tirade against Serena, Joachim, and the entire entertainment industry of America. The only good thing was that Mona was also mad, so it didn't look like my dad was a lone crazy person. She was yelling too.

It didn't take long for Serena to take off everything she had put on, even though I thought she wiped a little harder than she needed to. It wasn't my fault Mona had freaked out and my dad had wanted to pull me out right then and there. They said I looked *waaaay* too old and inappropriate and all sorts of other things I didn't really understand, but when they realized I was crying, they were quick to tell me it was totally not my fault, and everything began to settle down. That made me feel better.

Serena gave me some Visine for my eyes, and the redness went away pretty fast. After that, Mona stood by my side while Serena put a tiny bit of foundation on my skin, a trace of blush on my cheeks, and a hint of pink on my lips, and that was it. Serena kept muttering about the computer and the lights, like before, but Mona was firm. "I'll take my chances," said Mona.

While I got on my dress, I could hear Mona through the door as she lectured Joachim and his team.

"I want this done quickly; I want the utmost care taken that the model is not taxed or upset; I want it clean, wholesome, and pretty. And that's it. If any of it goes off track or gets too fresh or rude, you're fired and no one gets paid. Does everyone understand?" she said.

There was murmuring I couldn't hear, but I could tell that Mona had the last word.

After that, things *did* go quickly, and well. Patricia gave me a bouquet of white flowers to hold, and after a while they swapped it for a white basket tied with ribbons and filled with white rose petals I had to scatter. They had me barefoot, with a crown of daisies—all sorts of looks. I didn't realize there were so many props available at The Special Day for junior bridesmaids!

I know I was pretty stiff at first. Joachim kept trying to tell me jokes to get me to relax. My dad got in on the act and started goofing around, and after a while we were all laughing, and it went by pretty fast. There was a lighting guy name Frank, and when the lights got too hot, he'd give me a little break in front of the fan, which was nice. And Stella, on the computer, let me see the shots she thought were the best. Right as I started to feel like I was dragging, Joachim said, "We've got it."

Patricia had me change and wash my face. I put my hair back in a ponytail, and I looked like my regular old self when it was time to leave. My dad made me go around and shake everyone's hand and thank him or her before we left. He thanked Mona, too, and they shared a laugh about the near disaster with my makeup. I felt funny listening to them, because I had thought I looked good in the makeup—like a real model, even if I did look much older. But the way they reacted was like I had looked ugly. I didn't really get it, but it made my face burn when I thought about it.

We were the first to leave. I could see Patricia had at least an hour to go of breaking down the equipment and then the cleanup, and I felt bad for her. I asked my dad if we could stay to help, but he said no. Mona overheard and said, "The talent never cleans up, darling! Run! You've worked hard all day!" She gave me an envelope with my pay, and I gave her and Patricia hugs good-bye; then my dad and I left.

It was dark when we drove out of the mall, and I couldn't believe I'd spent the whole day at work! Back home, my mom wanted to know every detail, but I felt like so much had happened, I didn't know where to begin. I told her a little, begged off, and then went upstairs to flop onto my bed. I'd meant to read or play my flute, but my eyes must've drifted shut. The next thing I knew, my mom was gently squeezing my shoulder, telling me it was dinnertime.

The following week flew by, and the next thing I knew, it was late Friday afternoon, and I was at Katie's, getting ready to deliver double-fudge cupcakes to a birthday party, followed by a trip to the movies with all the Cupcakers. As much as I had enjoyed working the weekend before, it was fun to just be a kid this weekend. I'd be back at The Special Day in the morning, but only for a few minutes, to drop off Mona's order. There weren't any trunk shows this weekend, and I was actually kind of glad about it.

Katie and I were in the kitchen packing the cupcakes into their carriers, Mia and Alexis had gone home to change, and suddenly Mrs. Brown came into the kitchen. She was holding the local paper that comes out Fridays and kind of waving it around in the air.

"Emma, honey! Look! It's you!" she cried, her reading glasses slipping low on the bridge of her nose.

She spread out the back page of the first section onto the kitchen table, and there I was! A full-page ad of me, with my back to the camera, looking over my shoulder, and the flower bouquet in my hands and a closed-lipped smile on my face. The top of the ad read, JUNIOR BRIDESMAIDS BY JADEN SACKS, and the bottom had, THE SPECIAL DAY, CHAMBER STREET MALL.

"Oh! There I am! You're right!" I giggled. I was embarrassed to see myself there like that; I'd kind of forgotten that anyone could see the ad once it came out. I didn't know what to say. Plus, it was, like, a whole page. I mean, my face was huge!

Katie stood there staring at the photo, her mouth hanging open in shock. She looked up at me. "Emma! You're a model! For real!" she said, breathlessly.

I shrugged, still grinning like an idiot.

Mrs. Brown gushed, "You look absolutely beautiful, honey. Simply gorgeous. I love it. I have to call your mom and tell her."

"But . . . I didn't realize . . . I mean, I know you said you'd be in the paper, but I kind of forgot. And here you are!" sputtered Katie, incredulous.

I laughed. "I didn't know when it would run, either. I just . . . I kind of forgot too!" I said. The truth was, I wasn't sure what to think about the whole photo shoot episode. Some of it was fun, some of it was funny, some of it was frustrating, and a lot of it was mortifying and upsetting, but Mona had given me one hundred and fifty dollars on top of my usual trunk-show payment! I hadn't really talked about any of it with Katie and the others, because I didn't know what to say. Now, I flipped over the paper to hide the photo. "Okay! Moving right along!" I said with a little laugh. (That's what my mom says to me sometimes when she wants to change the subject.) Katie was still looking at me oddly, like she wasn't sure who I was.

"Earth to Katie! Let's finish up these cupcakes so we can get to the theater. Alexis will not be psyched if we're late."

Katie kind of came to, shaking her head as if to clear it. "So that's all? You just turn it over and move on?"

I punched Katie lightly on the arm and resumed my cupcake packing. "What do you want me to do? Drool all over the photo? Hug it? Cry? Come on, Katie!"

She laughed a little and then began helping me again with the cupcakes. "I don't know," she said finally. "I'm not sure what I'd do if I was you!"

At the movies, Mia and Alexis raced over when they saw us. "Emmaaaaa! We saw your photo! It's amaaaazing!" Mia said dramatically. She kept looking at me the way Katie had before, like she was searching for something in my face. Like she didn't really know me.

Only Alexis was totally normal. "I hope you got paid a lot for it," she said. "It's a totally huge ad, and the paper's circulation is about forty-five thousand. I googled it. So figure—"

"Stop!" I swatted her. "Look, it was a once-in-a-lifetime opportunity. I did it. It's over. It was kind of interesting, kind of hard. I did make some good money. And that's it. I'm just me. Just plain Emma." I smiled and shrugged at them. "Same old, same old."

"Emma!" cried someone behind me. We all turned to look. It was Olivia Allen. Ugh!

Olivia is a girl in our class, and none of us like her. She's new, and she kind of used Mia when she first moved here; then she dropped her like a hot potato for the superpopular girls in the Best Friends Club. They're basically our enemies, which means we were *not* psyched to see Olivia and two of her henchmen, Bella and Maggie, here tonight.

"Emma!" She got closer. "OMG! We saw your *photo*! In the *paper*! We didn't know you were *modeling*!" she shrieked.

Well, it's not like we're friends, so how would you know anything I'm up to? I wanted to ask. But instead I shrugged. "Yeah, I guess so," I said, looking around uneasily, to make sure no one else had heard. "Just a little."

Olivia came over and then looped her arm through mine and kind of pulled me away from my friends and toward hers. "Tell me everything. Do you have an agent? How many go-sees are you doing each week? What's your portfolio like? Online or hard copies?"

I was overwhelmed. Why was she suddenly being so chummy? Was it just because of my ad? And how did she know so much about modeling?

"Actually," I said, removing my arm from hers. "I do trunk shows at The Special Day bridal salon, and they just asked if I'd do this one ad for them. So I said yes. That's all it was." I looked at the Cupcakers, who were all watching me solemnly as I spoke with the enemy.

"Oh!" Olivia looked disappointed. Bella and Maggie looked bored. "Well, if you ever want to talk shop, just let me know," said Olivia. "I've had lots of experience in that world." She rolled her eyes, like it tired her out just thinking about all the experience she'd had. I knew that was my cue to ask her what she knew and how she knew it, but I just couldn't bring myself to start a bragathon with her.

"Okay," I said. "I will. Um. Thanks. Enjoy the movie!" And I turned my back on Olivia and then grabbed my friends, walking us to the concession stand.

"What was *that* all about?" I muttered as soon as we were out of earshot. "Is Olivia Allen a model?"

"I think she might have been in an ad when she was younger," said Mia.

We walked past a couple of girls from the grade below us at school. I smiled, and one of them whispered to the other, "That's her!"

"Hi, Emma!" they cried in unison, then they turned away, blushing and giggling.

"I guess a lot of people read the *Gazette*!" said Katie, impressed.

"Maybe we should run an ad for the Cupcake Club!" said Alexis.

I laughed. Two girls—except this time from the grade above us—said hi to me while we were buying our popcorn, and then a bunch more girls said hi to me when we got into the theater.

"I'm telling you, Emma. You're the new Romaine Ford," said Alexis.

"I feel like we're out with a celebrity!" Katie squealed.

I swatted her. "Stop!" But it was kind of true. I did feel . . . special. It was fun being recognized and spoken to. Even the attention from Olivia was kind of pleasant. *This must be what it feels like to be famous,* I thought as the lights dimmed and the preshow silence-your-cell-phone announcements started.

Suddenly, a boy's voice rang out of the dark. "Emma Taylor's a hottie!" and a bunch of people laughed.

My face instantly grew hot as I squirmed in my seat. I felt people looking at me, but I kept my eyes on the screen, like I hadn't heard.

Alexis, who was sitting next to me, reached for my hand and squeezed it. She seemed to be saying, *Don't worry* and *Isn't this exciting?* all at once. I squeezed back, saying, *Yes*, *No*, and *Thanks*.

CHAPTER 5

Bambini di Roma

On Saturday afternoon I came home from orchestra practice and found my mom in the kitchen paying the bills.

"Hi, Emma!" she said brightly. "How was it?"

I got an apple and told her all about practice and our pieces and the new assistant conductor. She grilled me about what I still had for homework (everything), and I had to tell her my plan for getting it all done.

Finally, she put her palms flat on the table and took a deep breath. Looking down at the table, she said, "Sweetheart, Mona called with an opportunity for you. She said the head of publicity at Miller's called her for your contact info. They'd seen the beautiful ad in the *Gazette* yesterday, and they want to ask you to do some modeling for them, in-store and maybe in print." She looked up at me. "She wanted to know if she should give them our number."

I took a bite of my apple and then chewed. I thought about the photo session and mean Serena, and my dad embarrassing me. But then I thought about the money and all the nice feedback at the movies. Miller's department store was big and really chic. They had cool ads, and not just in the *Gazette*, but in big local magazines, and sometimes billboards, too.

"Yes," I replied, not meeting her eye.

"Emma," said my mom.

I looked up.

"Do you really want to do this?" she asked.

"Yes," I said again.

She sighed. "What do you like about it?" she asked.

"Um, the money. The . . . attention," I added, feeling shy saying it.

"Don't we give you enough attention? Are you feeling neglected, sweetheart? Oh, I knew it! I just knew—"

"Mom! Stop! It's not about you guys. It's about me! It's fun being recognized. It's fun being fussed over. It's fun being all girlie for a day, okay? And they pay me for all that! What's not to like?" Besides mean makeup artists and unpredictable popular girls and people shouting at the movies, even if they are saying nice things—for now. But I didn't say any of that.

Mom nodded, thinking. "Well, I can see the appeal when you put it that way. Your dad and I will need to discuss it, and we'll have to set some guidelines. Like, local work only. That will probably be one. And only on weekends. And one of us will always go with you. Hmm . . . I think I'd better go online and do a little research on how to be the mother of a model!"

She reached over and gave my hand a squeeze. "I'm sorry if I sounded negative. It *is* exciting, sweetheart," she whispered.

I smiled. "I know," I said.

"And we're proud of you."

"Thanks."

Just then my brother Matt walked in, bursting the bubble.

"Dude. Everyone's talking about your picture," he said, opening the cabinet and taking out a glass with a clatter. He poured himself a tall drink of milk.

"Oh yeah?" I asked casually, then added, "I hope they're saying nice things?" I wasn't exactly fishing for compliments, but I wouldn't have minded if he wanted to pass any along.

"Yeah. Josh Samuels thinks you're totally hot. He's carrying the page from the paper around in his knapsack. And Brewer Jones said you looked hot too."

"Oh." Josh and Brewer aren't exactly the coolest guys in the world. And they're not particularly cute either. They're just normal.

"What about Joe Fraser?" I asked. "Has he said anything?"

Matt chugged his milk. After he finished, he wiped his milk mustache with the back of his hand and then let out a huge burp.

"Matthew!" scolded my mother.

Matt grinned. "Nope. Joey hasn't said a word. Want me to tell him you were asking what he thought of it?"

"Matt, if you dare . . . !" I leaped out of my seat and lunged at him.

"Children!" said my mother sternly. "That's enough."

Matt cackled and dodged out of the way. "I'll tell him you're framing a copy of the ad for him for his birthday, and you're signing it 'Love and kisses, Emmy'!" Matt dropped his glass in the sink and scooted out the door.

"Mom!" I protested.

"Emma." She sighed wearily. "This is something I cannot control. You remember me mentioning that just this sort of thing might happen. Makes you think twice, doesn't it?" She looked at me knowingly.

"Oh, whatever," I said. I folded my arms across my chest and looked away.

"I know, but it's hard to have your cake and eat it too," said my mom with raised eyebrows.

I hate know-it-alls.

That night my mom and my dad and I had a meeting. We listed the pros (good money, nice feedback, work experience) and the cons (hard work, overexposure, lots of strong personalities to deal with) of modeling and talked about the guidelines my mom had mentioned earlier.

My parents really were reluctant to let me expand beyond The Special Day. But I reasoned that the extra money would be handy, and I promised I would put at least half of it in my college fund. I pointed out that work experience is always important and that I'd be learning to get along with all types of personalities. Plus, they'd be there on the shoots with me! Finally, I think I just wore them down with my begging because they looked at each other, and my dad shrugged.

"Fine, we give in!" he said. "Right, Wendy?"

"Yes. But as your managers," she continued, grinning, "we reserve the right to turn down jobs and to take you out of any jobs we feel are not appropriate. Understood?"

"Yes! Oh, Mom, thanks! And Dad! Thanks, you guys, you won't regret it!" I hugged them both and then ran upstairs to let my friends know that I was officially a model.

My first job for Miller's was two Saturdays later, after lunch. They had in a new line of children's wear from Europe, and they hired four models to walk all around the store wearing it and carrying a little sign saying, BAMBINI DI ROMA, 4TH FLOOR. The other kids were younger than me, so they were allowed to walk together, but the publicity person wanted me out there on my own. I hated to say it, but it was kind of lonely and boring. Plus, the clothes were majorly babyish if you ask me.

My first look was a red smocked dress with a

white Peter Pan collar. I don't know how kids in Rome dress, but if they're still made to wear this stuff after they turned ten, I would think there'd be a mutiny. They put my hair back with a thick, black, velvet headband, which I also didn't like, but at least I didn't have to wear any makeup. The people working with me were nice but very professional. They barely remembered my name, and they certainly didn't chat with me the way Patricia always does. It was okay, though. No one was mean or anything. It was just work. They were professionals, and they just assumed I was too. Which I was!

They gave me my sign to carry, and I left my mom upstairs and then took the elevator down to the ground floor to walk around. I knew how to do this: Make eye contact, smile, hold up the sign a little, and twirl. It wasn't hard.

Only it was hard.

No one really looked at me.

I smiled harder and twirled more often, but I began to feel like I was invisible. My mom was still upstairs in the lounge, doing some needlepoint and waiting for me. I felt I could leave and no one would notice. At one point I crossed paths with the other models, in their little threesome. They were being shepherded by the publicity lady, and people were fawning all over them, like, "Oh, aren't they cute?" and "Isn't this outfit darling?" It made me cranky just watching, but I am, after all, a professional now, so I smiled and waved and twirled myself right on to another floor.

I realized my mistake only a second too late.

"Emma!" a voice squealed.

I was in the teen department.

I spun around, face-to-face with none other than Olivia Allen.

"Hey!" I said, trying to drum up some enthusiasm.

"Hey yourself!" cried Olivia, kind of swatting my arm (a little hard, if you ask me). "You said you only model for that bridal place!" She narrowed her eyes, but smiling like she was being friendly.

"Yeah, well . . . Miller's made me an offer I couldn't refuse," I said, joking.

"*Really,*" said Olivia, more as a statement than a question. Oops. I guess she believed me. Whatever.

Bella, Maggie, and Callie joined her side. *Do these girls ever do anything alone?* I wondered. "Hi," I said weakly. They were dressed to the nines in all sorts of chic ensembles. (Why are they clothes shopping if they look this good already?) I was suddenly aware of my childish outfit, so I started edging away before anyone could say anything.

"Okay, so . . . ," I mumbled.

"Wow, isn't runway work just draining?" asked Olivia, all concerned. She looked at her friends, and they all nodded sympathetically, like they did it all the time and were exhausted just thinking about it.

"Well, I don't know that this is really *runway* work," I said. But Olivia wasn't actually interested in what I had to say. Although she posed her statements as questions, all she really wanted to do was share her own experiences. She continued.

"Well, your feet will be just killing you at the end of the day." Olivia glanced down at the ruffled white ankle socks and black patent leather Mary Janes the publicity people wedged me into. Her nose wrinkled in distaste. "When you do TV work, there are lots of breaks in the trailer, and they have all kinds of snacks laid out at the craft services table. Yummy bagels and cookies and all sorts of treats. And they'll bring you anything you want if they don't have it there, you know. You just ask, and your wish is their command."

"Wow," said Bella appreciatively.

Olivia continued to nod dreamily.

I wanted to burst her bubble by asking her

exactly what kind of work she'd done to earn being treated like Angelina Jolie on set, but I didn't think it would be appropriate for a store employee to be rude to a customer. Also, I didn't want to prolong the conversation and end up getting caught chatting on the job.

"Well, I need to go. It's time for my next look," I said, glancing at my wrist where my watch usually lives. (They made me take it off upstairs because it didn't go with the outfit. Probably because the six-year-olds who'd usually be wearing this outfit can't tell time!)

"Of course. You're working. We shouldn't interrupt at all. I, of all people, understand," said Olivia solemnly.

"Right. Thanks, um . . . bye," I said.

But of course as I tried to edge away inconspicuously, two grannies accosted me and trapped me there for five full minutes, feeling the material of my dress and asking all about Bambini di Roma. I tried not to look at Olivia and her group, but they hadn't budged. The other three stood rapt while Olivia apparently imparted all her knowledge about the wide world of modeling.

As I finally left for good, Olivia called out, "Bye, Emma! Have fun! Talk soon!"

I was confused. Olivia was being totally nice, so why didn't I trust her?

The afternoon went slowly as I worked my way through eight Bambini di Roma outfits. My mom smiled supportively whenever I came back for an outfit change. She fed me some snacks and brushed my hair and gave me a hug each time. I wished I could stay with her. Or better yet, drag her to the teen department to shop with me. But we didn't have time. By the time I finished at five o'clock, we needed to get home, so she could cook dinner, and then we had to run over to see my oldest brother Sam's basketball game.

At the end, the publicity lady handed me an envelope with a check for two hundred and fifty dollars! I couldn't believe it. I smiled and shook her hand, like my dad had told me to, and said good-bye.

The lady paused, and then in a low voice she said to me and my mom, "I don't usually do this, but you are such a dear to work with and just so lovely looking. My very good friend is a big modeling agent in the city, and she asks me to keep an eye out only for exceptional talent to refer to her." She reached in to her desk drawer and pulled out a shiny gold business card that she handed to my mom. "Why don't you give her a call if you aren't already working with an agent. She's tough, but she's the best in the business. I'll tell her to look out for your call. Thanks again, Emma. It was so nice meeting you, and we will certainly be in touch with more work for you very soon."

"Thank you. It was a nice opportunity. And thanks for the card," I said.

In the elevator I leaned against my mom and read the card.

Alana Swenson

Representation

(913) 555-3798

"Huh. We'll have to google her," I said, clueless.

CHAPTER 6

The Big Time

*T*yler Jones, Randi MacNeil, Josanna, *and* Mallory Cordite! *All of them!*" I cried incredulously. I was reading from the Internet to my mom as she made dinner. I'd searched Alana Swenson as soon as we got home, only to find out she was basically the biggest modeling agent in New York, representing every major model I'd ever heard of. "Wow!"

"That *is* amazing," agreed my mom, then added, smiling, "*I've* even heard of some of them."

I sat, also smiling, and shaking my head in disbelief. The Swenson Group's home page was just a phone number. I guess that's all she needed.

The phone rang, and I saw on the caller ID that it was Alexis.

"Hey! How did it go?" she asked.

"Good! Actually, bad. It was really boring, but I did a good job, I guess."

"Of course you did!" said Alexis. "What else is up?"

"Well, they gave me a business card for an agent. I'm trying to convince my mom to call her," I said, glaring meaningfully at my mother.

"Not till I speak with your father!" she sing-songed for the tenth time.

I made a sound of aggravation. "What are you up to?" I asked Alexis.

"Not much. Homework. Just calling to make sure you're coming over to bake tomorrow. We've got that baby shower in the afternoon for Mrs. Kramer's daughter."

"Right! I almost forgot. Yes, I will totally be there," I said, smacking my forehead. I mentally reviewed the mounds of homework I had upstairs. "What time?"

"Eleven, okay?" she asked.

"Yup. Sure. No prob. See you then."

We hung up, and I groaned.

"What?" asked my mom.

"Work, work, work," I said.

My mom said nothing. Right. Be careful what you wish for.

"I can't go to Sam's game," I said.

"Oh, honey! That's too bad. It's the semifinals!"

I shrugged. "Homework. I need to get it done tonight, so I can go bake tomorrow. Sorry."

"You don't have to apologize to me. It's Sam who will miss you."

"I'm sure!" I snorted. "Not a game goes by where Sam doesn't seek me out in the crowd."

"Well, I'll miss you, then," my mom said, knowing that to contradict me on this was pointless since I was right. Though we do try to make it to everyone's games when we can, with the amount of sports that go on in this family, there are a lot of missed games too. It's okay. Sam really wouldn't mind.

As I closed my laptop to go upstairs, the phone rang. My mom peeked at the caller ID and said, "It's for you, sweetheart."

SPECIAL DAY, THE, it said.

"Hello?" I answered.

"Darling, I have the most divine news!" It was Mona.

I smiled. "What?"

"Jaden Sacks has given us her line to carry—permanently. It's just incredibly exciting! We're all pinching ourselves!"

"Congratulations, Mona! That's great news!" I said. I was really happy for her. She'd worked so hard for this.

"I know. I'm thrilled. Anyway, we're going to have a launch party and runway show here at the store, one month from today, and I wanted to make sure my top model wasn't booked. I think Ms. Sacks herself will be coming! Oh, it's just too exciting to think about!"

"Sure! I can be there, no problem. I'll double-check with my mom, but I'm sure it's okay." I noticed my mother looking at me. "Thanks for asking me!"

"Also, darling, it will be quite a crowd, and there probably will be some press, so let's go ahead and amp up the cupcake order. Maybe do something over the top, okay?"

"Great! We'd love to!" I couldn't wait to tell Alexis. A big cupcake order, and press!

"Okay, darling. Now that I'm in your book, I feel much better. Have a fabulous night. Kiss, kiss. Talk soon."

"Bye!" I said, and hung up.

"What's up?" asked my mom.

"Mona got the Jaden Sacks account! She's going to carry the line for good!"

"Great!" said my mom. "And more work for you?"

I nodded happily. "I'm going to model at the launch, a month from today, and Mona wants a big splashy cupcake order for the party."

"That's wonderful, dear. I'm so happy for you."

I hugged myself a little, feeling great, and picked my laptop back up. "I've got to let the others know."

"Okay, I'll call you for dinner in a little while."

Upstairs, I shot out a quick e-mail to the group to let them know about our new job. Alexis replied instantly, saying we'd brainstorm during our baking session at Mia's tomorrow, and I got to work on my homework. There was quite a lot of it.

At Mia's the next day, we were all buzzing with ideas for the Jaden Sacks launch party. Alexis suggested minis with Jaden Sacks's logo (it's an intertwined *J* and *S* inside a heart) on them, which I thought was cute but might be hard to execute. Mia suggested we create a stencil in the shape of the logo and just sift pale blue sugar through it onto each cupcake, and we agreed that would be really cool. But it was Katie who reminded us of our early days and of one of our ideas for Mia's

213

mom's wedding, which had been to do a cupcake tower with tiers, so it looked like a wedding cake. And that was it, we were sold.

As the Kramers' cupcakes baked, Mia sketched a design on a piece of paper, and we all crowded around her, offering ideas and details. Katie thought fresh flowers would look pretty—maybe with some ivy hanging down—and we agreed, but Alexis cautioned us about cost, reminding us we didn't want to lose money on this project. In the end we were set on a plan, and Alexis promised to cost it out and get Mona's sign-off on it.

"Girls! Yoo-hoo!" Mrs. Valdes was home.

"In here, Mom!" called Mia.

"Oh, I'm so happy you're all here, *mis amores*! I have some great news!" Mrs. Valdes was beaming, her dark hair piled atop her head in a gorgeous bun, and a fitted dark-gray turtleneck sweater and black leggings completing her casual-chic weekend look. She was such a glamorous mom.

Mia looked up, and her mom reached to wipe a trace of powdered sugar off her cheek.

"I just ran into an old magazine colleague of mine, and we had a long chat. She was filling me in on what she does these days, and guess what? She's a food stylist and photographer. She's just starting up her own studio in the city, so she offered to take some photos of your cupcake creations for free if she could use them for publicity!" Mrs. Valdes clapped her hands happily and did a little dance in place, tossing her head from side to side.

"Awesome!" I cried, and all us Cupcakers hooted and high-fived.

"Now, maybe we can do a website!" said Alexis. "I've been pricing it out for a while, and this could be just the thing that makes the numbers work— free publicity photos!"

"When would we do the shoot?" asked Katie.

"Whenever you like, but the sooner the better. And weekends are fine!" said Mrs. Valdes.

"Cool! Thanks, Mami!" Mia gave her mom a big hug. "Our cupcakes are going to be models! Just like Emma!"

We all laughed.

"So what should we make for the portfolio?" asked Katie eagerly.

Mrs. Valdes laughed, then said, "I'll leave you to the important part. Just let me know what day you'd like for me to set it up." And off she went to make herself an espresso at the fancy machine on the counter.

We began brainstorming, with me taking notes.

Alexis decided we needed to make ten examples of our "greatest hits," and we started to list them. Among them we had clown cupcakes that we did for little kids' birthdays (with an upside-down ice-cream cone as a clown hat on top); Jake Cakes ("dirt with worms" cupcakes, like we made for my brother Jake's birthday); caramel cupcakes with bacon frosting (my invention); minis, like we make for Mona; little "gift" cupcakes, like we made for Alexis's sister Dylan's sweet sixteen; the tiered wedding cake idea; Millionaires, which had expensive ingredients; and more. We started to realize it would be a lot to coordinate, and some of the cupcakes would be hard to transport (like the tiered wedding cake), so maybe we wouldn't do them all. But as Mia pointed out, a lot of them we could assemble at the studio, so it was really only a matter of bringing in the supplies. We narrowed it down to ten and then voted to confirm it.

This was going to be so much fun! We ordered pizza and then spent the day finishing the Kramers' cupcakes and refining our plan for the shoot. Of course, Alexis wasn't wild about spending a lot of money on supplies for cupcakes we wouldn't be selling, but we pointed out that business development is priceless, and she relented.

✿

It was late afternoon by the time we'd finished with the Kramers and everything, and I headed home for Sunday dinner. I found my parents at the kitchen table, peeling potatoes, and the timing was perfect for us to discuss Alana Swenson. My mom had already filled in my dad, so all I had to do was beg.

"Please, Dad! Don't you see what a great opportunity this would be?"

My dad sighed. "I guess I'm unsure of your motivations. Is it the money? Are you interested in fame? Do you enjoy the process? Is it more fun than the other stuff you do and so you don't mind making sacrifices? It would be easier for me if I understood where you're coming from," he said.

I had to stop and think about all that for a minute. He raised some good points. After a moment I said, "All of it, I guess. I love making money. It's fun to be all girlie and get dressed up and be around pretty clothes and stuff. It's exciting to have people see your picture in the paper, and it would be neat to have some more of that. I don't know about fame. That seems like a lot of work. But I'd like to be recognized, anyway, as a model. That would be cool." It felt weird saying it—like, kind of embarrassing—but it was true. I looked

217

over my shoulder to make sure Matt hadn't snuck up behind me to eavesdrop and then torture me with my confession later. But the coast was clear, thank goodness.

"And the sacrifices?" my dad prompted.

I shrugged. "I already make a lot of sacrifices for work. I'm used to it," I said. "Dog walking, Cupcake Club, babysitting, The Special Day . . ."

My dad and mom looked at each other, and both seemed to be thinking.

Finally, my mom said, "Well, I guess we should at least give it a try. Emma, you certainly have a great work ethic, and I'd like to encourage that. Let's see what this Alana Swenson says, and we'll take it from there. But here are the ground rules: A parent will always go with you. The work has to be age appropriate. You will put ninety percent of your earned money into savings, and you can keep ten percent to spend." My mom was ticking things off on her potato-peely fingers. She looked at my dad. "What am I forgetting?"

"Good grades," he offered.

"Right. Your grades must stay above a B plus average, or we take a break from the modeling. And that's not just because we're worried about it eating into your study time, though we are. It's because your schoolwork and brain development matter more than your looks, and they always will. That is our priority in this family. And no big egos, okay?"

I was so excited, I would have agreed to anything. I jumped up and hugged them both. "Great! Thanks, Mom. Thanks, Dad! I can't wait! Can I go tell my friends?"

My dad laughed. "Sure. They can say they knew you when . . ."

But my mom said, "Honey, I don't mean to be a killjoy, but let's not get too far ahead of ourselves. We haven't even spoken with this Swenson person yet. . . ."

The next day my mom spoke to Ms. Swenson while I was at school, and it went well. She relayed the conversation to me when I got home, and I guess it was a pretty short one. Ms. Swenson said her friend from the store had called her to tell her she'd given us the business card and to look out for us since I was "beautiful" and "very natural" (!!!!). Ms. Swenson told my mom to e-mail her five casual, nonprofessional photos of me with no makeup or hair styling, in certain poses. But she said that this was just a formality: If her scout thought I was a fit, then I probably was. We'd meet as soon as possible and get things rolling (her words). And that was the whole conversation!

Needless to say, I wanted to take the photos and e-mail them in immediately, but my mom said since my dad was a great photographer, we'd have him come home early from work the next day and take the photos in the backyard. Also needless to say, when I told the Cupcakers this news, they all insisted on coming over for the shoot, and Mia said she'd have her mom put a few looks together for her to bring to me before she went to a meeting in the city.

At lunch the next day, Mia, Katie, Alexis, and I were sitting together (of course), discussing the outfits Mia had packed for me, when Olivia Allen came walking by with her crew.

"Hey, Emma, how's the modeling going?" she asked, all interested and cool. She waved breezily at Mia and ignored Katie and Alexis, as usual. Mia had been Olivia's first friend when she moved to Maple Grove, but Olivia had dumped her in favor of the more trendy popular girls, Callie, Maggie, and Bella. Now she acted kind of friendly to Mia but never called her or invited her to anything. Mia didn't care anymore, but it made me mad on her behalf.

"Oh, it's going . . . ," I said, letting my words just trail off vaguely. I didn't want to let her in on any more information, but unfortunately Katie didn't get my hint.

"Emma has an agent! A famous one!" said Katie.

I glared at her for blabbing, but she didn't notice.

Olivia's eyes widened, and she turned back to look at me a little more carefully this time. "Well, my goodness, that's exciting!" she said, sounding like a grown-up. "I doubt I would have ever heard of any of the agents around here, but try me. Who is it?" She arranged her face into kind of a bored expression.

Now I was annoyed, and this made me competitive. I couldn't wait for her reaction. "Alana Swenson," I said, all casual.

Olivia's eyes nearly popped out of her head. Her face turned bright red. "Did you say Alana Swenson? Are you *kidding* me? She's the top agent in the world! I am *freaking out* right now!"

And she did look like she was freaking out.

Olivia spluttered, "I need to go call my mom! I mean, I . . . I nearly signed with Alana a couple of years ago, but then . . . well, my mom thought I was getting overexposed or something. . . ." She blushed and looked away.

Right.

"Do you have her number?" she pressed.

"It's at home," I said, shrugging.

"Oh, right. Wow. Okay. Uh . . . I've gotta go. Talk to you very, *very* soon," she said. And she was off, with her gang tagging along.

"I can't wait," I said to her back as she disappeared from sight.

"Typical Olivia Allen, hot and cold," said Alexis. "One day she's your best friend; the next day you're dead to her. She likes to keep 'em guessing."

"Trust me, I'm not guessing!" I said, and we all laughed.

"You know the only modeling she's ever done was a baby food commercial when she was, like, one year old," said Mia quietly.

"Whaaaat?" I couldn't believe that! "Are you sure?"

Mia nodded. "I mean, I guess she might have been trying off and on since then to get more work, but that's the only actual job she's ever had. She sent me the link on YouTube."

"Oh, we have *got* to see that!" said Alexis. "Priceless."

"Wait, but if the commercial is, like, twelve years old, then how come it's on YouTube?" asked

Katie. "YouTube wasn't even invented then!"

Mia rolled her eyes. "Olivia put it up, of course!" she said.

"Oh boy." I was embarrassed for Olivia now. "Shoot me if I ever get that cuckoo about modeling, okay? Promise!"

"We will, don't worry! If you get too big for your britches, well . . . just watch out!" Alexis wagged her finger at me.

I laughed. "I knew I could count on you." But inside I felt a little pang. I wish I could have them around during the jobs. Modeling was kind of lonely. Oh well. At least the money was good.

CHAPTER 7

Alana Swenson

After school the girls came to my house, we all had a snack, and then Mia dressed me up. The outfits were cute, with Mrs. Valdes's signature touches— great scarves in gorgeous colors, a fun slouchy hat to crush on my head, cool earrings—and other than that, totally age appropriate (as my mom would say) clothes that I would normally wear. I was psyched. The looks were great, and Mrs. Valdes and Mia had organized each outfit with coordinating accessories zipped into a Ziploc bag and taped to the hanger. It couldn't have been easier to get dressed!

My dad came home as I was ready in my first look and my mother was fighting off Mia, who had a tube of dark lipstick in her hand.

"She said no makeup!" my mother protested,

laughing as she tried to grab the lipstick from Mia's hand.

"Please, Mrs. Taylor! A strong lip would just complete the whole look!" Mia giggled, dodging out of my mom's reach.

"A strong lip!" My dad laughed incredulously as he walked into the room. "That sounds like something you'd get from an enemy in the schoolyard!"

"Oh, Dad!" I said. "You're hopeless!"

"Let's get this show on the road!" my dad instructed, hoisting his camera.

Mia gave up on the lipstick, and we tumbled out into the backyard where my mom had hung a white flat sheet over the back fence. The light was pretty good, according to my dad, since the sun was kind of low in the sky. He took a bunch of photos of me in the first outfit, with the Cupcakers all oohing and aahing as I went through the poses Alana Swenson had asked for: three-quarter turn, head-on, looking up, head shot, and full body. My mom would later send her my measurements.

We worked our way through the three outfits Mia had put together, and I tried to be patient with my dad, pretending he was a professional, just like Joachim, but it was not easy. Just as we were

225

finishing the third outfit, the phone rang, and my mom went inside to answer it.

"Honey, it's someone called Olivia Allen? I told her you were in the middle of something, and she said she just needs a phone number from you?" my mom called from the back door.

The Cupcakers and I all looked at one another in shock.

"OMG!" I said. "The nerve!"

Alexis was shaking her head.

"Pushy, pushy," said Katie.

"What are you going to do?" asked Mia.

I thought for a second. "Just tell her to google it. It'll come up," I called back to my mom.

My mom gave me the thumbs-up, but was back in a flash. "She wants to know if she can use your name."

Now my jaw dropped at the nerve. "NO!" I yelled so emphatically that my mom raised her palms in the air, like, *Sorry, I'm just the messenger.*

"Wow!" I said to my friends, shaking my head.

"Over here, Emma! Stay focused!" called my dad, then muttered, "I can't believe I actually just said that."

"Yes, *focus*, Emma, for goodness' sake!" said Alexis, all fake businesslike. She made a funny face at me, and seeing her, so did Katie. Pretty soon my friends were all hamming it up, and my dad told them if they were going to work so hard, they should be in the photos too.

"Hey! A group shot for our website!" said Alexis.

Mia laughed. "Of course. All for business!"

"Well, you never know," said Alexis as my dad snapped away, the four of us in different silly, cute, and serious poses. It was really fun, and I have to say I liked it better when I wasn't the only one in the frame.

Later, after everyone had left, I got an IM from Olivia. It said,

Swenson wants me too! Yay! Modeling buddies!

I wanted to throw up.

Two days later I was sitting in Alana Swenson's waiting area with my mom after having taken the train into the city after school. I couldn't believe how fast things were moving, but I was pretty psyched. I hadn't seen Olivia at school since she'd told me she was also signing with Alana Swenson, so I planned on mentioning her to Alana to see what she said. I had a sneaky feeling what Olivia had said wasn't true, but I couldn't be sure.

My parents and I had selected five photos the night my dad had taken them, and my mom had e-mailed them. We heard back from Alana that very night. She replied to my mom's e-mail, asking her to call her assistant in the morning to book an appointment. I think my parents were kind of rattled by the speed of the whole thing too, but they were trying to act like they were in control.

Alana Swenson's waiting area was windowless, stark, and modern—all black and gray rugs and upholstery, and very hushed, except for the phones, which purred and buzzed nonstop. There were six beautiful young women at a long counterlike desk, answering the phones. The women were all different ethnicities, like a United Nations of model wannabes, and they all wore headsets and spoke so quietly into them that I couldn't hear a thing they were saying.

We were the only visitors.

Exactly thirty seconds after our appointment time, a door opened and another beautiful young woman silently beckoned us with a curved finger. We stood and followed her down a quiet hall, dim and spare, passing closed doors on either side until reaching the final closed door at the very end of the hall. The woman tapped on the door and opened it, and I had to wince at the instant brightness.

There were wraparound windows and gold everywhere—gold desk, gold-tiled floor, golden lamps, gold painted walls—the whole room glowed gold.

And sitting at the desk in a gold swivel chair was a tiny woman with golden hair pulled back into a tight bun, and gold-framed glasses on her tiny nose. She was the size of a child!

"Hello, Taylors! I am Alana Swenson!" Despite her size, she had the raspy, booming voice of a very large person. I was totally caught off guard. I wanted to laugh, but managed it down to just a big grin.

"I know, I know, none of this was what you expected!" she boomed. "That's the point! Have a seat! You are lovely looking! Trina was right. I'm glad she sent you. This won't take long."

My mom and I sat in two additional gold swivel chairs in front of the desk, and Alana proceeded to hand us paperwork (agent contracts, agency rules, this week's list of open calls, my website's username and password) and briefly explain it all. There will be go-sees, where I am invited to try out for a job. I will be told what to wear and where to go. The client will let Alana know if I get the job. My money will be sent to Alana, who will take twenty percent and send me a check for the rest. Alana was talking very quickly, and my mother was nodding and writing everything down in her notebook.

"All right! Any questions?" Alana asked.

I didn't have any. "It all sounds great!" I said, hoping to appear perky.

"It's hard work," Alana pointed out.

Right.

"What about school?" asked my mother.

Alana shrugged. "With looks like hers, this one will make more money than any education could give her." Alana laughed—"Heh, heh, heh"—like she was drowning.

My mom's jaw dropped, but then she recovered. "I meant, the go-sees are after school and on weekends, right?"

Alana's phone buzzed. She put her hand to the receiver to answer. "Not always. Any other questions?"

My mother and I looked at each other. I shook my head.

"Uh . . . ," said my mother.

"Alana Swenson," said Alana, picking up her phone, she waved and mouthed *Bye* at us.

We stood up and found our escort back at the door to take us out.

"Thank you," I said over my shoulder. Alana waved again.

Moments later we were out on the street, and my mother and I looked at each other and then burst out laughing.

"Was that for real?" I asked her.

"No, I think it was a scene from a movie!" she said.

"OMG." We stood for a minute and caught our breath. I couldn't stop thinking about what Alana had said about school. "Mom?" I began.

"No. I know what you're thinking. Listen, sweetheart, you're certainly beautiful, but no one is that beautiful. School comes first, and it always will. Look, you don't even know if you like modeling yet. Let's take things one step at a time."

"Fine," I said. And I have to admit, I was a little relieved.

It wasn't until the train ride home that I realized I'd never had a chance to ask Alana if it was true about Olivia. Oh well. I'd find out sooner or later.

sparkle

CHAPTER 8

Modeling Buddies

The next couple of days I rushed home from school to see if I'd received any assignments from Alana, but there was nothing. My mom said to be patient and that it was better to ease into things, but I just wanted to get started.

It wasn't until Friday that I finally ran into Olivia in the cafeteria. She looked caught, like a deer in headlights, when I spied her.

"Hi, Olivia," I said. I couldn't wait to get to the bottom of her Alana story.

"Oh, hi, Emma, I'm just running out. . . . I'm late for a meeting with my lab partner. . . ." She scrambled a little, trying to get away from me, but I wasn't going to let her get off that easily.

"So what's up with Alana Swenson? I've

been meaning to ask you, but I haven't seen you around."

"Oh, you know." Olivia shrugged. "She was supernice. She said to send in my photos and she'd take a look, so . . ."

Olivia was acting like she was still waiting to hear back, but I knew how quickly Alana responded to things. Olivia must've been rejected. "So what did she say?" I pressed. I didn't want to be mean, but I also was annoyed at Olivia for lying and trying to kind of steal my thunder.

"Well . . . they're pretty busy right now, so, you know . . ."

"It didn't work out?" I asked flat out.

"No, she said to check back, though, maybe when I grow a little."

Bingo! Rejected! Just as I suspected.

"Oh, okay. Well, keep me posted, anyway," I said, "and good luck!"

I am not a mean person, but I hate liars, and it felt good to call Olivia out on her lie. That said, I did feel a little sorry for her. Being rejected stinks, and when it's for something as personal as your looks, well, it has got to be hard.

"Yeah, I think I'm hitting some open calls this weekend, if you're interested. I'll have my mom call your mom, okay?" And she took off before I could say not to bother.

I sighed. Oh whatever.

When I got home after baking minis for Mona at Katie's all afternoon, my mom was already back from work and all a-chatter about the great conversation she'd had on the phone with Mrs. Allen! Ugh! Apparently, Mrs. Allen was quite the expert on modeling and children's careers (having had *so* much experience with adorable Olivia as a baby), and my mom was fired up with information and plans.

"So if you're interested, I thought it would be good practice, and you could go in with them tomorrow and kind of do a dry run for something that doesn't really count, you know?"

"Wait, you and Mrs. Allen are all buddy-buddy now, and you want me to go on an open call with *Olivia*?" I spluttered. I couldn't believe it. From not wanting me to model to now shoving me out on any old call. "Mom!"

She looked at me as if really seeing me for the first time, and then she sat down heavily in a chair at the kitchen table and put her head in her hands. "Oh, dear. I can't believe it. Just listen to me!

I'm turning into what I promised myself not to become—a stage mother!" She lifted her head and looked at me with a smile. "Sweetheart, do whatever you like. Mrs. Allen just got me all whipped up, but honestly, it's none of my business. If you'd like to go, you should go. If not, don't. It's totally up to you." She shook her head as if to clear it and then stood up to make a cup of coffee.

Now it was my turn to sit at the kitchen table. *Would* it be good practice? *Should* I do it? It might be better than going alone the first time. But spending a day with Olivia Allen? That sounded insane. And what would my friends say? I rested my chin on my hand and thought.

We didn't have any cupcake plans for the next day. I could knock off a lot of my homework tonight. Plus, Mona didn't need me tomorrow. I would be sleeping at Mia's tomorrow night, but I'd be back in time for that. I could actually do it.

"Okay," I said quietly.

"What, sweetheart?" asked my mom, nibbling on a cookie.

"I'll go."

"Oh, Emmy, you don't have to do it on my account. I was a blithering idiot when you came in here. Mrs. Allen talks so fast and got me so amped up. Really, you don't have to go."

"No, I think it's a good idea. Look, they at least have some kind of experience, and it might be less scary than going on my own the first time. I'll go."

My mom eyed me warily. "You're sure?"

I nodded. "Yup."

And that's how I ended up on the train to the city the next morning, with Olivia and her mom, after I'd made my weekly delivery of minis to Mona.

Mrs. Allen was friendly, but very hyper and wired. She had this big bag filled with snacks and activities and all sorts of grooming supplies. Once my mother had called her last night to say I'd "love to join them" (overstatement), she had e-mailed my mother the open call description, as well as instructions on what I should wear and how I should be styled. It was superorganized and generous, but there was something a little "compulsive" about it, to use my mom's word.

Olivia was actually unusually nice, but kind of quiet. I think her own mom scared her a little, which was sad. She was much better one-on-one than when she was trying to impress her cronies. We chatted on the way in about famous models and their careers, and fashions we liked (I'm not all that into fashion, but thanks to Mia, I can fake it for a while). I told them about the Cupcake Club, and Mrs. Allen looked very impressed.

"Why don't *you* start a business like that?" she said to Olivia, but her voice had a little bit of an edge to it, and Olivia winced. I looked away and pretended I hadn't noticed.

The open call was at a big loft downtown in kind of a desolate neighborhood. They were looking for models for *Teen Look* magazine, which was major. Inside, the loft was packed with girls our age, and we had to sign in at a desk and take numbers. We'd be seen in groups of three, and luckily, Olivia and I were in the same group. Just seeing all these kids was really intimidating. I knew there'd be no way they'd pick me from all this competition, but I knew it would be a good experience. We settled onto a bench to wait, and Olivia's mom pulled out some magazines and handed them to us. I was impressed that she had thought to pack something to pass the time.

Olivia and I chatted a little bit, but then fell silent, just watching the crowd around us. It was better than a reality TV show. There were girls of all shapes, sizes, and colors, and a wide range of prettiness, if you ask me. And the mothers! I was so glad my mom wasn't there to witness it, because I think she would have made me quit then and there.

The mothers were yanking their daughters' hair with hairbrushes, painting on makeup, adjusting the girls' clothing, roughly grasping and maneuvering them. It was like the mothers were taking out their nerves on the daughters. I didn't know where to look.

The people running the tryout were calling in groups of girls, but it was still moving very slowly. Olivia and I sat for two hours before they even got close to our number. We mostly observed and made quiet comments to each other now and then. Olivia was pretty good company. Not too braggy without an audience, and nice enough. We didn't click completely, so I doubted we'd ever really be friends, but she was perfectly pleasant.

From the minute we got there, Mrs. Allen was in her element, chatting with all the other moms in various degrees of annoyance about "the biz," as she called it. Everyone had advice and inside information, and it was all delivered with so much urgency, it was making me nervous. She only seemed to notice us occasionally and handed out some dried apricots and seltzer water to keep up our energy, but other than that, it was like we weren't even with her.

Finally, finally, our group was called, and Olivia's mom snapped to attention; brushed Olivia's hair one last time; grabbed her by the shoulders; squatted down to look at her, eye to eye; and said one word: "Sparkle." Then she swatted Olivia on the bum, gave me kind of a closed-mouth smile, and in we went, with one other girl.

Inside the room was a long table filled with grown-ups. They asked for our names and ages and our representation. I could see they were impressed when I said, "Alana Swenson." Two of them looked at each other and nodded, and a third raised his eyebrows really high and made a note on his clipboard. The other girl mentioned another agency. I felt bad for Olivia when she said, "Self-representation for now," so I pretended not to hear.

Olivia went first. They had her stand in front of a white sheet and take some test photos. They called out the poses to her, and she did them naturally, like she'd been doing this all her life: "Three-quarter turn, profile, smile, serious . . ." And then they said, "Thank you! We'll be in touch!" and she was sent out the door. The whole thing took about two minutes.

The other girl went next, and they did the same. Then it was my turn.

"Emma," said one of the women at the table. "How old are you? Where are you from? Do you play any sports? Can you sing?" and all kinds of questions like that. They took lots of photos of me, and it took almost three times as long as it had for the others. At the end they said, "We'll call you with the details of the shoot on Monday." And someone gave me a business card, and then I was out the door too.

Outside, Mrs. Allen was packing up, and Olivia was watching the door anxiously. I was pretty sure I'd been picked, but I didn't know the lingo or anything, so I wasn't sure what to tell the Allens.

But I guess because I'd been in there so long, Mrs. Allen already knew.

She gave me another tight-lipped smile and said, "All finished finally?" I wanted to say, "No, I have to go off to the shoot now," but I didn't, of course. The Allens had been nice to take me, and I felt bad by how it had worked out. Olivia hadn't been picked, and I was pretty sure I had. I shoved the business card deep into the pocket of my white jeans and knew I wouldn't look at it until I was home.

We had a quiet taxi ride to the station, but when we got to our seats on the train, Olivia's mom had a slew of things to say to Olivia, like, "Were you relaxed? Did you smile? I mean, did you *really* smile, and *sparkle*, like I told you? Because they can tell when you don't really want it. I mean, the camera doesn't miss anything, Olivia."

Olivia took it in silence for a few minutes, but then she burst out, "Jeez, Mom, I did my best! What else do you want from me?"

"I want you to try. That's all. If you'd only apply yourself, and just stick to things . . . You just need a work ethic. Look at Emma, with her cupcake business, and now this . . ."

Olivia looked out the window, and I excused myself to go to the bathroom. I couldn't just sit there and listen. I felt terrible for Olivia.

After that, it was a quiet ride home. I mostly stared out the window of the train. No magazines or apricots were offered, to me or to Olivia, and I was bored and hungry. I couldn't wait to get away from the Allens.

I'd never looked forward to seeing my mom so much in my life.

CHAPTER 9

Acting Natural

At school on Monday, I ran into Olivia first thing. She was with her crew, of course: Maggie, Callie, and Bella.

Olivia was all smiles. "Hey, I have a really good feeling about that open call on Saturday, you know?" she said loud enough for everyone to hear.

I stared at her for a minute. *Is she kidding?* They hadn't given her one scrap of encouragement. But no, she was serious.

"Yeah. Right. Well, we'll see, I guess!" I said, trying to be cheerful.

She crossed her fingers and waved them in the air at me. I did the same back and went on my way. Weird.

But that evening, when my mom listened to

the messages on our voice mail, there was a call inviting me in for a shoot on Saturday! It would be three hours, and they'd pay me a thousand dollars.

My mom and I whooped and high-fived. But then she said, "Wait, do you want to go? It's for *Teen Look*, right? Is that interesting to you?"

"Mom, who cares?!" I said. "It's a thousand dollars!"

We fell silent and stared at each other. Then we started laughing again. "Oh my goodness!" said my mother, wiping her eyes. "That's a lot of money!"

Suddenly I remembered something. "Wait, but I have my cupcake shoot in the city the same day!"

My mom's eyebrows knit together in concern. "Can we do both? What's the schedule for the cupcake shoot? This one is from nine to twelve."

I quickly called Mia and discovered our cupcake shoot was for the afternoon, from one to five p.m., and I told her I'd get back to her with a plan. When I called back later, she proposed we all drive in together and they come to watch my shoot. I agreed, saying my mom would check to see if they could watch, but they could certainly drive in with us, and it was all settled.

❧

On Wednesday we had an official meeting of the Cupcake Club, and it felt good to be back. We'd all been a little busy lately—Alexis with our web design, Mia and Katie with school, and me with the modeling stuff—so the cupcake business had slid a little. Except for our weekly delivery to Mona and our big plan for her Jaden Sacks launch party the following Saturday, we didn't have any other jobs booked right now.

"It's okay," I said. "Sometimes it's slow, but just think about the times we've been swamped and how we'd wished it would quiet down. It will pick back up again. I'm sure of it."

Alexis nodded. "We just have to use this quiet time for business development. The website will be great. I can't wait to show you what I have so far." She flipped open her laptop and proceeded to walk us through the site layout.

"And here's where our portfolio will go," she said, "and here would be a photo of us. . . ."

"Oh, my dad has great shots from that day. I'll e-mail you some, and you can pick the one for there, okay?"

"Great." Alexis nodded again.

After the site tour, we made our shopping list for

the supplies for Saturday, then divided it up, since we had so much to get. We agreed to meet after school on Friday at my house to pack everything up and do our baking for Mona and the cupcakes for the shoot, then everything would be ready to load in my mom's minivan the next morning. Leaving our meeting, we all felt organized and efficient. It was a good feeling.

At home, my mom had three new messages about go-sees from Alana! One was tomorrow, one was after school next Wednesday, and the other was next Saturday—during the Jaden Sacks launch! And, of course, that go-see was the biggest one. It was for Icon, one of my favorite stores. The money they were offering was insane (five thousand dollars!!!), and my mom and I just stared at each other, dumbfounded. How could people make so much money just standing around having their picture taken?

"But I can't go," I said, coming back down to Earth.

"Emma, that's a lot of money to turn down," my mother said. "Are you sure?"

"I promised Mona two weeks ago. It's a really big day for her. I can't back out now!"

"Could you have someone else go to Mona's

in your place? Like Olivia Allen?" my mom suggested.

"No. No way. I owe it to Mona." I felt very strongly about this, as hard as it was to turn down the Icon shoot. Plus, to be honest, there was no way I was going to even suggest Olivia take my place at my beloved The Special Day.

"Well, that's too bad. But you *are* doing the right thing. I know."

We sat quietly for a minute.

"Now, I just need to figure out the logistics of getting you into the city tomorrow for this go-see!" said my mom.

Oh boy. "Sorry," I said. "We don't have to go. It's such short notice."

"No, I think we should, especially since the Icon one won't work out. We don't want Alana to think you're not interested. I can make it work. I'll just have Jake go to the Smiths after school. Dad can organize dinner," said my mom, thinking out loud. "Matt can come home alone. Sam's working. . . ."

I guess there's more to modeling than just standing around in front of the camera after all.

The next day, my mom and I drove into the city because, even though parking is expensive, it would allow us to leave as soon as we were done rather than waiting for a train.

The go-see was at a studio in Chelsea, and it was very professional. They'd told me to come dressed like a typical junior high kid (well, that was easy) and to bring my portfolio (my dad had gotten it made at Staples, with big printouts of the photos he'd taken). We were one of the first to arrive, which was lucky, because about fifty more girls filed in after me, and I knew some of them would be here for hours. My mom was asking me all sorts of questions since I'd done this once before. It was kind of funny to have a role reversal where I was experienced at something and she was clueless. She seemed more nervous than I was! After about twenty minutes of sitting there with all the other girls scoping me out, I began to get a little nervous too.

I was called fourth, and my mom came in with me. We introduced ourselves and gave our representation info, and Alana's name again drew impressed looks of approval from the three people sitting on a long sofa against the wall. But no one said anything. I stood there feeling superawkward as they just stared at me, and finally I just looked away and pretended I wasn't there.

After a minute that felt like an eternity, the photographer and his assistant called me over and asked me to stand on the backdrop. Then they had me do the usual poses, which took about two minutes. Then the photographer thanked me. The people on the sofa still hadn't said anything.

I stood for a second. Was that it? Three whole minutes? My mom looked at me uncertainly.

"Thank you! Next!" called the photographer. And we were out the door again, portfolio in hand.

"Well, that was fast," my mother said as we put our jackets on in the elevator.

"Yeah. Kind of weird."

"Was that how it was last time?" she asked.

"No. They asked questions and everything. They actually talked."

"Maybe you just don't have the look they need for this."

"Yeah," I said.

We fell silent.

"You sure you want to keep doing this?" she asked finally.

I nodded. "For now."

"Okay. . . ." And we walked back to the parking garage, and went home.

✿

Saturday morning was chaos at our house, and early. I was tired. All this running around was catching up with me, and all I wanted to do was relax in front of the TV, but I had a huge day ahead of me.

The Cupcake Club had shopped, organized, and baked the night before, and I'd gotten up early today to shower and blow-dry my hair. I'd been told to dress as I normally would, so that was easy, and I was ready when the Cupcakers arrived at seven. We'd have to drop the minis at Mona's on the way into the city, and then my mom would drop me and the Cupcakers at my shoot while she parked.

There was a lot to load into the car, and in the end, we had to sacrifice the tiered wedding cupcake stand that we were planning to use for the Jaden Sacks launch. We'd just have to shoot that next weekend at the event instead.

Luckily, everything went according to plan, and we made it to the *Teen Look* studio with only a few minutes to spare.

I checked in at the front desk and they escorted us back to the studio. Mia was in her element, drinking it all in—the editorial offices, the framed covers on the wall, the racks of clothing samples in the halls—and Alexis was buzzing happily in such a busy work environment. Katie was wide-eyed, saying, "I can't believe I'm at *Teen Look!*" I had to giggle.

Polly, the lady running the shoot, was nice and superstylish. She had masses of long, dark ringlets, and was dressed from head to toe in black, including towering black platform boots that would have been impossible for me to walk in. The bracelets on her arm went *clackity-clack*, and her earrings went *jingledy-jing*, and she smelled amazing, like a cloud of flowers was following her.

She introduced me to the photographer and the stylists, who were all supernice and friendly, and she showed me the buffet, which was all laid out with bagels and spreads and fruit salad and juice. She told the Cupcakers to help themselves too, which was generous. All I could think of when I saw the buffet was Olivia and how she'd love to be here. I felt bad right then, but not for long, because I was quickly whisked off to change into my first look by a stylist named Shoshana.

I waved at my friends and they waved back, their mouths stuffed with breakfast foods. Still smiling, I opened the dressing room and came face-to-face with the ugliest, weirdest outfit I have ever seen.

It was hanging on a mannequin, and it was made up of so many elements, all I could think was that it would look better on a hobo lost in the Arctic Circle.

There were thin, brown leather pants, with a kind of raw edging that looked like an Inuit had sewn them in a rush (we learned about Inuits in social studies last year; they live in the Arctic and dress in heavy stuff, so you can just imagine). There was a gray cotton waffle undershirt that was ripped and distressed; with a plaid button-down overshirt in silk; a big shaggy vest made of fake white fur; a huge orange fur hat; gigantic platform Ugg-type boots; and masses of necklaces made of wooden and glass beads.

"Wow!" I said. "Is that for me?"

"Yes, isn't it amazing? It's from Slim Adkins's new line. It's genius. People are raving about it," said Shoshana.

"Really," I said. I was thinking more of getting sick about it. It all looked pretty heavy. It was a lot of fake animals for one person to carry on her body.

"Yes, let me just break it down so you can get started."

Shoshana took the look apart and began handing me the pieces. I never change in front of people; I just feel insecure about it, so I stood there and waited for her to finish.

"Do you need something?" she asked, stopping what she was doing.

"No." I was confused. *Why?* I wondered.

"Okay, then get going! We only have Miles until noon, so we've got to make the most of it. He costs a fortune."

"Wait. . . . You want me to change *now*? *Here?*"

Shoshana looked at me like I was insane. "As opposed to where?" she asked, suddenly not as nice as before.

I felt myself blushing a deep red and was furious at myself. "Oh. Okay. Usually I have privacy when I change," I said. I was proud of myself for saying it, but I was beginning to shake a little with nerves.

"O-kaaay. . . . A little unusual for a model to want privacy, but whatever . . ." I could tell she was annoyed, and I was embarrassed. She rushed off all the clothes from the mannequin and kind of flung them at me. "Call me when you're decent," she said, rolling her eyes and then stepping out.

"Thanks," I said, wanting to cry. I got on the pants and the waffle shirt as fast as I could, then I called "Ready," and Shoshana came back in.

It took another ten minutes to get everything on, and then she rushed me out to the hair and makeup lady. That took another half an hour, and

I knew my friends must be getting restless. Finally, I was ready, and they sent me back into the studio.

My mother had arrived from parking the car, and when she saw what I was wearing, her eyes widened in horror, but she didn't say anything. I think she would have said it was not age appropriate, but honestly, I'm not sure how old you'd have to be to pull off this look. I could hear my friends suck in their breath. I looked like a freak. They'd put red eye makeup on my eyelids, up to my brow bones, and made my skin really shiny. I had white lips, and my hair had been waxed into dreadlocks that dangled out from under the fur hat. I had to take baby steps or I'd fall over in the boots, and the pants were actually supertight on me.

But at last I was in front of the camera. The music was thumping, the lights were hot, and my friends were watching. It was all pretty uncomfortable.

Miles started asking for poses, and I was going along with it, but I felt so weird and stiff and so not like myself that I knew I wasn't photographing well. He kept saying, "Okay, relax. Just shake it out. There we go. Okay, I won't bite you! Don't worry," and stuff like that, but I just couldn't get into it. "Okay, Emma, let's just get a real, genuine, relaxed smile. We just need one for the keeper!" It started to be embarrassing, and I could sense he was losing patience but trying to be polite.

Finally, after about twenty agonizing minutes, he stepped away from the camera and went to look at the computer to see what he'd gotten so far. Then he called over Polly, and they went out of the room to chat.

In the meantime the Cupcakers were silent, just watching me. And so was my mom. I could sense they were all worried about me and feeling bad, which made me feel worse.

Finally, Polly came in, all businesslike, and said, "Miles is taking a quick break. I think we'll try one more look, something a little less out there, and see how it goes."

So back I went to try on something else. But this time, though it wasn't all dead (fake) animals, I thought it was even *more* out there. They put me in a sparkly miniskirt, a bathing suit kind of a top, leg warmers, a cape, and chunky heels. I looked like Wonder Woman on Halloween. They changed the eye shadow to blue and teased my hair up huge. This time, when I went back into the studio, my friends laughed in surprise. I had to giggle too.

Miles came back in, and he began shooting. But

my giggles wouldn't go away. I don't know if it was nerves, or because my friends were there, or because I knew I'd already blown this job, but I could not stop laughing.

"Glad you're having a good time, now," said Miles at first. "Okay, a few serious shots, then." But I couldn't do it. By this point I was laughing so hard, I was almost crying, and I think that given the chance, I might actually cry. "Okay, Emma, I just need a real, genuine smile. Just for for the keeper shot!" But I just couldn't do anything but giggle. Oh no! Miles and Polly conferenced again, and Polly came over with a look of regret.

"I'm so sorry, Emma, but I think this just isn't going to work today. We love your look, but maybe another time, when you're a little more experienced."

"I am so sorry," I said. "I just—"

She put an arm around me and gave me a little sideways squeeze. "It's okay. It's hard to start at the top. We'll get you again later, when you're a little more seasoned."

"Thanks. Really, I am sorry. And you were so nice."

"You should see how some girls come in here," said Polly, walking me back to the changing room.

"Some are spoiled brats with terrible attitudes, some are exhausted from partying all night, or worse, still partying. It's refreshing to have to deal with inexperience!" She laughed. "Thanks for coming. We'll send you a kill fee if we don't end up using any of the photos."

"Thanks." I stuck out my hand for her to shake, and Polly looked pleasantly surprised.

"Great meeting you," she said.

"Same," I agreed. And then sulky Shoshana helped me undress in silent disapproval, leaving automatically when I got down to the bathing suit.

Back in my normal clothes, I thanked everyone and grabbed some baby wipes from the makeup bench to remove my makeup. There wasn't much I could do about my hair, though.

I went back out to the studio to grab my mom and my friends, but they had already left and were waiting for me back in reception.

"Let's go! Quick!" I said, feeling like I was making a narrow escape.

They dashed after me, giggling, and we fled out onto the street in relief. I was laughing again, hard, but inside I was horrified by how badly I'd blown the job. I cringed thinking of how Polly would call

Alana, and Alana would fire me as her client, and it would be awful.

But maybe not that awful. This business was hard, and I could see a little bit of why the models got paid so much.

You spend a lot of time and energy, all to be poked, prodded, and evaluated. You have to get to places at a moment's notice and have the look down right. You have to deliver punctuality, professionalism, courtesy, all with a pleasant attitude. You have to be healthy and strong and fit and have a certain look, as well as no modesty or sense of privacy whatsoever. It was a lot, and I was glad to be done with it for the day.

"Let's discuss all this later, okay?" my mom whispered as my friends chatted away. Thinking of Mrs. Allen and her public reprimands of Olivia, I was grateful and nodded.

My friends used my mom's hairbrush to get my hair back down to normal, and then we set out to grab a quick bite of lunch before our next appointment. None of my friends said anything else about the *Teen Look* shoot, and for that I was also grateful.

our new website!

CHAPTER 10

Model Cupcakes

By the time we hauled everything from the mini-van up to the food stylist's studio, it was just before one o'clock. The stylist met us at the door, and we introduced ourselves. Her name was Debbie, and she was older, like a grandma, and a little chubby, with short gray curls, a huge smile, and dimples in her pink cheeks. Her studio was quiet and old-fashioned looking, with brick walls, a big open kitchen that had vintage appliances and a big marble island in the middle of it, and soft-looking wooden floorboards. There was a fireplace off to the side, with a comfy old table and mismatched chairs around it, and classical music was playing over the sound system. She directed us to where to put our supplies, and she offered everyone hot chocolate, which we all accepted, even my mother.

While my mom talked to Debbie about how she'd opened this studio and what other kinds of work she did, we unpacked everything and laid it all out. Then it was time to start.

"Okay," said Debbie, handing around the mugs of cocoa, "the first thing we do is create our shot list, with a brief on each shot. I think you're planning ten shots, right?"

Alexis nodded. She's our natural leader on Cupcake Club business. "Yes. I've written down the cupcakes' names, and we can do them in any order. We did cut one at the last minute because we couldn't fit the display in the car. . . ."

We all giggled, and Debbie smiled. "Well, maybe we can figure out something else to show it on." She looked over the list, and then she said, "Okay. Let's go to the cupboard and pick out some pretty plates and napkins and background color sheets. I think we want to mix it up a little, so we'll shoot maybe half of them in the natural light that's about to start coming in over by the window, and the rest here on the counter with my task lighting. Why don't we have each of you, including your mom, choose one cupcake and pick out a background and props for it, then we'll line it all up on the counter and regroup."

This was going to be fun!

Katie was in ecstasy, looking at all the great kitchen props. I couldn't stop drooling over the top-of-the-line KitchenAid mixer, and I could tell by the gleam in Alexis's eye that she was calculating how much money could be made in a business like this!

We made our selections and created little piles, then we worked on index cards for each shot, listing the props, the cupcake name, and whether it would be natural or stage lighting, and what color background.

Debbie chatted with us the whole time, telling us all the old-fashioned tricks of food styling, like how they used to use Elmer's Glue instead of milk in cereal bowls for cereal ads, and how they don't really cook meat but brown it with a blowtorch, and how ice cream in ads is really just a mix of lard and sugar, so it won't melt under the hot lights. Meanwhile, we each built our cupcake presentations. (My mom needed some guidance on hers, but she managed to pull it off in the end, saying she had a new appreciation for how hard we worked in the Cupcake Club!).

Debbie surveyed the cupcakes, telling us they

were beautiful and explaining that when there were multiples to choose from, the chosen food item is known as the "hero," because it's the one that gets shot. She also instructed us to add some height to the cupcakes whenever possible, because height makes things more interesting in photos. Then she explained how she'd be spraying the cupcakes with cooking spray, to make them shinier, and shooting them at an angle, with the cupcakes filling the frame whenever possible.

Finally, it was time to shoot.

Debbie set up the shots quickly, but then she must've looked through her camera lens a hundred times before pushing the button to shoot. She'd go back and forth, adjusting the lighting, the angle, the background, using tweezers and other little tools to shape and prop and generally primp the cupcakes.

"It's like you this morning, Emma!" said Alexis, laughing as Debbie shot a multicolored cupcake with a tall heap of rainbow frosting on top. "We're shooting a portfolio, and this cupcake is our little model!"

"Yeah, with the teased hair and everything!" I agreed.

"That was ridiculous," said Mia, with scorn in her voice. "No one dresses like that."

It was easier to talk about it this way while we were working and no one was actually looking at me.

"Did you like any part of that, Emma?" asked Katie.

I could feel my mom waiting for my reply. "I would have liked it better if the clothes weren't so weird. The money is great, but I probably won't get much of it for today," I admitted, then added, "And my agent might fire me."

"Then she doesn't deserve you!" said Alexis sharply.

Tears pricked at my eyes. I loved my friends. And I loved being in business with them. The Cupcake Club was hard work, but it was fun, and we were a team. Modeling was a lonely business. And I had to wonder, Was it appealing just for my ego, so I could say I was a model? Did I need money that badly? Did I even enjoy it? So far, the answers weren't good enough. I'd really need to think hard about it this week.

Our afternoon was cheerful, relaxing, and productive, especially compared to my morning. Debbie got so many beautiful shots, I actually thought Alexis might cry. At the end, Debbie promised to e-mail the best shots to Alexis, and we signed a release allowing Debbie to use the shots for publicity and on her website. (She said she'd give us credit, and we said we'd do the same.) Then we packed up, cleaned up, and headed home.

I actually fell asleep in the car on the way home and didn't wake up until our first stop to drop off Alexis. By the time we'd dropped off everyone, I was refreshed.

"Thanks, Mom, for everything today," I said from the backseat.

She looked in the rearview mirror. "It was a pleasure. I adore your friends, and I am so impressed by how hard you all worked and what a great team you are."

"It kind of stank, this morning. . . ." I wanted to discuss it, but I didn't know what to say.

My mom pressed her lips together. "That just wasn't a good match. I'll have to speak to Alana about it. If you want to keep doing this, that is."

"I think so. . . ." I wasn't as sure as I had been. I didn't know if I wanted to stay in just to prove something or if I actually liked it.

"If that's the case, then you *will* have to be more professional. Maybe you could take some classes or something," said my mom. "I also think it's a mistake to bring your friends. We certainly won't do that again."

"We kind of owe Olivia one, though . . . ," I said, feeling guilty.

"Of course. But that's different. She isn't there to giggle with."

I thought of Olivia's mom and her "sparkle" directive. "That's for sure," I agreed, and sighed.

Back home, there were three messages from Alana, asking my mom to call her.

"Uh-oh," I said, listening to the third one.

My mom grimaced, and dialed. "Alana?"

Boy, she must've picked up on the first ring. I braced myself, waiting to hear shouting through the phone. I tried to read my mom's expression, to see if I could tell what Alana was saying. Finally, my mom got a word in edgewise.

"It's not your fault. No, don't be silly. She's fine." My mom looked up at me, smiling and making a surprised face. "Well, yes, the outfits were inappropriate, but Polly was very nice. No, don't worry about it. Please. Whatever money you can get is fine. Thanks. Talk soon. Bye."

My mom hung up the phone and stared at it in shock for a second before looking up at me. "Alana was furious. At *them*! Polly called her to explain what happened, and Alana freaked out that they'd taken a child and tried to dress her as an adult, and on and on. She wanted to know if you were 'scarred for life' and insisted she will get every penny of the original fee for you. Wow!"

I grinned. "No wonder people are impressed when they hear she's my agent. She's fierce!"

"We're lucky," said my mom. "Now let's make sure we deserve her."

For Wednesday's go-see, my mom learned that it was an open call, so she made me invite Olivia, who was thrilled. Ugh. Even worse, my mom had no one to pawn Jake off on, so he had to come too!

We took the train into the city, and the call was at a big casting company's office. There were all sorts of commercials and ads being cast at once, so there were hordes of kids in different staging areas. It was overwhelming. One whole group was dressed as elves, which was kind of funny, and another was all in ballerina outfits. I felt like I was in a dream.

Olivia and I got our call numbers and studio assignment, and my mom and Jake tagged along to the holding area. It wasn't that big of a group waiting, and I didn't understand why until the door opened at one point and I got a flash of what was inside. Dogs. Lots of them! I suddenly feel great, because I am a dog expert! If this job calls for working with dogs, I have already nailed it!

I smiled at Olivia. "Dogs," I said confidently.

"What?" she asked, a look of fear creeping over her face.

"It must be a dog food ad or something. There are tons of dogs in there!" I announced happily.

Olivia paled and sank down into her chair. "I hate dogs," she whispered. "I'm afraid of them!"

And sure enough, when we're called and ushered in, the room was alive with pooches. I dropped to my knees to play with the first ones to come to me, but Olivia backed up against a wall, terrified. Jake followed me into the room and got down on his knees too, laughing hysterically when the dogs began to lick his face. My mom signed us in and sat on a chair to wait for our test shots.

Olivia was called first. She inched up to the backdrop, and a handler brought some dogs over to her on leashes. I could see that she was trying not to look scared, but it was not working.

"Okay, just smile and relax, please," said the photographer.

But as I watched, Olivia could not relax and she could not smile. After, like, three shots the ad person said to Olivia, "Okay, thank you!" Olivia looked stunned that she was already done. "Thanks!" the lady said again when Olivia wasn't fast enough to move off the backdrop.

"That's it?" Olivia asked as she walked off.

"Uh-huh. Next?" the lady suddenly called, and I stepped in.

She handed me the dogs' leashes and asked for a pose, but I was distracted by the animals that wouldn't seem to do as I said. They were pulling me one way, while the photographer was in the other direction, and suddenly I felt something warm on my leg. No! A dachshund just peed on me!

"Sorry! Thank you!" the agency lady said, and now I'm hustled off the backdrop and handed a wad of paper towels. *What?* This was my moment to shine! Dogs loved me! But it was not to be.

I mopped my leg and noticed the ad lady and the photographer conferring for a minute. Then the ad lady went over to my mom, and they chatted briefly. My mom called over Jake from where he was wrestling with a bunch of dogs, and I am mortified. Here we were, unprofessional on the shoot again. This time I'm sure they'll call Alana and then she'll fire me. *Why does Jake always have to ruin everything?* I thought angrily.

But suddenly Jake was shrugging, and they were changing his shirt. He was on the backdrop laughing with a bunch of adorable golden retriever puppies rolling all over him, and they were taking his picture. Olivia and I stood in shock, watching, as Jake nailed the job we'd both come in for.

By the time we were on the train back to Maple Grove, Olivia and I were in stitches, laughing over being upstaged by a little boy with no front teeth, and my mom was moaning about having two models in the family. Jake was clueless about what it all meant. He just had fun playing with the doggies, and he said he didn't mind if his picture ended up in a magazine!

The night ended with me thinking maybe it would be better if I left the modeling career to Jake, who seemed to take it all pretty lightly.

LAUNCH ☆ PARTY!!

CHAPTER 11

Jaden Sacks!

$\mathcal{M}$ona called me in a complete panic on Thursday afternoon.

"Darling! I'm in a pinch! Jaden Sacks wants oodles of bridesmaids at the launch, and I've only signed up you! Help! I need some more gorgeous tweenagers!"

I laughed. "How about the Cupcake Club, since they're already planning on coming? At least I know they're free!"

"Sounds great to me, but would you be able to send me a photo? Jaden Sacks's publicity team likes to approve the models in advance, to make sure they're consistent with the company image. Not too flashy, you know?"

"Sure. I just happen to have a great photo."

We hung up, and I e-mailed Mona the link to our new demo website. In the section About Us, there's a really pretty and fun group shot from the session with my dad. An hour later, Mona called back. "Book them, darling! They're approved!"

But that night, as I was lying down to go to sleep, my stomach dropped.

Olivia!

I should have invited her too. I didn't want to, but I kept thinking about her mom, and I kind of felt bad for her. Going on all those casting calls is tough for anyone. It would be a nice thing to do.

I climbed out of bed, switched on my light and laptop, and dashed off a quick, kind of neutral e-mail to Olivia, asking if she could e-mail me a head shot, since I might know of a job for her. Of course it was in my in-box first thing the next morning when I checked, and I forwarded it to Mona with the subject line "One More" and crossed my fingers.

At school, Olivia accosted me, again in front of her friends, asking me about the job we're booking and have I heard back about the dog food one yet. Her gang was all ears, impressed.

I tried to make it sound like she had a chance

for the dog food one, which was a flat-out lie, and I prayed that Jaden Sacks didn't like her look. I was a little mad that I had tried to do something nice and she was just acting like regular Olivia.

It turned out, though, that Jaden Sacks thought Olivia was, according to Mona, "just divine." If she only knew.

On Saturday, as Icon's five thousand dollars sat in their bank account rather than my pocket, we all trooped over to The Special Day, cupcakes and tiered stand in hand. My dad drove us, because he said my mom has gotten to see more of me lately than he did, and he wanted to grab some snapshots of the big day, anyway.

Mona and Patricia and their team were even more aflutter than I've ever seen, and all the furniture in the store had been pushed against the walls, to make room for the crowds. Olivia was there waiting for us with her mother, and between the two of them, it was hard to tell who was more ecstatic. I felt good about calling and including her after all, mostly because it might make her mom a little nicer to her.

We scrambled inside; set up the huge cupcake display, which Mona swooned over; and then headed back to have our hair done. Mona hired a professional hair stylist for the day, and we all lined up to be lightly worked over by the curling iron.

Then Patricia whisked us away for our look lineup. I retrieved my slip from its usual hanging spot and put on my first dress. It was a floaty, linen dress, with just a tiny bit of stitched detail at the hem, and a wide, pink sash. I loved it. It could not be more comfortable to wear, and pretty! It was something I would have picked out for myself. As Patricia finished tying a big bow in the back, I slipped on white ballet slippers and headed out to show my dad.

But when I got out to the main salon, I saw him chatting with Mona and another woman I didn't recognize. I started to approach them, and then Mona spied me and waved me over, calling, "Darling, come!"

"Darling! Isn't she divine?" she said to the other woman. "This . . . is Jaden Sacks!"

"Oh! Oh my gosh! Hi! Wow! It is so cool to meet you! I'm just . . . I love, love, love your dresses! I wish I could wear them every day. Like, even to school!" I knew I sounded silly and I was gushing, but it was all true. Jaden Sacks smiled.

She wasn't as old as I would have thought—maybe in her late thirties. She had golden hair to her shoulders, cut in a swingy kind of shag, and she was tan, with bright blue eyes. She was very petite, and when I shook her hand, I was surprised by how light and thin it was. She had real artist's hands—graceful and delicate. She grinned warmly and her eyes sparkled, and I felt like we were sharing a great joke, like we were instantly friends.

"I have a lot to thank you for!" she said, in a surprisingly girlish voice.

"Me?! Why?"

"Your ad was a huge hit! Our flagship store got one hundred and seventy-two calls looking for the dress you wore in that ad. One of the reasons I was hoping to meet you was to see if you and Mona would mind if we bought the shot and ran it nationally."

"What? Really?" I thought of Olivia and her "national ad" information. "Great. I mean, you'll have to speak to my agent. . . ." I looked around for my dad.

"Oh my gosh! An agent! They start so young these days!" Jaden joked. "Who *is* your agent? You?" She looked at my dad, who was standing behind me.

But he shook his head. "No, I'm her father. Emma's agent is someone called Alana Swenson."

Jaden put her head in her hands, like she was devastated, but she was joking. "Of course it is. She wouldn't let someone like you escape her radar! I'll call her on Monday. She owes me a lunch, anyway, since we used only Swenson girls at our last runway show!"

"I bet she loved that!" I said, laughing.

"Oh, she did." Jaden laughed back. "Ka-ching!"

Patricia came scurrying up to say the bridal models were all ready and the bridesmaids nearly so and did we want to open the doors yet. I turned to look outside, and there were so many people standing beyond the doors that I couldn't even see past them. Wow! I gulped.

"I'll let you go. Congratulations! See you after!" I said to Jaden. And I scurried back to the dressing room.

Mrs. Allen was there, whispering directives to Olivia, but Patricia booted her out, and Olivia relaxed after that. The next half hour went by in a blur as we did our fashion show before a couple hundred people, and then we could relax as we mingled.

The Cupcakers thought the whole thing was

a hoot, but they were exhausted at the end.

"This is really hard work!" said Alexis. "Just being on your feet this long is tiring!"

"Yeah, and all that smiling," said Katie, who seems to be smiling all the time, anyway.

"I loved it!" said Olivia, and it was true. She had seemed happy. Maybe runway work was the thing for her. I wouldn't mind too much if Mona ended up using her too. It might be nice to have a little company at the trunk shows. "Of course, it's nothing like a national ad shoot for TV, when they have all the buffets lined up. . . ."

I groaned, and everyone laughed.

Olivia looked up and blushed.

Before we all changed, my dad, who'd been taking pictures all day, asked the Cupcakes to come outside, and he got some great shots of the Cupcake Club with Jaden Sacks and Mona in front of the store.

The pictures turned out so great that when he e-mailed them to Jaden and Mona later, they picked one to run in an ad in the *Gazette*.

A month later my family had a big Sunday dinner to celebrate Jake's dog food ad in the new issue of *Parents' Life* magazine and the full-page ad in the *Gazette* of all the Cupcakers with Mona and Jaden.

The best part was at the bottom of the bridal ad. It said:

jadensacks.com

thespecialdaysalon.com

thecupcakeclub.com

I had dialed back on my modeling career a little by then. My mom had told Alana we'd only do tween stuff, and only on weekends, and only with at least a week's notice. And Alana was fine with that.

Olivia worked a trunk show at Mona's with me one weekend, and it was fun to have her there. She was a lot nicer when she was alone, and she was a lot more relaxed when her mom wasn't around. I could kind of see how Mia liked her at first, and I kind of felt badly that her mom could be so hard on her. We went on our lunch break together, and it was my treat, with money from my last photo shoot. We had apricots and seltzer water from the Fruit & Nut stand, and cupcakes for dessert!

But the next Monday at school, she was back to her old self again. As I walked to my locker, I could hear her talking about the fashion show at Mona's.

"Emma was okay, but anyone could tell she was inexperienced," she was saying. Bella and Callie were hanging on to her every word. "I was the star of the show, if I do say so myself. Everyone was staring at me, and I heard Jaden asking Mona who I was. That's why I wasn't in the print ad. They wanted to save me, so I could do an ad by myself, without being lumped in with all the, well, regular girls. Poor Emma! I'll probably have to replace her at The Special Day, but it was going to happen eventually. She's just not 'model material.'"

I couldn't believe it! After all I had done to try and help her out. I was steaming. I walked right up to her and tapped her on the shoulder. Olivia blinked and looked startled for a moment, but then went right back into her act.

"Oh, Emma, I'm so sorry! I didn't mean for you to hear that," she said. She touched my arm lightly. "But maybe it's better coming from a friend, you know?"

I looked at Bella and Callie, who just stared at me and nodded sadly.

"I think you're right, Olivia," I replied, "that sometimes criticism is better coming from a friend. But you aren't my friend. I tried to do something nice for you after you didn't get booked on any jobs and after Alana Swenson didn't take you on as a client, and I asked Mona to include you in The Special Day event. I'm sorry you weren't in the ad that ran. They were looking for someone less fake-model looking and . . . well, someone with a bit of sparkle."

I felt a little bad right then, because Olivia turned really pale and looked like she wanted the floor to swallow her up. I almost started to say something about being a baby model as her last job, but I stopped. I had said enough to make my point. There was no need to stoop down to her level.

I smiled my best "model" smile and turned to walk down the hall, like it was a big runway. I thought of my mom, who thought I always sparkled no matter what, and I kept walking toward my friends, who didn't care if I was a model or not. I thought of going to The Special Day and putting on the pretty dresses with my friends Mona and Patricia and just having fun. I thought of how excited I was that the Cupcake

Club had booked a bunch of new jobs, thanks to our website. I smiled a real, genuine smile. And then I laughed. Because if Miles was there, I know that smile would have been "the keeper."

Alexis
gets
frosted

CHAPTER 1

Back to Reality

*W*inter break was over and it was back to reality.

I happen to love reality, but my friends weren't so thrilled about it this morning.

Katie still looked half asleep, and Mia was grumpy. Emma was pleasant if a little quiet, but I was raring to go. After all, ten days without school or friends or the Cupcake Club is a long time! By habit, and without even planning it, all of us Cupcake Club members had convened at Mia's locker this morning to catch up before homeroom.

"Why can't it be winter break forever?" Katie was moaning. She leaned against Mia's locker like she couldn't spend the energy to stand up on her own.

"Where is my new assignment notebook?" Mia

wailed, quickly pawing through her tote bag.

I smiled, not wanting to gloat about being all organized and ready. I'd had all my school things laid out since yesterday: my outfit, my books, my pens, and my day planner. Failing to plan is planning to fail, I always say! (But I don't say it out loud too much or my best friends get annoyed.)

"Cupcake Club meeting today after school?" I asked, trying not to sound too cheerful since everyone else was kind of down.

They all looked at me blankly. Then Katie said, "How can you even think that far ahead?"

"We can meet at my house . . . ," I offered. "I have some cool quartz rocks I got on the trip I want to show you."

Mia sighed and slammed her locker shut. "No notebook." Then she looked at me. "Sure, I'll come. It will give me something to look forward to on this horrible first day back," she said.

"Obviously, we'll all be there," said Emma, snapping out of her trance.

"Of course we will," agreed Katie.

Mia was looking carefully at my face.

"What?" I asked. It is kind of annoying to have someone peer at you like that.

"Do you have any balm or cream you can put

on that peeling skin of yours?" she asked.

I'm not much of a cosmetics person, even though I periodically try to get into it. It just seems like too much work, and I hate carrying extra stuff in my bag. I shrugged. "No. Does it look terrible?"

"No . . . just kind of painful," said Mia. "Here." She reached into her tote bag and took out a huge cosmetics case, then she opened it and rummaged for a minute before pulling out a small tube of face cream. "My mom got free samples at the mall. You can keep it till the peeling stops. Just remember to reapply every hour on the hour."

"You know, you really should be more careful about sunscreen on the slopes," said Katie.

"I know, but who would have thought Utah would be so sunny?!" I said. My face had really hurt for days out there, between the sunburn, the windburn, and the dry air.

We reached a turn in the hall and separated for homeroom. I stopped in the bathroom first to apply the cream when Olivia Allen, our resident mean girl, came in. She took one look at me and then began to snicker.

"Does your face hurt? Because it's *killing* me!" she said, and laughed to herself.

"Ha-ha," I said. "Not." I can take a joke, but a

bad one? From someone I don't like? About my appearance? Please.

"What did you do, fall asleep reading a book in the sun?" she said, all serious and fake-concerned.

"No, it's from skiing," I said. I ignored her kind of bratty tone and looked away, busying myself putting the cap back on the cream and stashing it into a pocket of my backpack.

"So, you were reading while skiing? Now that's impressive!" she said sarcastically.

I was confused. "I wasn't reading," I said. "I was skiing."

"Oh, but I know how much you love to geek out on your homework, so I just assumed—"

"Good morning, girls!" said my homeroom teacher, Ms. Dobson, as she went to wash her hands.

I looked at Olivia for a second longer. She was smirking, amused with herself. Why was she going after me all of a sudden? I mean, Sydney Whitman, our former mean girl who moved away to California, was one thing. But Olivia Allen had never before directly attacked me like this. It was surprising and upsetting. My face was flushed, and my ears burned at the tips, which made them even redder, if that was even possible. I kept playing Olivia's comments over in my head, the words "geek out" rattling around like pinballs in a machine. Am I a geek? Is that what people think of me? I was too mortified to even work out what my comeback should have been.

When the warning bell rang to head out to our homerooms, I kept my head turned away from Olivia, hoping she wouldn't say anything else. She must've been satisfied with her morning's work, because she just grabbed her bag and calmly strolled off. I stalled a little to put a good amount of space between us in the hall.

I couldn't wait to tell the other Cupcakers what had happened. Maybe they could help me figure it out.

The morning started off well after that since I had math (which I love) with my favorite teacher, Mr. Donnelly (who rocks). My next class, though, was English, which is not my favorite. We're reading Charles Dickens's book *Great Expectations* and learning about life in Victorian England. Today, Mrs. Carr announced we would each have to complete an independent project with a visual presentation component that shows what it was like to live in Victorian England. *Ugh. Math is so much easier than this,* I thought, heading to gym class.

I was lost in thought as I walked to the locker room. What on Earth would I make? I am not crafty or creative, like Katie, who is obsessed with baking, or Mia, who is obsessed with fashion. When we do Cupcake Club stuff, I am mostly in charge of the business side of things—marketing, invoicing, purchasing, and all the numbers stuff. I knew I'd have to brainstorm for this project with my friends. I just hoped their ideas weren't too wild, because I did not have the skills, patience, or interest to do something over the top.

We didn't have time to talk about it during gym class, so I was still distracted at lunch when I got on line for food, but suddenly, I realized someone had jostled me and cut me in line. I looked up from the silverware rack to see the unmistakable back of Olivia Allen.

"Hey!" I cried out in protest.

Olivia turned back to look at me. "What?" she asked, all innocent.

"You just cut ahead of me!" I sputtered.

Olivia laughed. "Alexis," she said, all fake sweet. "I know you have a hearty appetite, what with all those cupcakes you eat, but can you let other people have a chance at the food too?" Then she turned and kept moving along.

I was speechless. To so rudely and blatantly cut me, and then to insult me on top of it? What a jerk! I fought the urge to bash her over the head with my tray. Luckily for Olivia, she headed off to the salad bar while I stopped for the hot meal. I wished I'd had something clever and mean to say to her to put her in her place. I'd have liked to see her blush and shake for once!

By the time I got my food, I was in a red rage. I sought out my friends and stomped over to join them.

"Uh-oh!" said Emma, spying me. She has been my best friend since we were toddlers, so she can always spot my mad face a mile away. "What happened?"

I slammed my tray down hard on the table. "What happened? What happened? I'll tell you what happened! I hate Olivia Allen, *that's* what happened. She is an evil witch, and she is after me!" I proceeded to tell the others all about Olivia's unwarranted attacks on me so far today. They were appropriately shocked and angry on my behalf, and I began to calm down. By the end of my retelling, I was mostly mad at myself for not coming up with a comeback or beating her down in some way.

"If she was so eager to get her lunch, that line-cutting piggy, then she should have gotten to the cafeteria a little faster!" I snarled.

My friends hooted and clapped. "That's what you should have said to her!" said Mia, laughing. "'Line-cutting piggy'! That's great!"

"I know," I muttered, digging into my fish taco. "I always think of things like that too late. I'm an idiot."

"You're *not* an idiot," said Katie kindly. "You're the opposite. Anyway, would you really want to be the kind of nasty person who always has a sharp comment or comeback ready to go? That's a terrible way to lead your life."

I nodded. She had a point. But still. "Maybe I'd like to be the person who sometimes has a comeback, instead of the person who never does," I said. "Oh, and to make matters worse, I have to do a visual component for my presentation on Victorian England for English! What the heck am I going to make?" I wailed.

Mia clapped her hands. "Ooh. What about a costume? I could help you dress up like a Victorian lady. That would be so much fun! The high, tight waist; the long, full skirts; the lace-up shoes . . . !"

"No, you should do a diorama of, like, people

selling stuff from carts. . . . You know, Victorian business practices!" suggested Emma.

"Hmm. That would be fun to research," I said, already imagining the diorama.

"No, what if you did a diorama out of gingerbread!" said Katie, always thinking about food. "Like a Victorian house, but in gingerbread!"

"Yessss!" cheered Mia and Emma.

"That is totally it!" added Emma.

I thought for a minute. "I think that would be really, really hard, even if it is a cool idea," I said.

"We'll help you!" offered Katie. "It'll be fun!"

"Yeah," Mia chimed.

"Well . . ." It is hard to turn down your three best friends, whom you already know you work well with in the kitchen, when they're offering their help on a horrible project like this.

"And Olivia Allen will be so jealous when she sees it, her eyes will pop out of her head!" said Mia.

Well, that sealed the deal for me!

"Okay!" I agreed. "Thanks, you guys! You really are the best." I pictured Olivia's jaw dropping as I wheeled some massive and spectacular creation into class. All the kids would be oohing and aahing. It would be glorious!

"Hey, wake up, you two dreamers!" Mia laughed.

Katie was also lost in thought. "Wouldn't it be cool to do gingerbread houses from all different eras? Like, imagine a log cabin, *Little House on the Prairie* style. That would be fun to make."

"Oh, I always wished I'd lived then!" said Emma wistfully. "I would have loved those pioneer days."

"Uh-uh, not for me. I'd have liked the nineteen seventies! Just think of the clothes!" Mia sighed. "The whole gypsy-peasant look? I would have totally loved that!"

"I think the nineteen fifties had cool clothes," said Katie. "Those cute Peter Pan collars and the swirly skirts that stick out? I would have looked great in those."

"What about the sixties? All the hippie stuff?" I said.

"We still have a bunch of those kind of clothes from my grandma," said Mia. "My mom saved them because they were so chic."

"It's funny when you see pictures of how your mom used to dress when she was your age, right?" said Emma. "My mom was our age in the eighties, and her clothes were a disaster!"

"I know, but at the time they thought they looked great!" Mia laughed.

I tried to picture my mom back then. We don't

have too many pictures of her when she was a kid because she hates clutter. I've seen some at my grandparents' house, but now I was wishing I'd seen more. I made a mental note to ask her when she got home from work tonight.

I looked at my watch. It was time to go. I dreaded seeing Olivia again. My reserves were worn down, and I knew I'd probably burst into tears if she was mean to me again (more from my frustration at not knowing what to say back than anything else!). "Back into battle," I said sadly.

"Come on! You're tough, Becker!" said Emma. "Don't let her get the best of you."

"Yeah, and you've got us to back you up!" said Katie, making a fist so puny, I had to laugh. "What?" she protested. "I'm tough!"

Mia added, "We've got your back, and all she's got is some ragtag band of hand-me-down jerks from Sidney Whitman."

I laughed. "Yeah!"

"Okay, so buck up!" added Mia, rubbing my back supportively. "And remember, fun Cupcake Club meeting at your house today, to look at your new rock thingies."

"Okay. I'm ready! I can do this!" I said, pumping myself up.

And, of course, because I was ready, I didn't run into Olivia again—not for the whole rest of the day! Typical! But still, I couldn't help but wonder what the deal was with Olivia. Why was I suddenly "enemy number one" to her? I forced myself to stop thinking about it and thought about my three smart, beautiful, funny friends instead. Thank goodness for Emma, Mia, and Katie!

CHAPTER 2

Think Pink

We didn't have a whole lot of business in the pipeline, since we were just back from vacation, but we did have our regular client, Mona at The Special Day bridal salon to bake for this Friday, as well as a baby shower coming up the following weekend.

For Mona, we always bake mini cupcakes the width of a quarter, filled, and topped with a burst of frosting. We try to stick to neutral colors and flavors, like white and vanilla, so nothing stains the wedding dresses in her shop.

We needed to buy some supplies, so we voted on a cash disbursement to me, the purchasing agent (I do love titles!), and I would go after school on Thursday to pick up the ingredients we'd need to restock.

As for the baby shower, it was for Emma's little brother's old preschool teacher, Mrs. Horton, so we could be creative. We'd brainstorm now and do test baking at our regular baking session on Friday.

"I'm thinking of those alphabet blocks as a decoration. Like, do the whole alphabet in cupcakes, with each letter frosted on to a little block shape," said Katie.

"Cute!" agreed Emma. "What flavor?"

"It would be cool if we could do a cookies-and-milk flavor somehow, like snack time at school," offered Mia.

We were quiet a minute while we thought through the logistics of that.

"Graham cracker something . . . ," I said.

"With a cream filling?" added Katie.

"Or we could do an apple-cinnamon thing and cream-cheese frosting and then decorate the cupcakes with a little piped red apple with a green fondant stem and leaf? Like, apples for the teacher?" said Mia.

"That's a good one too!" I agreed.

"Yum," said Katie. "Maybe with applesauce in the middle!"

Emma was writing it all down. That way, if I had to get extra supplies for our test baking session on Friday, I'd have all the info I needed.

"Ooh, applesauce," said Emma. "What about baby food cupcakes, since it's a baby shower? Like carrot cake, applesauce cake, sweet potato . . ."

"Broccoli cake?" asked Mia, wrinkling her nose in distaste. "I think we're on the wrong track with that one!"

Emma laughed in agreement, but this was how brainstorming worked. One weird idea can just take off or spark another idea that's actually better. It's like when Emma thought of bacon cupcakes and we all laughed, but they became one of our biggest hits.

"Hey, would you guys mind if I got some gingerbread supplies too, with my own money, of course, while I'm at the store? Then maybe we could get started on it?" I asked.

"Great idea!" said Katie. "I can't wait!"

I smiled, grateful for her support.

"Get started on what?" asked my dad, coming in from the back door and hanging his briefcase and raincoat on a hook.

"Dad! What're you doing home so early?" I asked. I was happy to see him, but it was a surprise. My parents don't usually get home until six or later, and it was only five now.

"Your mom and I have to run to a reception at the new health-care center that my company helped raise money to build. It's just cocktails, so we won't be long, but I want to get in and out as soon as it starts. These charity events are exhausting. I'd rather do the real work than stand around making small talk! Now, what do you girls have cooking?" he asked.

My mom is a health-food nut, so my dad is always scrounging for samples or volunteering to be our tester for things, since he rarely gets baked goods or treats. It's kind of pathetic, but we're grateful to have him as our number-one fan.

"Actually, we're talking about Alexis's class project for English. She's doing a gingerbread house diorama of a Victorian house," Emma said.

"Neat! I can help you if you need anything," my dad said, folding his arms and leaning against the counter. Then he snapped his fingers. "Oh! And also, Mrs. Becker's birthday is coming up, and I'd like to order some cupcakes for her. I've decided we're going to have a little lunch party that day. So, maybe four dozen? We don't want any leftovers. . . ." He grinned.

I smiled at him. "I'm on to you, you know!" I scolded, wagging my finger at him. "Mom doesn't like cupcakes! This is just an excuse so you can have some!"

My dad pretended to be shocked. "Me? What? I don't like cupcakes!" He made a grossed-out face. "Can't stand 'em! No sirree, not me."

We all laughed. Even my friends know how much he loves them.

I shook my head from side to side, still smiling. "What kind?" I asked.

My dad tapped his foot and looked up at the ceiling while he thought. "Well . . . I know the bacon caramel ones are her favorite . . . ," he said, acting all casual.

"Dad! Those are *your* favorite!"

"Me? No way! I told you, I hate cupcakes!"

At this point my friends and I were all laughing really hard when my mom walked in. "What's up?" she asked, smiling as if she wanted in on the joke.

"Dad's just teasing us," I said, then asked slyly, "What are your favorite kinds of cupcakes?"

"Oh, I'm not a big cupcake person . . . ," she said.

At this my friends collapsed into helpless fits of giggles because it was so perfect. My dad pretended to be all exasperated, but he was laughing too.

"She's just kidding because she's actually a

cupcake monster, but she doesn't want you to know it," he said, elbowing her.

My mom said, "Now I am totally confused."

"Really, what kinds of cupcakes do you like?" asked my dad.

My mom thought for a second. "Maybe like a strawberry shortcake kind of thing? Something light and fruity, that's for sure."

My dad raised his eyebrows and gave me a significant nod, like, *Got it?*

I winked at him and gave him a small nod back without her seeing me.

"Why?" asked my mom.

"Just taking a poll," said my dad. "Come on, time to head out."

My mom groaned a little. She didn't want to go either. "See you girls in a bit," she said reluctantly. "You know what? Let me just run and brush my hair. . . ." And she dashed off.

My dad looked down at his shoes and said, really quietly, "And if you felt like making any of those strawberry shortcake cupcakes in caramel, of course . . ."

"Of course!" I said. "All our strawberry shortcake cupcakes come with a side of bacon caramel cupcakes. Right, girls?"

"Absolutely," agreed Mia, smiling.

My dad smiled in relief. "Great!"

"Okay, back to business. This Friday, we have the usual order for Mona, and we're trying the apple-cinnamon and milk-and-cookies cupcakes to see if we should make them for Mrs. Horton's shower next weekend. Then that *same* weekend, for my mom's birthday, we'll do strawberry shortcake and bacon caramel. Two dozen of each." I looked meaningfully at my dad, who nodded, like he had no stake in it whatsoever.

"Now, who wants to help me sketch out a house design for the gingerbread house? We could go look online for images first, and then I could show you my rocks in my room," I said.

Everyone was game, and Mia offered to sketch out the house and figure out the measurements with my help, since I am the math whiz. Katie would figure out how much gingerbread we needed, since she is the baking whiz.

"Have fun, Mr. Becker!" said Emma as we left the kitchen.

"I wish I was staying home and eating cupcakes instead," he said sadly, and we all laughed.

After my parents left, we found some neat images that we printed out, but it was going to be hard to guess the dimensions. Mia started sketching at my desk, and the rest of us turned back to discussing our cupcake jobs as Emma and Katie turned my new quartz geodes over and over in their hands.

"What should we do to make your mom's cupcakes pretty?" asked Katie. "Like, what's she into?"

I was embarrassed for a second because I didn't really know. "Well, she likes things very neat and orderly, so we could make them, like, really perfect looking. . . ."

"And healthy!" said Emma.

I nodded. "Yeah, like low-fat cupcakes with some really light frosting."

"Do you want to decorate or style them in some cute way?" asked Katie.

"Well . . . she's into Sudoku. . . ."

Katie wrinkled her nose in distaste. "Numbers all over our pretty cupcakes?"

I nodded. "I know . . . not everyone loves numbers as much as I do." But what else? "She likes murder mysteries . . . and movies, as long as they're not gross-out comedies."

Katie thought for a second. "Well, maybe, what was she into when she was a kid? Since cupcakes are kind of kiddish."

"You know, I'm not really sure. We don't really

talk about when she was a kid that much."

I could feel Emma looking at me. "You know her favorite color, though, right?" she asked quickly.

"Oh, yes. Pink!" I said, relieved.

Emma did a little clap. "Perfect, then. We'll make the cupcakes pink. They'll be really cute."

Right then I felt grateful to Emma, like she had saved me. But I was still uneasy about my answer. Between not knowing how my mom dressed in the eighties and not being able to come up with what she was into when she was a kid, I felt like I had some homework to do, like I was behind. Everyone else seemed to know all about her mom's child-hood, except me.

"Ugh!" Mia crumpled up yet another sheet of paper and then chucked it over her shoulder.

"What's the matter?" I asked.

"It's just really hard to draw something and make it look three dimensional when your only reference is a flat photo."

"I can't even imagine," I agreed since I am not artistic at all.

"I should go," said Emma, making absolutely no move to leave.

"Me too," Katie piped up. But she did stretch and stand up.

"Your rocks are really cool, Alexis," said Emma, handing the geodes back to me.

"Thanks," I said, looking inside at the pink crystals that looked like diamonds.

"I'll keep trying at home," said Mia. "I know I can come up with something."

I smiled at her gratefully. "You're the best. Thank you *so* much."

"It's nothing," she said modestly.

"Your dad is so funny," said Katie as we walked down the stairs. I winced because her dad basically disappeared after her parents got divorced. Katie doesn't talk about it that much, but I know she sees my dad and Emma's dad around all the time and involved, and Mia's dad always makes time to see her, even though he lives in the city and is divorced from Mia's mom. It's got to be hard for Katie.

"He's such a joker," I said, kind of dismissing it. I love my dad so much, but I don't want Katie to feel bad.

"You're lucky," she said.

"Thanks" was all I could say. We had arrived at the back door. "Thanks for everyone's help," I said. And then, because I couldn't let it go, I added, "I'll try to find out some more about what my mom

304

was into when she was a girl. I can't believe I don't even know."

"Pink!" said Emma, and she smiled. "Think pink!"

"Right," I agreed, and smiled back. "She was into pink."

CHAPTER 3

Yessss

That night when my mom came into my room to tuck me in (it sounds so babyish, I hate saying it, but my mom still actually tucks in my covers!), I had to ask.

"Mom, what were you into when you were my age?"

"Me?" It was like she was surprised I was asking and wasn't sure how to answer. "Well ..." She stared into space for a minute.

"Mom?"

"Oh. Well, I liked ballet. And also my dollhouse."

I propped myself up on one arm. "Your dollhouse? Weren't you a little old for that at my age?"

She winced a little. "Yes. I probably was. But it was so relaxing to work on it, and it was a great project for my mother and me. After Grandpa died when I was eight, she and I moved into a tiny apartment for a few years, just us two. And we worked on this dollhouse and went all over looking for bits and pieces for it. She even bought a kit to electrify it and figured out how to do it all by herself." She smiled at the memory. "It gave us a lot of focus, and I think comforted us, since we missed Dad. Plus, moving from our big beautiful house into the little apartment, we were still able to decorate and shop for our 'house,' but on a much smaller scale. I loved it."

"So why did you get rid of it?" I asked.

My mother looked at me in surprise. "I didn't get rid of it! It's at my mom and Jim's house." My grandmother remarried when my mom was sixteen, and she actually had two more kids, my aunt Margy and my uncle Mike, who are much younger than my mom and lots of fun.

"It is?" I asked, confused. "How come we've never seen it?"

My mother laughed. "I did show it to you girls one time when Dylan was three and you were one, and you two were just grabbing everything and trying to eat it, so I left it there. I'd always meant to bring it here when you girls got old enough to be interested, but you never really were into dolls or anything. Then I kind of forgot about it."

"Can I see it?" I asked.

"Sure," said my mom, shrugging. "I didn't think you were into dollhouses, though."

"I'm not." The one she had bought me when I was eight had sat in a corner of my room untouched for two years before we donated it to the pediatrician's waiting room. "But I'm into knowing more about you when you were a kid!"

With a smile, my mom brushed my hair off my forehead. "I can call Granny and see what her schedule is. I'll find a time to take you over there. Maybe this weekend."

"Thanks," I said, snuggling down into my covers. "Also I want to see pictures of how you dressed in the eighties."

"Oh no! You definitely don't want to see those!" My mom laughed.

"Why?"

"They're awful! Clothes were hideous back then. Except for one little yellow gingham dress I had, with a green pear-shaped patch pocket." She looked all dreamy. "I loved that dress!"

"Hmm. Sounds great." I yawned. "Tell Granny I'd like to see those photos too."

"Why this sudden interest in my past?" asked my mother, turning out the light. She stood in my doorway, just a tall, slender figure backlit by the light from the hall.

"Just interested . . . ," I fibbed. Obviously, I couldn't tell her about the cupcakes, but it was more than that, anyway. It was about my friends knowing way more than I do about their moms and also about wondering how she handled things when she was my age. Like, I wondered if anyone was ever mean to her, like Olivia Allen was to me today. But it was too late to get into that tonight. My mother is all about fixing problems right away, and she'd have the light back on and my dad in here and we'd all be chatting it through, using strategies she learned in her parenting class. It would be misery. I kept my mouth shut. But I made a mental note to find out a little more about what my friends knew about their moms, so I could make sure I was up to speed.

In English the next day, Mrs. Carr went around the room and asked each person to say what they're doing for their project. Lots of kids are doing costumes because, let's face it, it's the easiest. The best student in our class, Donovan Shin, is making a diorama of a Victorian slum. That should be amazing. Olivia is doing a costume of a rich lady of the time, of course. When it got to me, I kind of mumbled; I knew my plan was going to be hard to do, and I almost hated committing to it by saying it out loud.

"A diorama," I said quietly.

"A diorama?" asked Mrs. Carr, confirming she'd heard me right.

I nodded. "Of a house," I added miserably.

"I'm sure it will be lovely," said Mrs. Carr with a smile. "Next?"

I spaced out, hoping Mia had come up with some kind of blueprint last night. I hadn't seen her yet today to ask.

Suddenly, Olivia leaned forward from where she was sitting diagonally behind me and said, "I'm surprised you didn't figure out a way to bake something fattening and call it a project."

I turned around in shock, feeling like I'd been slapped and also mortified because, of course, I am baking something for the project.

"What?" was all I could think to say. Brilliant, as usual.

"Olivia, do you have a comment you'd like to share with the class?" asked Mrs. Carr loudly.

She became my favorite teacher right then, even though I still hate English.

Olivia blushed a little at being called out, which was awesome!

"N-no," she stammered. "I was just saying I'd hoped Alexis would be baking a treat for us since she's such a good baker and all." She shifted in her seat uncomfortably, and I turned around to look at Mrs. Carr and shake my head a little, like, *No, that is not what she said.* Mrs. Carr caught my gist.

"Let's keep our comments about other people's plans to a minimum, shall we?" suggested Mrs. Carr.

I turned for one last triumphant look at Olivia, and she was glaring at me but now with a full blush on her face. But my moment of victory passed as it suddenly sank in that Olivia would only be meaner to me now, just to get back at me. I shrank down in my chair and stared straight ahead, bracing myself for the worst.

What had I ever done to Olivia to deserve this abuse? It was so out of the blue! Like she'd come back from the break and decided she hated me. Ugh. The class couldn't pass fast enough now! I had to get out of there.

A few minutes later, when Mrs. Carr's back was to the class, I felt a scratching on the back of my arm. I looked down and it was a note, being passed from Maggie, behind me to my left. Maggie used to hang around with Sydney Whitman in the Popular Girls Club. When Sydney moved away, the club was renamed the Best Friends Club, and Olivia started hanging out with Maggie and Bella. The weird thing about this group of girls, the Best Friends Club, is that on their own, they're not all that bad—usually. It's only when they're together that they're awful.

Glancing up at Mrs. Carr to make sure I was safe, I quickly reached back to snatch the note. Then casually, over the course of a few minutes, I slowly opened it up without making any noise, and read what it said:

You should be careful what you say about people if you don't want them to get angry at you.

What? Olivia was angry at me? Because I said something about her? I couldn't even begin to imagine what it would be. And how could something I said hurt someone as powerful as Olivia Allen? Lowly old me?

Now I was stressed.

I didn't write a return note, and as soon as the class was over, I flew out the door to gym class without looking back.

After gym though, I still didn't even want to go to lunch and potentially face her there, too. I felt like I was on the run, like a character on a TV show. I grabbed a sandwich and then told my friends I had a meeting of the Future Business Leaders of America, and I took off to eat my lunch alone in the math lab. It was depressing, but at least I felt safe. After school I commandoed out of the building and raced home without running into anyone. It was like I was in the witness protection program.

At home I IM'd my BFFs to say I wasn't feeling well, and even though I felt bad for lying, I knew it would buy me some time alone. I just had to figure out what I'd said about Olivia, and in the meantime, how to stay the heck away from her.

To distract myself, I really focused on my homework and did a great job, and I made a little headway on a spreadsheet I'm working on for the CC that details the specific quantities of ingredients needed for each of our standard cupcake designs.

At six fifteen, my mom dashed by with a quick hello as she changed out of her work clothes and went into the kitchen to make one of her super-healthy dinners for us. I was just glad to be left alone.

When they called me down for dinner, I went, but I was still distracted by the drama of my day.

As soon as I sat down, my older sister, Dylan, said, "I thought you were sick."

"What?" I could feel my cheeks pinken into a blush.

"I saw Emma at the library a little while ago, and she said you'd rushed home because you didn't feel well."

My mom put down her fork. "What's the matter, Lexi? Do you have a fever? Your cheeks are all pink."

She stood up and came over to press her lips to my forehead, which is the annoying and mortifying way she checks to see if we're feverish. (For some reason my mom is always obsessing that we might have fevers. Always has, always will, for reasons unknown.) I tried to squirm away, but she had me in a tight grip.

"No, no fever," she said, returning to her seat, visibly relaxed. She picked her fork back up and began eating again. "What is it? Your allergies?"

"Yeah," I said.

"'Yeah'?" my mom repeated, and raised her eyebrows a little at me. She hates when we use that word. "There's an *s* on the end of that word, correct?"

"Yessss," I corrected myself. "Just itchy eyes and a runny nose and stuff." I was thrilled for the excuse she'd thrown me, even though it wasn't nice of me to fib to my parents.

"It's going to be a bad year for allergies. All this dryness. No snow this year to fill up the groundwater," said my dad.

"I know. It was the worst skiing year on record," agreed my mom. "Those poor ski-resort owners. You know the Campbells canceled their trip. . . ."

I tuned out what she was saying as something in my mind began buzzing. Snow. Skiing. Ski resorts . . . OMG!

"Oh no!" I moaned out loud without meaning to.

"Sweetheart!" cried my mother. "What is it?" She looked at me all wide-eyed and scared.

"Oh, nothing. Sorry." I felt sheepish. "Just something I forgot to bring home for homework. I have to call Emma."

Everyone looked at me suspiciously. Not only am I a bad liar but I'd thought up a bad lie. I'd never forgotten something I needed in all of my life. I am the most organized person I know!

"Oookay," my mom said skeptically.

I started to stand up to call Emma, and my father said, "Not right now, young lady. It's dinnertime." And he pointed back to my chair.

"Sorry," I said. Then I wolfed down the rest of my dinner, and asked to clear my plate and be excused.

"Wait!" said my mom. "One thing I forgot to tell you before you go! Granny said we could come out Saturday morning to see the dollhouse and all the photos. She's thrilled to get things organized and lay them all out for you." My mom smiled.

"Thanks, Mom," I said. I tried to muster up some excitement as I scraped my plate into the disposal, but all I could feel right now was dread.

"Wait, what's all this about Granny?" asked Dylan, and I left my mother to explain. Dylan would hate to miss out on anything with our grandmother because she gives us great old things all the time, like clothes and records and stuff, which Dylan loves.

I took the stairs up two at a time and grabbed the cordless phone from the hall table as I sprinted by. Inside my room I frantically dialed Emma's number without even stopping to think what I usually think, which is that my crush—her brother Matt—might answer the phone. Which he didn't, luckily.

"Alexis?"

I love caller ID.

"Thank goodness you answered. I figured it all out."

"Wait, the gingerbread house?"

I could hear the confusion in Emma's voice.

"No! Olivia Allen!"

"Oh. What?"

"I know why she's after me. Remember when we were in the hall talking the day we got out for break about my ski trip? And Maggie and Bella were there? And Maggie was asking where we were going and everything, and she said something about how Olivia used to be, like, a professional skier in the Alps or something?"

"Yeah . . ."

(*Yessss!* I thought, channeling my mom, but I didn't say it!) "Well, remember how Maggie said something that wasn't really nice about Olivia, and we were kind of surprised because we thought they were BFFs?"

"Oh yeah! Something about how it always has to be the best with Olivia or whatever?"

"Right!" I agreed, feeling relief she remembered too. "So then I said some joke about, 'Well, she probably thinks she's an Olympic skier, but she's really one of those people who just wears the outfits and sits in the lodge all day.' Remember that?"

"Uh-huh," agreed Emma, giggling. "It's true!"

"Well, I was just trying to make Maggie feel better, because she was obviously annoyed at Olivia for some reason, and I thought I'd just chime in. But then I said something like, 'I can't stand those kind of posers!' or something."

"Oh," said Emma, now not giggling.

"Uh-huh. And I think Maggie told her."

"That traitor! You were just trying to make her feel better."

"Well, all I did was make myself feel worse!"

"What can we do?" asked Emma.

I loved that she said "we"! "I don't know. But you're the best," I said.

"Yeah, but you're still number one on Olivia's hit list."

"Yessss," I agreed sadly. "Yessss."

CHAPTER 4

Quack

I resolved to confront Maggie first and to find out why she had ratted me out to Olivia. My nerves wavered, though, when I saw her walking in the hall with Callie. They were all dressed up, looking stylish and chatting intently, and I was too scared to interrupt them as they sailed by, oblivious to my existence.

My luck was with me, though, because I ran into Maggie in the bathroom just before homeroom.

"Uh, Maggie?" I started, approaching her at the sink. My voice was kind of shaky. So not the image I wanted to project! I cleared my throat and then tried to establish some presence and poise, as if I were delivering a business presentation.

"Hi," she said in kind of an oh-it's-just-you tone of voice. She peered at herself in the mirror and took out her makeup case.

"Listen, I just . . . I'm wondering . . . Why did you tell Olivia that dumb joke I made about her and skiing?"

Maggie turned and looked at me blankly. "What?" she asked.

"You know, the note you passed me yesterday. About being careful about what I say about people?"

"Yes, but it wasn't me who told her. It was Bella." Her face darkened, and she turned back to the mirror. "She said it was both of us—you and I—talking about Olivia. She's a total tattletale, just trying to suck up to Olivia."

Isn't that what you do? I wanted to ask, but I didn't think the timing was quite right.

"So, wait . . . Why isn't Olivia mad at you too?"

"She was," said Maggie, kissing her lips together to spread her clear lip gloss. She studied herself critically, took out a brush, and began to run it through her hair.

This was like pulling teeth! Now exasperated rather than intimidated, I said, "So why isn't she mad at *you* anymore?"

Maggie put her brush away, zipped her case shut, and stowed it into her bag. "Because I apologized," she said briskly. And she turned on her heel and left me there, gaping.

Great, I thought. *Now I have to apologize to Olivia?* I couldn't even picture it. And since she'd been so mean to me, part of me didn't even want to. Like, why should I be nice and kiss up to her, after all the mean stuff she's said this week? She should apologize to me!

I felt that horrible dread in my stomach that I'd been feeling the past two days, ever since Olivia started being mean to me. I looked in the mirror Maggie had just vacated and saw my pale face, worried eyes, and set jaw. I looked scared and unhappy.

I took a deep breath and rearranged my features. Then, looking over my shoulder to make sure no one was around to see, I smiled at myself. I read in some self-improvement manual of Dylan's that if you smile, it tricks your body into thinking you're happy. But it wasn't working. I smiled harder. Still nothing.

Sighing, I frowned and felt better.

Well, at least I had a game face. Maybe that would scare Olivia away.

And I had math right after homeroom. That would be fun.

Except that it wasn't.

In math class, Mr. Donnelly announced we'd be merging with the other two sections to form teams for the school's math rally. He said we've move around classrooms for the next couple of days, and then he read the list of who was on which team.

See if you can guess who was on mine.

The good news was I got to stay in my classroom. The bad news was that Olivia came in and sat one row away from me. When Mr. Donnelly handed out the sheets of practice problems for us to work on, he broke us into groups of four or five kids and had us all move our desks into little circles, so we could talk. That left me staring right at Olivia Allen. Ugh.

Kids were chatting about their weekend plans when Olivia asked loudly, "Alexis, do you do anything besides math homework and baking on the weekends?"

All the other kids turned to listen, because they could tell by her tone of voice that something was brewing. Kids love a good drama. But I didn't want to be the star of it.

I took a deep breath and then I looked her in the eyes and replied, "It depends on what my boyfriend is doing. He's in high school." I had no idea how I came up with that! I felt my face turn red with the lie, but I also had to hide my grin. It was the first time I'd had any sort of comeback for her, and I was thrilled, even if it was a fib. *Maybe if you practice enough, you can get kind of good at comebacks,* I thought.

I looked down at Mr. Donnelly's practice sheet as if to say, *This conversation is finished.* I could feel the other kids watching Olivia to see what she would come up with next, but seconds passed, and she didn't say anything. I was so proud of myself, I wanted to burst!

Finally, she said, "Good luck with that. I think it's illegal."

I shrugged without looking up, like, *Who cares what you think?* I turned to this kid, Aubrey Peterson, next to me and asked if he wanted to quiz me. I felt light-headed, like I was floating. It must've been the adrenaline from my fear, but I was pleased with myself. By the end of class she hadn't said another word to me and I had come back down to Earth.

Maybe I'd made things worse in the long run

by winning the battle but not the war. I mean, how was I going to come up with a boyfriend in high school? But it didn't matter. It had felt great. And even if she threw worse stuff at me now, thinking I was tougher than I looked, it didn't matter. I'd always savor my first victory.

At home in bed that night, I mentally replayed the whole scene in math class. I was proud of myself for my bravery and my cleverness. But as the minutes ticked by in the dark, my pride shrank and my fear grew. I was ashamed of myself for lying and being mean, and I knew my fighting back had only fanned the flames of Olivia's anger. I dreaded the wildfire I was sure to face from her soon.

On Thursday I snuck around school like a hunted animal, peering around corners and slinking down halls. I skipped lunch with my friends again and ate alone, then at dismissal, I raced out of there and literally ran home. I was relieved I'd avoided Olivia again, but it was no way to live.

By dinner I was exhausted. I guess I didn't say much, or maybe it was obvious I was tired and stressed, because my mom came into my room after she did the dishes and sat on my bed.

"What's up?" she asked.

I wasn't sure I wanted to get into it with her. As I said, she can get a little too intense about problem-solving sometimes. I sighed.

Then I spilled the beans. All of them.

"Wow," said my mom. "I'm sorry you've been going through all this. I wish you'd told me."

"Yes, but it's just been kind of snowballing, getting bigger and bigger. I didn't realize it was my new way of life."

My mom was looking thoughtful. "You know, there was a mean girl in my class when I was your age. . . ."

"I know. Susan! You always tell us about her!" I rolled my eyes.

My mom smiled. "Well, she comes in handy in a lot of lessons. Anyway, mean people take a lot of energy, and it's not worth it. And they can make you act mean too, just to protect yourself. That can be a terrible feeling, because then you're losing yourself. It sounds like that's what happened yesterday."

I winced, thinking of how proud I'd been of my comeback yesterday but how bad it had made me feel later.

"You know, most of the Olivias in the world

are really just insecure, and their mean streak comes from being hurt."

I rolled my eyes again. "Excuses, excuses," I said. "Everyone is insecure, Mom!"

She nodded. "Come on, though. Olivia is obviously hurt. And you were mean in what you said about her and skiing. Think of it this way: You're the one who's lived here all your life, and you're the one with the tight-knit group of friends, who really knows yourself and has a strong identity and a good reputation in the school, right? And then you insult her behind her back, questioning her claims about her athletic abilities, all when she's new to the school and trying to establish herself. How do you think that makes her feel?"

It was weird to flip the problem on its head like that, but it was true, when you looked at it from the other side. I felt bad now.

"I guess she's probably hurt," I said, ashamed.

My mom sighed. "You did start this, Alexis, and I didn't raise you to be a mean girl. But I *really* didn't raise you to be a victim, which is what Olivia's retaliation is turning you into. Right?"

I nodded.

"Look, you don't want to waste your time feeling bad, or being mean or hiding. Those are all negative states. You need to apologize to Olivia and to get that out of the way. I think it will clear the air with her, and it will take care of your conscience. No more sleepless nights!" she said.

I nodded again. Reluctantly. I dreaded apologizing. How soon would I have to do it? I wondered. And where would I do it? And what would I say? Ugh.

My mom prodded me out of my daydream. "So, you'll get the ball rolling with an apology and let me know what happens? I support you all the way, sweetheart." She leaned over and gave me a kiss and a hug. "Now we'd better get to the store to stock up on those ingredients you need for tomorrow."

"Oh right. Hey, Mom," I said. "What ever happened with Susan? I mean, did she stop being mean to you?"

Standing in the doorway now, my mom paused. "As you know from other stories, she was awful, and she had a crowd who hung on everything she said. She picked on me. So one day I just couldn't take it anymore. I screwed up my courage, and I confronted her and told her that I didn't appreciate it, but that, really, her behavior had no effect on me whatsoever. I asked why I was so fascinating to her that she was spending so much time watching and commenting on what I was doing."

I gasped. "What happened?"

"Well, I guess Susan found me less interesting after that. We stayed away from each other, but she never singled me out again."

"Huh," I said.

"Something to think about," Mom said. "But don't think about it too much, Alexis. You are great the way you are. You have wonderful friends, a family who loves you, and one big, bad Olivia shouldn't get in the way of any of that. You need to act like a duck."

I had to smile. It's one of my mom's favorite things to say when Dylan or I get ruffled: Act like a duck and let it roll off your back.

"Quack!" I said, and my mom quacked back, and grinned.

Of course I didn't see Olivia at all the next day. I'm not sure if she was even at school. But I marched around bravely, my head held high, ready for action, ready to change my situation.

At lunch I sat front and center with the Cupcakers, and even though we saw Bella, Maggie, and Callie, there was no Olivia. Typical. Just when I have my nerve up, she's nowhere to be found.

We chatted about our baking session later in the day and the fact that I'd made no progress on my diorama plans, but I promised to figure something out over the weekend. We only had the coming week and weekend to work on it, so if I didn't figure it out now, I was sunk.

"I guess I could always ask Mrs. Carr if I can switch to a costume," I said glumly.

"Yay!" said Mia, but Katie gave her a dirty look that silenced her.

"I'll work on it too, Alexis," said Katie. "It's too cool of an idea to bag. You know, let's at least try to make some gingerbread this afternoon and see how hard it is to work with. We're not giving in to costumes yet!"

"Thanks."

"By the way, speaking of costumes," said Mia. "I was talking to my mom about the eighties clothes and everything, and I found out she was the wardrobe mistress for the school productions all through middle school and high school! Isn't that typical?!"

We all laughed, and Emma said, "Guess what I found out about my mom? She played the flute! Just like me! Except she quit, and she always regretted it, and that's why she wanted me to play."

Katie said, "How about this: My mom was

329

allergic to eggs and milk when she was a kid, and she never even ate a cupcake until she was fifteen!"

We were all still laughing. I didn't have much to add. "I'm going to my grandma's tomorrow to see some old photos of my mom and her dollhouse from when she was a kid."

"Cool! I love dollhouses!" said Katie.

"I'll take a picture and then e-mail it to you," I promised.

We were quiet for a minute, picturing everyone's moms as kids. Then Emma snapped her fingers. "Hey! You know what could be really cool? If we did a time capsule. We could put in tons of things about us and even stuff about our moms. Then we'll bury it for our kids!"

"That's a great idea!" I said, and everyone agreed.

We spent the rest of the meal brainstorming about what to put in and how to get it, and lunch flew by. We planned to meet up again later at Emma's to bake and finish our plan.

CHAPTER 5

House Hunting

After school I stopped off at home to pick up some supplies, then headed over to Emma's, but not without taking a few minutes to brush my hair, change out of my school clothes and into something cuter, and put on just a tiny dab of lip gloss and some earrings. Hey, you never know who could be over at the Taylors', with all those cute brothers of hers. But hopefully the love of my life, Matt Taylor, would show up at some point.

At Emma's, we set up three workstations. We only need one person to make Mona's minis since we could all do it with our eyes closed at this point. Emma did that since Mona is her special friend. Mia took on the baby shower samples. She had the two different recipes to try—apple cinnamon and milk and cookies—and Katie and I played around with the gingerbread.

It was easy enough to make the dough, but the hard part was getting the sheets of baked gingerbread just right. Katie had found an amazing website that had recipes along with instructions on how to build elaborate gingerbread houses. We had to figure out what mine would look like and then we could start making templates for the pieces.

The back door slammed and my heart leaped. Was it Matt?

"Hey, Cupcakers," greeted Matt, dumping his gear in his locker at the back door. "Smells like Christmas in here!"

Yes! It was him! I willed myself not to blush.

"It's because we're making apple-cinnamon cupcakes for a job and a gingerbread mansion for Alexis's class project," Mia said.

Matt went to Mia's side to inspect the cupcakes, then he looked at me. "Alexis's class project? Alexis has everyone working for her now?" he teased. "Why am I not surprised by that?"

And the blush I'd been fighting rose up my neck and cheeks as I giggled.

"She's the CEO!" said Mia.

"In training!" I protested.

Matt came over to inspect the printed ginger-bread house instructions and our dough. "This looks hard!" he said.

"I know," I agreed glumly.

He looked at me. "Couldn't you do something easier for your class project? Like a costume or something?"

"That's what I said!" singsonged Mia.

I groaned and put my head in my hands.

"Run along, now, Matthew! You're scaring her!" said Katie, shooing him away.

He laughed, grabbed an apple and a pear from the fruit bowl on the counter, and headed up to his room. "Let me know if you need any computer help!" he called back over his shoulder.

"Thanks," I replied listlessly.

Katie was reading the directions aloud now. "We need to roll the dough out to a quarter-inch in thickness and then cut it into the shapes we need. I'll cut four equal squares for walls, and we can put aside two to add windows and another to add a door, okay?"

I watched her work and noticed how easily it came to her. Her hands did what she wanted them to, and things turned out beautiful looking as well as delicious.

Katie slid the tray into the oven to bake and then continued poring over the instructions. It wasn't that interesting to me, and I felt bad, like Katie was doing all the work for me. But she did seem to be enjoying it. And it had been her idea in the first place.

I went to check on Mia's progress, and things were looking good. The cakes were baking and smelling great, and she was whipping up two kinds of frosting. The one for the apple-cinnamon cakes would be cream cheese, with caramelized apple chunks on top, and the other was a fluffy vanilla cream, for the cookie cakes. I sampled both and liked the cream-cheese one better.

"You could use this with any kind of fruit, you know," said Mia, looking around the kitchen. "Caramelized bananas would be delicious. Pear. Even pineapple."

"Yum," I agreed. The word "pear" stuck in my mind for a minute, and then I realized why. My mom's dress! Maybe we should do a pear cupcake for her! And we could cover a platter in yellow-and-white gingham fabric or paper and then arrange the cakes in a pear shape; maybe pipe little green pears on top of each one! That could be cute.

I checked on Emma and Mona's minis. She

was ready to frost, so I jumped in and helped. We finished quickly, and then it was time for my gingerbread to come out.

Everyone gathered around to watch Katie handle the bread. First, she lifted the walls off the tray and then set them to cool on a wire rack for just a minute. Then, one at a time, she trimmed them to make the edges perfect (gingerbread expands a lot in the oven), and then she popped the scored areas out with a knife. The finished product looked great.

While they cooled, she readied her supplies. She had made a bowl of icing, which would hold everything together. It was white, but we could dye it any color we wanted when we did our real project. She also had a cardboard base where she'd drawn the outline of the house, like a blueprint. In the middle of the outline she set two unopened soup cans. The cans would prop the walls up while the icing dried, so they wouldn't fall over.

"Katie, you've thought of everything! Thanks!" I cried.

Katie smiled modestly. "I think this is really fun. Maybe if we get good at it, we could start a sideline in fancy gingerbread houses!"

"We could charge a lot of money for them," remarked Mia.

"I'll have to run the numbers on that, because they're pretty labor intensive," I added.

"What does that mean?" asked Emma.

"It means it takes a lot of hours to build them, and at a certain point, it's not worth it. Time is money."

"But you're the one who always says, 'If you're going to hang out with your best friends, you might as well be making money while you're doing it,'" Emma pointed out.

I grinned. "I'm glad someone's listening!"

"Oh please," said Mia, laughing. "We all know your mottoes by heart. 'Failing to plan is planning to fail!'" she said in a chipper voice.

"'Business first!'" cried Katie.

"'Knowledge is power!'" added Emma, laughing.

"All right, stop! This is embarrassing!" I said. My face was red, but it was funny, and it felt good to have friends who knew me so well. I looked over my shoulder. I just didn't want Matt to hear them!

"We have to make sure we get all those little Alexis quotes into the time capsule," said Emma.

I rolled my eyes.

"You *are* a character, Alexis," said Mia, shaking her head and still laughing.

"Thanks. I think," I said.

Katie deemed the walls sufficiently cool, and we began assembling them. It wasn't easy. The icing was slippery, and the walls were surprisingly heavy, and it took a little getting used to. Katie thickened up the icing with more confectioners' sugar, so it was a little pastier (I wouldn't have thought of that but was glad she did). That did the trick.

We very quickly had the four walls standing, and with the little door and windows cut out, it looked really cute.

"So once it's built, how long do you wait to decorate it?" I asked.

"Overnight," replied Katie.

I did some calculations. "We'd have to bake Tuesday, build Wednesday, decorate Thursday. Which means I need the plans ready by Tuesday morning."

"Monday," corrected Katie. "Because you'd need to print them out, then cut them out so they can be traced, and I bet that takes a while. Don't forget, you'll also need a good shopping trip to get all the supplies. We'll probably need a trip to the baking store at the mall. Maybe this weekend."

I smiled at her. That place was heaven for Katie, and she didn't get to go too often. Again, I was grateful for her use of the word "we."

"Okay. I guess we have our work cut out for me," I joked.

"We sure do!" agreed Katie.

We finished and then packed Mona's cupcakes for delivery the next morning. Then we called Matt down for a taste test of the two kinds of sample cupcakes (my idea). He was happy to oblige.

The cookies and milk was first, and he liked it, but didn't rave.

The second he bit into the apple-cinnamon one, though, it was the clear winner.

"Wow. Oh! This one is off-the-chart good!" he said with his mouth full. "It's insane! You've got to make these." He crammed the rest of the cake into his mouth. "Can I have another?" he asked with his mouth full, gesturing toward the plate.

"Please?" prompted Emma, exasperated. Her brothers drive her crazy.

I gladly handed him another, "please" or no "please." It was fun to see someone enjoy our cupcakes this much, and it was extra special that it was Matt, whom I secretly love, but also because he's helped us out so many times. He's a big supporter of the Cupcake Club, which I appreciate.

"How's the house?" he asked, turning to look at it.

"Pretty good!" I said. "Katie's a whiz!"

Katie blushed modestly.

"The hard part's going to be making the blueprints or templates or whatever," I said.

Matt nodded, swallowing his last bite. "I can help you with that," he offered.

"Really?"

"Sure, no prob," he said. "I have a CAD program we can run. It will be easy."

"Okay! Thanks! What's CAD?"

"Computer-aided design. It turns your ideas into blueprints."

"Cool."

"I'll just need the design," he said.

"Right," I agreed.

"You do have the design, right?" he prompted.

"Well . . . not exactly," I admitted.

"But she will very soon!" Katie said brightly. "Right?"

"Right," I repeated miserably.

"Uh-oh!" said Matt.

❖

Trudging home from Emma's, I tried to think of how I could get some kind of plans or measurements together for the gingerbread house. I'd looked online for hours but couldn't find anything close to what I was hoping. There had been a few kinds of houses that looked good, but they were so complicated—so professional—I couldn't begin to even *think* about taking them on.

I'd have to ask my parents at dinner, to see if they had any ideas.

When my mom called me to come in for dinner at seven, I was lying on the sofa in the den (which is also my mom's home office), watching my favorite show, *Celebrity Ballroom*, and sorting paper clips by color from a big bin into a small tackle box. It was very relaxing. I almost couldn't pry myself away.

At the table, I must've sighed one too many times, because my mom stopped eating and then looked at me carefully. "What's up, sweetheart?" she asked.

Dylan was out, so my mom and dad and I could speak freely without worrying about Dylan butting in or ragging on me.

I knew my mom was assuming this had to do with Olivia, and I was glad to say it didn't. "It's my class project," I said morosely. "We have to do a presentation with a visual component on Victorian times for English class."

"Well, what are you doing?"

"A Victorian house made out of gingerbread," I said.

My mom and dad both burst out laughing.

"Sorry, honey," said my dad. "It's just . . . Of all of a parent's worst nightmares . . . The class project thing . . . And to have it be something so intense like that. It's just funny to us."

"Like when Dylly had to do that Alaska project!" My mom laughed.

"And she insisted on making an igloo out of sugar cubes!" added my dad, howling.

"A huge igloo!" My mom roared with laughter. "Two thousand sugar cubes!"

"And the glue!" They were gasping with laughter now.

"I'm glad you think this is funny," I said, without even cracking a smile.

"Wait, is this something the teacher assigned or you picked?" asked my dad, mopping his eyes with his napkin.

"Well, I kind of picked it. It was Katie's idea."

"Can you change it?" asked my mom hopefully.

I shook my head, picturing Olivia's face when I brought in my fantastic creation. No way would I change now.

"You couldn't do a costume?" she asked.

I made an aggravated sound. I wished they would ban the word "costume" from the English language for a week!

"And how far have you gotten?" asked my dad.

I shrugged. "Nowhere."

"And when's it due?" asked my mom.

"Next Friday," I said.

"At least it's not due tomorrow!" remarked my dad, and the two of them got to hysterically laughing again.

I stood up. "Until you two can control yourselves, I will be leaving the table. Thank you for dinner," I said.

"No, stay, stay. We're sorry, sweetheart. We won't laugh again," my dad replied.

"We promise," added my mom.

They could barely suppress their smiles, but I sat back down again, anyway. *How could two individuals be so annoying?* I wondered.

"So what's the first step?" asked my dad.

I sighed heavily. I could barely describe it. "I need to find a Victorian house to use as a model for the gingerbread house, so we can put the measurements into a CAD program and create templates for the gingerbread."

"Oookaay . . . ," said my dad, thinking.

My mom bit her lip, staring into space.

"There's a Victorian out on Route 20," said my dad to my mom. "You know the one?"

She nodded, but she was still distracted.

"Maybe we could go knock on their door, ask if we could measure?" He shrugged.

"No. I've got it!" My mom snapped her fingers, grinning. "I have *got* it!"

"What?" my dad and I asked in surprise.

"My old dollhouse! The one we're going to see at Granny's tomorrow! It's a Victorian!" She folded her arms in triumph. "We'll just measure that!"

"Oh, Mom!" I cried, and I threw my arms around her neck. "Yay!"

"Let the games begin!" said my dad.

CHAPTER 6

The Little House

The trip to my grandmother's only takes about an hour. It's too bad we don't go more often, but with everything we have going on, it's hard to find the time to get out there. Usually she just comes to us, which she says she loves, because she gets to see us "in our own environment."

But my granny's house is really neat. It's old and it rambles. It's not supertall; the second story has only two of the bedrooms in it, and both are kind of in the eaves, with little dormer windows bumped out, and window seats. But there have been so many additions to the back of the house over the last two hundred years that it twists and turns and teems with hidden nooks and crannies. It's great for hide-and-seek.

As it turned out, Dylan had cheerleading practice and couldn't come. (I think she never really had any interest in coming—she just wanted to be invited.) So it was just my mom and I who went, which was better, anyway. When we got there, my granny and granddad (who isn't really my granddad, but I call him that because he's the only one I've ever known) were eagerly waiting for us. He had already gone to the Milburn Deli and bought sandwiches, coleslaw, and hard-boiled eggs, plus Cokes and chips and peanut butter Kandy Kakes for dessert, which we always have when we visit. It's junk food heaven (kind of my mom's worst nightmare!) and delicious.

First, we ate at the kitchen table, and afterward, while Granddad cleaned up, Granny, Mom, and I headed into the dining room to look at all the photos they'd laid out for us. I was dying to see the dollhouse, but I didn't want to seem pushy, so I kept my mouth shut for the moment.

"Lexi, look at this adorable picture of your mom," said Granny, holding out a photo. I took it and carefully inspected it, surprised by what I saw. It was my mom in the now-famous pear dress, but what surprised me was how messy she looked. My mom is always as neat as a pin—not a hair out of place, her clothes perfect, everything under control. But here, in the pear dress, her hair was wild and her knees were dirty, and one sock was falling down, and on the other foot, her shoelace was untied. And she had a big red mustache, like she'd been drinking red juice.

"Mom!" I said. "I can't believe it! Is this really you?" I held the photo toward her. She took it and looked, then she laughed.

"What a mess I was!" she said.

My granny peered over her shoulder. "You were adorable. I still have that dress somewhere. I just couldn't put my hands on it for today. I'll keep looking."

I took back the photo and then studied it again: my mom's wild looping curls (the same ones she carefully blow-dries straight every day), her dirty face (the one that now has always-perfect makeup on it), her messy outfit (ahem).

"What happened?" I asked. "When did you get so neat?"

My mom laughed a little, like she was embarrassed, but my granny said, "After your granddad died—your grandfather Jack, I mean—your mom grew up a lot, and quickly."

"I had to!" she protested.

My granny chuckled. "Well, I don't know about that. It wasn't like you didn't have anyone to look after you. You still had me!"

"I know, but I didn't want to make any trouble or more work for you," said my mom. "And you always had that motto. . . ."

My granny waved her hand, laughing. "Oh please! I only said that a few times."

"What? No! You said it every day!" protested my mom.

Now this was fascinating stuff. They sounded like me and my mom. Or maybe more like Dylan and my mom.

"What was the motto?" I asked.

"'You can't lay down and die just because he did,'" said my mom. "That's what she always said."

My granny gave an exasperated huff. "I only said it a few times. And I was saying it more for myself than for you." She turned to me. "Your mother was a wild and carefree child, but when her dad died, she became very serious and hard on herself. She felt she had to be perfect and look perfect, so no one would feel sorry for her. It broke my heart. She already was perfect." My granny reached over and gave my mom a hug.

Now my mom was kind of teary. Wow. This

was heavy stuff. It would definitely not be going in the time capsule!

"Oookaay . . . ," I said. "Awk-ward!"

They laughed.

"Sorry, sweetheart," said my mom, grabbing a Kleenex out of her bag and then blowing her nose.

"All right, who wants to see the dollhouse?!" my granddad boomed, coming into the room, clueless to all the girlie drama going on.

"Me!" I yelled, relieved to be getting out of there. I am so not one for crying or being all huggy or anything. Plus, I was dying to see if this little house would solve all my problems.

"Let's go, champ!" said my granddad.

In the finished basement rec room, the dollhouse was set out on a waist-high table, with a sheet over it. My granddad said, "Close your eyes. I want you to get the full effect, just at first."

So I closed my eyes, and I could hear him rustling, then I heard a click and another click, and when he told me to open my eyes, the overhead lights were out, but the dollhouse was lit up and glowing like a real little home!

"*Oh!*" I gasped, and rushed across the room to see it.

It was three stories tall, with a wraparound porch, a stained-glass window, a turret, wrought-iron balconies, and very beautifully decorated rooms—seven in all, not counting the porch, which had wicker furniture and fake plants and flowers on it.

There was a kitchen and a formal dining room on the lowest level. Then a master bedroom and living room on the second floor, and at the top, a children's room, a bathroom, and a playroom with a little crib in it.

All the rooms were wallpapered in tiny patterns, there were beautiful needlepoint and knitted rugs on all the floors, and embroidered curtains at every window. The living room furniture was upholstered and actually looked comfy, and the master bedroom had a bed with an upholstered headboard and a high canopy.

I heard my mom and my granny enter the room.

"It still works!" cried my mom.

"Actually, Jim got it working again," said my granny.

"It didn't need much," said my granddad modestly. "Just some wiring that had frayed, and a new battery system."

Listening to him talk, I began to formulate a

plan. "You're pretty handy, right, Granddad?" I said.

"Uh-oh!" He laughed. "What am I in for now?"

But I explained my project and what we needed, and he was thrilled to help. He had run a big construction company for many years, so building was his thing. I don't know why I didn't think of enlisting him earlier.

My granny scurried upstairs to get some paper, a pen, and a measuring tape and ruler. Meanwhile, my mom gave me a tour through the miniature house.

"Oh! I'd forgotten all about this! Look! Look at the tiny little plate of brownies, here in the kitchen! Gosh, we spent hours on this, my mom and I. And look at this! It's a real photo of me that my mom put in this itty-bitty frame. Wow. This really takes me back. I feel like I'm a kid again!"

I looked at my mom, smiling, her hair slipping out if its ponytail. She had a little smudge of dust on her chin, and her eyes were shining. For a second, I could picture her as a kid. I smiled at her. We would have been really good friends if we were the same age. I just know it.

"Hey, you need a plate of cupcakes for that kitchen!" I said, and we laughed.

❀

My granddad helped me with the measurements, and it took about an hour. He gave me all kinds of instructions, which I wrote down, for Matt on how to input things into the CAD program. (Actually, he offered to do it himself, because he has CAD too, but I wasn't about to pass up an offer from Matt!)

Along the way, my mom and my granny got bored and went upstairs for coffee. I asked them to pull together a few photos I could have for my time capsule, plus anything that showed how my mom used to dress, just out of curiosity.

When we'd finished with the measurements, I threw my arms around my granddad and thanked him. He had really saved the day.

"Oh, I remember all about school projects," he said, laughing and shaking his head. He winked at me. "Seems like they were always more work for the parents than anyone. Am I right?"

I laughed. "Usually, yes!"

"Now, if your friends have any trouble along the way with this, you'll call me up, okay? I can come and help you."

"Thanks. That's really nice of you."

We went upstairs to find my mom and my granny.

"Honey, anytime you want that dollhouse over at your place, I'd be happy to drive it in my pickup," said my granddad.

"Thanks! It's true. It wouldn't fit in our car," said my mom thoughtfully.

"Bring it home, Mom!" I cried. "I love it!"

She laughed. "I guess I should have tried again after that first time, with you and dollhouses. Maybe you were just too young and I was too eager to wait until you were the right age for it."

I shrugged. "Anyway, it *is* really cool. And you should have it nearby. Maybe you'll work on it again!"

"I'll talk to Dad about it. See if we can find a spot. Anyway, look at these horrible photos Granny found for you."

I sifted through the clutch of photos, laughing at the outfits my mom had on. The clothes were pretty ugly back in the eighties: plaid wool pants, stretchy leotardlike turtlenecks in rust colors. Ugh. Uncomfortable! Every time I giggled at one, I would hold it up for my mom to see, then she'd groan.

Then I came to a photo of her in a ballerina outfit—pink tights, pink leotard, ballet slippers, and her hair up in a tight bun.

"Hey! Was this for Halloween?" I asked.

My mom looked at it. "No, that was my ballerina stage."

"Stage?" Granny hooted. "That was a long stage! What was it, six years? Seven?"

"Wait, you were a dancer?" I asked my mom. I was shocked. "I mean, I knew you loved ballet, but I thought you loved watching it! I didn't know you *danced*! How come you never mentioned it?"

FYI, I am a great dancer. Not ballet, but I take modern dance after school a lot, and I am obsessed with ballroom dancing. My dad and I love to dance together. And I love the *Nutcracker Suite*, which my mom takes us to see in the city every year. You would think the fact she'd danced for so long would have come up. It seems like everything else has.

My mom waved her hand. "Oh, you know. I'm sure I mentioned it somewhere along the way. I didn't bring it up much, because I didn't want you girls to feel pressured to follow in my footsteps. You both tried ballet and weren't interested."

That was true. But still!

"She was a wonderful dancer," said my granny. "So graceful. So disciplined!"

I laughed. "That's not exactly a surprise!"

Granny looked thoughtful. "I think she liked

the structure, the rigidity. It gave her confidence. Right, honey?"

"Something like that," agreed my mom. "I really just liked to dance, though."

"Mom! You should do it again!" I cried. "Why did you stop?"

"Well, with ballet, you get to a point where you really have to commit to doing it full-time, and I didn't want to do that," she said. "Plus, a lot of the other dancers were mean." She winked at me. "It wasn't that healthy of a lifestyle, and very competitive."

"But you're competitive!" I said.

My mom laughed. "Thanks . . . I think! I guess I just channeled my competitiveness into school and then work. . . ."

"And Scrabble!" I reminded her. She never lets us beat her at that game, even when we were young.

"Right! And Scrabble!"

"Wow." I sat there, shaking my head in disbelief. I'd learned a lot about my mom today. "We've got to do this more often!" I declared.

My mom and my granny laughed.

"Anytime!" said my granny. "We love having you here!"

"We love being here," said my mom.

"Granny, can I take a couple of these and scan them for a project I'm working on? I'll return them to you," I said.

"Of course! What's this project, now?"

"A time capsule," I said. "My friends and I are making one, all about ourselves and a little bit about our moms, too." For some reason that second part was embarrassing. Like we were a fan club or something. I glanced sideways at my mom to see what she'd think.

"That's so sweet," she said, and I felt my shoulders sag in relief.

"You and your friends are just full of the best ideas!" said Granny.

"I know," I said with a grin. And I pocketed the photo of my mom as a ballerina, and the one of her all messy in the pear dress. They seemed to sum up everything anyone would need to know about her childhood.

On the way home in the car, I was kind of tired, so I mostly thought. I was surprised by some of the stuff I'd learned about my mom today. Well, some of it was unsurprising, like the perfectionism and whatever, but it was weird to learn new things about my very own mom after all these years. It made me wonder what else there is that I didn't know.

"Mom? What else don't I know about you?" I asked finally.

She laughed. "Oh, honey, I have no secrets. It's just … Things come up as they come up, you know? It's not like it's easy to work things from my child-hood into everyday conversation. They just come up as needed."

"Like Susan?" I said.

She laughed again. "Yes, like Susan."

"How did your dad die again?" I asked quietly. I can never remember this information. It's like I block it out.

"Meningitis. It was really sudden. They think he got it from a mosquito bite," she said.

"What's meningitis?"

"An infection that rapidly travels to your spine and then shuts down your body. Its main symptom is a really high, sudden fever."

Aha! No wonder my mom was always obsessing over whether we had fevers.

"Was it really hard for you guys when your dad died?" I asked. I didn't want to make her sad, but I felt so sorry for her after hearing what Granny said about her today.

She was quiet for a second, then she said, "You

know, it was really hard. My dad was a great guy. I felt vulnerable. All my friends had two parents, and I only had one. And I was scared that if something happened to Granny, then I would be without any parents at all. But it worked out okay. We were really lucky Granny and Jim found each other. He's been great for all of us, and he's a great granddad to you girls."

"He's really nice," I agreed. It was time to change the subject; enough of the sad stuff. "Mom. One more serious question."

"Mmm-hmm?"

"Why the heck did you dress like that in the eighties?"

CHAPTER 7

Friends and Enemies

When we got back late Saturday afternoon, I called Matt. I know, can you believe it? I just picked up the phone and then called him. Of course, my heart was fluttering the whole time, but I *did* need his help. Or I wanted his help, anyway!

We caught up for a minute and then I told him about the dollhouse. He was really psyched for me, saying it was a lucky break we'd be working off a model that was to size.

"Okay, so you're e-mailing me a photo of the house, and all the room dimensions, right?" he summarized.

"Yes. If you need any more info, I can either call my granddad or put you two in touch, or you can e-mail him directly."

"Cool," said Matt. "He's nice. I remember him from your holiday party."

"Yeah. I mean, yes!" I corrected myself, thinking of my mom.

"All right, so, I'll be in touch. Probably Monday, okay? I know you're in a rush."

"Thanks. There're lots of free cupcakes in this for you," I said.

"That's okay. Don't worry about it. I can use it in my portfolio." Matt is always trying to grow his digital graphic design business, so he takes on assignments from the Cupcake Club for posters and flyers, or this sort of thing. Then he uses them in his portfolio to show potential new clients what he can do. It is just another level that we connect on—as businesspeople, I mean.

"Great. Thanks!"

"Bye."

Next, I called Katie and explained my encounter with the Victorian dollhouse. She was thrilled, which made me feel really good. I e-mailed her the dollhouse photo, and we made a plan to visit the baking supply shop the next day. We'd work off the photo to find appropriate decorating supplies.

"This will be so much fun!" she squealed before we hung up.

After my calls, I felt much more in control of the project (even though it was really in Matt's hands now), as well as extremely lucky to have such generous and helpful friends. I spent the time until dinner researching Victorian-era houses online and working on my notecards for my presentation, and I got a really good chunk of work done. Not bad for a Saturday!

On Sunday morning I got up really early and basically finished the oral presentation component. I'd left a few spots where I'd have to see the finished model in order to insert a couple of facts, but I was in good shape. *Eat your heart out, Olivia Allen,* I thought.

I knocked off my other homework to clear the decks, and since I had a little time to spare, I started a spreadsheet to organize our time capsule. I had a sandwich, and then my mom took me to pick up Katie and then take us to the mall.

While she drove, Katie told my mom about what she'd collected for the time capsule so far.

"So, I have my tap dance shoes from when I was little, a recipe book with all my favorite recipes in it, and my stuffed bunny. The only bummer is that my favorite photo of me when I was little is with Callie," she said, looking at me sadly.

"Katie, that's totally okay!" I said brightly, trying to smooth over her still-hurt feelings from her falling out with Callie. (Long story.) "I mean, you can't just erase your past. It's what made you who you are today. And she was a big part of your life."

She shrugged. "But don't you think it's like I'm sucking up to her if I put her in our time capsule? And it's kind of disloyal to you guys."

"I don't mind," I said. And I was telling the truth. "She's not that bad on her own. I think she still likes you. Maybe you'll be friends again one day." I wanted Katie to feel better.

"Do you think so?" asked Katie hopefully.

"Yeah," I said. "I mean, yes. Your moms are still friends, anyway, right?"

Katie nodded and looked out the window.

I saw my mom glance at us in the rearview mirror, and I met her eyes. She made a worried face, like she felt bad for Katie but didn't want to interfere.

"You know, Katie, when my mom was little, there was a mean girl in her class named Susan . . . ," I began. And I met my mom's eyes again, and she grinned.

❀

361

At the baking supply shop, Katie was excited and full of ideas. Since I am traditionally the business end and not the creative end of the Cupcake Club, my only goal was to stay within the budget my mom and I had set. But it was fun to watch Katie brainstorm. She can pick up a package of black candy wafers and say, "Roof tiles!" Or black licorice whips and say, "Wrought-iron railings!" It takes me a second, but then I get exactly what she's talking about and how perfect it will be.

We'd decided the base, or sidewalk, around the house would be red brick, so Katie suggested we paint matzo with a solution of red food coloring diluted in water to simulate brick. We could use frosting to glue them down. That was pure genius and not expensive, which made me very happy. I wrote "food coloring" and "matzo" on a list I'd started, because they'd be cheaper to get at the huge grocery store on Route 48. Into the basket went the candy wafers and the black licorice whips, though.

Katie said we'd use royal icing to pipe all the pretty white details around the outside of the doors and windows. The Cupcake Club has its own pastry bag and fittings, so I wrote "confectioners' sugar" on the grocery list—the main ingredient in making royal icing—and we kept looking. Katie picked out a package of something called "isomalt sticks," which looked like wax glow sticks and were clear in color. We'd melt them and then pour them out to harden into flat sheets, she said, and then trim them to use as window glass. I thought it sounded hard, but Katie assured me it would be one of those final touches that would take the house from normal to amazing. She told me to add vanilla wafer cookies to the grocery list, so we could use them to make the front stairs. (Katie said we're going to skip doing stairs inside because it's too much work and not that important. I was relieved. If it's too much for her, it would be insanely hard for me!)

It didn't take us long to find everything we needed. Mom would take us to the grocery store next.

We were chatting happily as we spun out of the store and right into Callie and Olivia. Ugh. Why do we always seem to be at the mall at the same time as those girls? I'd been having so much fun, I hadn't given Olivia any thought in almost an hour. My palms were instantly sweaty, like I was gearing up for a confrontation, though I knew I'd avoid talking with her at any expense.

"Hey," said Callie cautiously. We all think she

still likes Katie but thinks she can't be seen being friends with her because it will affect her status in life or something. Callie didn't actually stop moving her feet, but she kind of slowed down and turned back to face us, like she might stop.

"Oh, hey," said Katie casually.

I could see Katie struggling with whether to stop and chat or keep walking. I wanted to keep walking—and not because of Callie!

Olivia gave me a dirty look and flounced her hair, but at least she didn't make some snarky comment. She didn't even break her stride.

We kept walking, and the encounter was over.

A little ways down the hall, we got on the escalator, and I finally breathed a sigh of relief. "Awk-ward!" I singsonged, but Katie was quiet.

"Katie?" I asked.

She turned reluctantly toward me, and her eyes had tears welling up in them. "Oh, Katie!" I cried, and then I tried to give her a hug. Hugging on escalators is not a good idea, by the way, and I recommend you never try it. But at least our nearly crashing to our deaths got Katie giggling, and her unshed tears only leaked a little.

"Sorry." She sniffled, but the crisis had passed. "I just couldn't believe that we'd just been talking about her, and then there she was, with her new life!"

"I know," I agreed quietly.

"And then . . . I had nothing to say to her! Nothing! And she used to be my best friend!" Katie's lip quivered.

"Well, I bet she would never have asked you to do a whole class project of hers, now would she?" I joked. "And she never would have made you march in a parade in costume, so she could be with her crush, huh? Would she? Now what kind of a friend is that?" These were all things Katie did for me.

Katie got giggling again.

"Anyway, how about me? I feel like I'm going to throw up whenever I see Olivia. I'm surprised she didn't figure out a way to insult me as she strolled on by! Like, maybe she could have said, 'Hey, Alexis, looks like you're having a hard time walking with that bag full of fattening supplies!'"

Katie grew serious. "Is she still doing that?"

"Totally," I said. My stomach clenched, dreading seeing her in school.

"It's funny she didn't do it just now, when there were other people around."

"I know. She's a sneak attacker," I said. Now I felt miserable. We had almost reached my mom's car. "And the worst part is, my mom thinks I need to apologize to her!"

"What?" Katie was shocked, but I couldn't finish the story now.

"I'll tell you at the grocery store," I whispered. "Hi, Mom!" I called in a fake-cheery voice, getting into the car. I gave Katie a serious look, and she nodded; we would not be discussing any of this with my mom.

At the grocery store we filled the cart with the items from the list I'd made, plus the gingerbread ingredients we'd need. Katie also threw in some waxed paper and a couple of other supplies that would come in handy.

As we walked, we discussed what I should do about Olivia. Katie understood my mom's point about apologizing, but she knows Olivia as well as I do. She knows that apologizing might only set me up as a permanent victim in Olivia's eyes.

"That girl does *not* need a new punching bag," Katie said seriously.

She had a point.

"But I need to apologize. It wasn't nice of me to say that. But it also doesn't justify the way she's been treating me. So after I apologize, then I want to follow it up with something strong, you know?"

"Yes, and at the same time. Like, you can't let the apology hang out there and then later do something strong, because she'll be gathering her strength, thinking she's beaten you after the apology. And then you'll never beat her. Let's think of a plan."

"Okay."

I loved that Katie was always helping me. She is a good friend, and I can't in a million years think of why Callie would have thrown her over for that mean and snobby group of girls. It really meant that something was wrong with Callie. Anyway, we didn't come up with a plan right then, but Katie promised to keep thinking about it, and obviously, I would too.

We finished our shopping and then checked out. The purchase was expensive, and I was not psyched. I like to make money, not spend it. Let me correct that. I don't mind laying out cash if I know I'll make some back on the outlay, but I hate spending money like this, knowing it will go to nothing. I tried explaining this to Katie.

"But you'll get a good grade!" she protested. "And you love good grades!"

"I know, but it's like buying a grade."

"Lots of kids buy grades. I mean, that's what tutoring is, isn't it?"

"Maybe . . ." (That made me stop and think. Maybe tutoring would be a good business to get into one day. Good hours, working with kids, doing stuff you already know how to do, being your own boss . . .)

"Earth to Alexis!" said Katie, and we laughed.

My mom took us for ice cream after the shopping, and we had a lot of fun.

We didn't run into anyone we knew, and that was just fine by me.

That night, as I lay in my bed in the dark, I thought about Olivia and why she makes me feel so bad. I think it's because she knows how to hit me where it hurts by accusing me of nerdiness and some kind of pigginess, as if all I do is think about food or sweets or homework. In general, I am having a great time living my life. I love school, I like working hard and getting good grades. I like running a business and making money, and I love my friends and family (except Dylan—not all the time, anyway). But I do sometimes wonder if I'm doing it all wrong. Like, maybe I should be out trying to run with the cool pack or not caring so much about doing well, but instead relaxing more and just hanging out. Maybe I'm trying too hard to be a little adult. Maybe I *am* a nerd.

Am I?

Do I care?

"Yes, a little bit" is the answer to both, but I'm not going to do anything about it. Like I said, I'm mostly happy in my life. Except whenever I see Olivia.

I rolled over, thinking with dread about what attack she would come up with tomorrow and whether it would be quiet and mean or public and humiliating. I thought about apologizing, but also what I could then do or say to gain back my power from her.

Sighing deeply, I tried to come to terms with the idea that it wouldn't be something I could plan ahead for; it would just have to happen naturally. In the wild.

CHAPTER 8

Duck!

I met Matt at school Monday morning before classes started. He was dropping off the plans so Katie and I could review them during lunch. It was a treat and a good omen. After all, if your week starts with a great interaction with your crush, you're starting from a position of strength. At least that's how I chose to see it (rather than that things could only go downhill from there).

He had the outer dimensions of the house plans ready to go and just had to put in the floor dimensions for the upper two stories. He said he'd have it for me by five o'clock today if I wanted to stop by after school. I wanted to hug him in gratitude, but I didn't have the nerve, so I just thanked him profusely.

"It was fun," he said. "The notes from you and your granddad were good. Very detailed, but I'd expect nothing less." He grinned.

"Thanks!" I said, choosing not to see this as a sign that he considered me a detail-obsessed nerd. I wished Olivia and her little flock would walk by me right now so they could see me laughing it up with Matt Taylor, supercutie! But of course they didn't. It did give me an idea, though.

I took a deep breath and screwed up my courage. "Hey, maybe when it's done, you can help me carry it to school on the presentation day? I think it's going to be a little heavy."

"Sure, just let me know when," he said, really easily, just like that.

Yessss! I thought. *Eat your heart out, Olivia Allen!* But all I said was, "Okay, thanks! See you later!"

After Matt left, I walked slowly to homeroom, happily daydreaming about when he and I get married and how we'd run a big successful corporation of our own and have a couple of children who are really smart and really good dancers . . .

After homeroom I heard someone behind me say, "I hope you got your fill at the baking store this weekend. I thought that place was just for old grandmas."

I didn't even need to turn around to see who it was. *Quack!* I reminded myself. *Quack! Quack!* But it wasn't working. I pretended I didn't hear her, but inside I was panicking.

Olivia continued, "Hey! I heard there's a new math store opening up. They're selling all the types of things that you love, like calculators and rulers and—"

"Quack!" I blurted, turning around to face her. She froze.

"Quack! Quack! Quackquackquack!!!" I yelled.

I knew I had just sealed my fate as a nerd for life, but I was so angry, I had totally lost control. The small, careful part of my brain that was still working knew that quacking was better than yelling bad words at Olivia in the middle of school, but even if it kept me out of trouble, it would mean certain social death.

People around us were staring, and I knew it must've made a strange picture, her cringing and me towering over her, quacking loudly and red faced. I was shaking, though, and I didn't care right now what anyone else thought. I was just trying hard not to smack her.

Finally, she snapped to and said, "What-*ever*, weirdo!" and walked on, her head held high.

I stayed put, to give myself time to calm down and to let her get a head start away from me. A couple of kids were giving me odd looks, and I was embarrassed. I took a deep breath and then went to the girls' bathroom, where I took some sips of cold water and splashed my face. I was exhausted after my outburst, and wished I could just go to the nurse and ask to go home. Instead, because I am not a quitter, I trudged off to math, where I knew my enemy awaited me.

In class, Olivia and I avoided eye contact, and when the bell rang, she slipped out of her seat, racing for the door while I held back. At least she wasn't trying to continue the fight. I wouldn't have had the strength to face her again. I made my way to gym and the safety of my friends.

Of course, by the time I'd reached them, they'd already heard about the incident from other people. I was mortified the story had spread so quickly. I put my head in my hands and rocked it from side to side.

"Alexis! Stop doing that! Right now!" Mia commanded in a serious voice as she quickly scanned the gym.

I lifted my head. "What? Why?"

"Because you're a hero, but you're acting like a

loser!" she said, looking sharply back at me.

"What?" I was confused. I was a nerd, and I knew it.

Mia sighed in exasperation. "Kids are talking about how you stood up to Olivia Allen in the hall and won. If you act like you lost, the story will start to change. Get it?"

"Sort of," I said.

"Just act proud," said Emma.

"Really?" This was weird, because I did not feel proud at all.

"Yes." Emma nodded. "Trust us."

Our gym teacher, Mrs. Chen, kept us too busy to talk during class so I couldn't tell them what happened in detail. Finally at lunch we all got to sit down and talk.

"Now, what happened?" Katie asked, and I told them the whole story, including how Mom always told me to let things roll off my back.

Actually, the timing was perfect, because right as they were roaring with laughter, picturing me having a duck meltdown in the hall, Olivia walked into the lunchroom. She looked directly at me and my table of friends, laughing our heads off, and she turned on her heel and left.

"You just won," said Katie, who'd been watching the door. "Did you see that?"

I nodded, but I didn't feel good about it. "It's not over."

"I think you're wrong," said Katie, shrugging.

"We'll see," I said.

We planned a meeting for later that day at Emma's and then, at my insistence, talked about other stuff for the rest of lunch. But deep down inside I let myself relax a tiny bit. Maybe I *hadn't* committed sudden social death.

"Okay, a few things on the agenda today . . . ," I began at Emma's kitchen table that afternoon.

"Quack!" said Katie, and she giggled.

"Quack, quack!" said Mia.

"All right, enough!" I cried.

"Sorry," said Mia with a smile.

I cleared my throat. "On the agenda—"

"Quack!" Emma peeped in a tiny voice.

"Stop!" I hollered, but I had to giggle.

"Quack! Quack! Quack!" They all were doing it at the same time.

I put down my ledger, where I keep track of everything. "Okay, you know what? Fine. Just get it out of your system, okay? We have a business to run here, and we need to discuss some other important items, so when you are ready to act like mature people and not like idiots . . ."

They quacked and laughed for another minute, and then we began for real.

"We have the shower this weekend, which we'll need to bake for on Friday, along with Mona's minis. We also have my mom's birthday, and I had a great idea. Since she's turning forty-four, we'll make forty-four cupcakes, eleven of each kind of the following: pear, something pink and ballerina-ish, the strawberry shortcake she requested, plus the bacon ones for my dad. It will be a little cupcake buffet. Okay?"

Everyone nodded.

"No duck cupcakes?" asked Mia with a smile.

"No," I said sharply. "Next, we have the time capsule project. I made a few notes on this." I pulled out some spreadsheets and then distributed them. "As you can see, there's a checklist and then a Q&A section. Everyone needs to fill in their answers to the questions, and everyone should provide one of each of the items on the checklist. Just let me know what you think needs to be added or deleted. It's only a starting point."

Emma was scanning the list. "This is going to

have to be a really big capsule!" she said.

"I know," I agreed. "I was almost thinking instead of putting the actual items in, we should just take a picture of them . . ."

"And we can put a printout of the pictures and a flash drive with everything on it!" finished Mia.

"Exactly," I said, grinning.

"Great idea! Then the capsule can be really small!" said Katie.

"And we don't have to part with the things we love," added Emma.

"Right. So is there anything I should add or remove?"

Everyone was quiet while they read their sheet. Then Katie said quietly, "The part about sworn enemies . . . Do you think we need that?"

I bit my lip. "I wasn't sure, but I thought it would maybe give us a chance to share what we've learned with future generations, like how to deal with bullies and mean girls."

"By quacking?" teased Emma.

"Very funny," I said. "Not."

Mia was thoughtful. "Maybe it should be a more open-ended question. Like, who was the meanest person you ever dealt with and how did you handle it?"

"An essay question?" I cried in dismay.

But the others thought it was a really good idea.

"I know who I'm writing about!" said Katie. (We all did.)

"Syd the Kid, à la Sydney Whitman, will be mine!" declared Emma. "Not that I can take credit for the Whitmans moving to California, but still, that solved it."

"Who's moving to California?" asked Matt as he ambled into the Taylors' kitchen from outside.

My heart skipped a beat. He was wearing a light blue hoodie that made his eyes look electric, and his hair was all wind-tousled and messy. So cute. Sigh!

"Hey, Alexis, I'm just going to run up and finish the plans. I'll be right down with the printouts," he said.

"Great. Thanks."

"So tomorrow is our baking day?" said Katie. "For the project?"

"Yup. Maybe at my house?"

Katie agreed, and Emma and Mia wanted to come too.

"You guys must have lots of other stuff to do. I think Katie and I can handle it. I feel bad taking up your time with my project."

But they insisted.

"Look, like Katie said, this could be a whole new line of revenue for us!" Mia pointed out.

"We wouldn't miss it," said Emma firmly.

That night I pulled my dad aside and told him about the plans for the cupcakes. I also told him about a few ideas I had for presents for my mom, including a spot for her dollhouse and having my granddad deliver it before the weekend.

My dad loved all my ideas and said I was very thoughtful, which, of course, I liked to hear. I don't know if he would have said it if he knew I'd quacked at someone at school today.

When my mom came to tuck me in, I couldn't bear telling her about what had happened with Olivia today. I knew she'd chastise me for being mean and also for not having apologized yet, and I didn't want her to be disappointed in me. But I could tell she knew I was holding something back by the way she kept asking questions but nothing directly.

In the end, she gave me a kiss and said she's always available for discussions.

Phew.

CHAPTER 9

Rallying

The day of reckoning had arrived. On Tuesday afternoon, it was time to bake the gingerbread and to begin the house. I felt like I was on one of those cooking challenge shows, with all the crazy ingredients assembled before me. Licorice whips, molasses, ginger, sprinkles, eggs, flour, cookies; plus rulers and knives and paper . . . It was wild.

But first, the gingerbread.

Katie and I made a triple batch in my mom's huge KitchenAid mixer. Mia and Emma actually sat at the kitchen table and did homework while we did that, because it was the "boring part."

When it was time to roll out the dough, and cut and score it, they came and helped hold the templates—which I'd cut out last night—in place over the dough, and offered opinions on how things should be laid out on the pans. This was deemed the "hard part." I only hoped it wouldn't get much harder than this. Compared to gingerbread architecture, baking cupcakes is a sweet walk in the park.

While we worked, we discussed the spreadsheets for the time capsule and made a plan to shoot the photos of our items on Saturday at my house, after my mom's birthday party.

Katie slid the trays into the oven to bake. We'd have to do about six rounds of baking before all the gingerbread was done. It smelled good, but it was not that appetizing looking, all shiny and brown. Katie laid out the next slabs of dough on waxed paper and tweaked them a little. I felt useless, watching her work.

"Any sightings today?" asked Mia. "I didn't see her in homeroom this morning."

I knew who she meant. "No," I said.

"She was absent," said Emma, not looking up from her notebook.

"What?" I was shocked. "How do you know?"

Emma looked up. "She's in my science class. Some kid told the teacher."

"I wonder if she was sick . . . ," I said.

"Or just scared!" cackled Mia.

"Don't even joke. I don't want to be a mean girl. You know that. After all, I'd be doing to her just what she's been doing to me, and look how bad it made me feel."

We were all quiet for a minute.

"Well, let's see if she has the sniffles tomorrow," said Katie, quietly cutting dough on the counter.

For whatever reason that got us giggling, and any discussion of Olivia was finally put aside. I did feel guilty, though, and I had been all day. I'd actually been looking for her at lunch, planning to apologize and just get the whole thing over with, but, as usual, when I want to see her, she's nowhere to be found.

The time passed slowly, and batches of dough went in and came out. Katie trimmed them carefully after they came out, to get rid of the puffiness they get from baking, then she laid them out on racks to cool. I was amazed by how she knew to do all this stuff and finally had to ask.

"Well, my grandmother likes to bake, and we bake a lot together. Every Christmas we make a simple gingerbread house. And my mom is really good with her hands, you know, because she's a dentist. Obviously, I kind of inherited that. The good with the hands part, not the dentist part. And then I went to that cooking camp and learned some stuff. And, you know, I watch cooking shows and go online to read about baking all the time. It's just . . . a lot of the skills transfer from project to project pretty easily."

"Cool," I said, thinking it was the same with my business skills.

Just then the doorbell rang, and it was the UPS guy. He handed me a package addressed to me, and I signed for it, wondering what it could be. Then I looked at the return address.

"It's from my grandma! She found the pear dress!" I said, shaking the box and hearing something soft shift around inside. "I've got to run upstairs and hide this," I said. And it was lucky I had, because when I came back down, my mom had arrived home from work and was chatting with my friends in the kitchen.

"Girls, I've got some bad news," she said, but she was smiling. "I've got to make dinner, so we're going to need to close the bake shop for the night."

"But, Mom!" I protested. "We're right in the middle of it!"

"I'm sorry, but I'm sure I speak for all moms everywhere when I say, it's time for dinner, and it's time for people to be doing their own homework at their own desks. Though I very much appreciate your friends helping you," she said with a smile. "I'm going to run up and change while you clear this up."

"Aargh!" I made an annoyed noise. "We're almost done!" I said, but she didn't even turn around.

"Here, let me just trim this one, and you take that one . . . ," Katie said, switching the trays around, and then—*crash!* Just as I was taking it from her hands, a tray fell to the floor, and the large slab of gingerbread split into three pieces. It was totally my fault, although Katie began yelling "I'm so sorry!" at the top of her lungs.

"No!" I cried. "We don't have time for error!" I dropped to my knees and lifted the tray back up. Biting my lip, I surveyed the damage. The others gathered around. "It's totally not your fault, Katie," I said.

"You can just make another one tomorrow, can't you?" asked Emma.

"No! I need to be building tomorrow. Because Thursday is decorating, and it's due Friday."

"I bet we can glue it back together with frosting," said Katie. She looked at her watch. "You know what, I do have to get home because I totally spaced that we have the math rally on Thursday, and unlike some people, it is *not* my best subject. I need to study."

"Okay. I totally understand. Thanks, you guys. Thank you all so much for helping me."

"It was fun!" said Katie, shrugging on her jacket.

Everyone cleaned up a little, but I shooed them out and did the rest myself. This way, I figured, if any more gingerbread broke, I'd only have myself to blame. I was so grateful to them for helping me, and I felt terrible that it was basically a three-night project. I knew I'd taken on too much—cheered along by Katie's enthusiasm and willingness to help—but now I'd have to see it through. However, I didn't foresee what would happen next.

Late that night, I was just about to shut down my computer when I spotted an IM from Katie. It said:

OMG Alexis I am so so so so so sorry, but my mom quizzed me on my math, and I did so badly, she said I have to come straight home from school tomorrow and study. She'll quiz me when she gets home, and if I do okay, I can come help you, but otherwise I have to stay home. I'm so sorry! Call me if you get this before 9:30.

I looked at my watch: 10:20.

I sat heavily on the edge of my bed. What was I going to do?

This was something that quacking would not help.

I was still sitting there ten minutes later, lost in thoughts of possibilities, when my mom came in to say good night.

"My goodness! You're not even in bed yet and it's ten thirty!"

I looked up, startled.

"What's wrong?" she said, sitting down on my spare bed to face me.

"I have to build this gingerbread house all by myself tomorrow, and I have no idea what I'm doing."

"What happened?" she asked, and I explained.

"Listen, sweetheart, do you absolutely have to do this immense and difficult project? Can't we just quit while we're ahead and help you with a pretty costume?"

"No!" I said forcefully. This presentation was going to kick butt. It had to.

"Okay, that's pretty definite," said my mom.

Then the two of us sat there for a minute, thinking.

Finally, my mom said, "What we need is someone who isn't at work, doesn't have homework, and knows how to build."

And at the exact same minute our heads snapped up, and we looked at each other. "Granddad!"

She jumped up from the bed. "I'm going to call him now!" she said.

"At ten forty?" I cried as she fled out of my room.

"They always stay up for the eleven o'clock news. Anyway, this is an e-mer-gen-cy!" she trilled as she ran down the stairs.

I sat on my bed, too nervous to chase her and listen in. I just focused all my energy on hoping Granddad would be free and able to come. I crossed every finger and toe and squeezed my eyes tight. Finally, I couldn't take it anymore. I left my room and tiptoed to the top of the stairs, where I could just make out my mom's end of the conversation.

"Yes, she gets out at three. That would be perfect. Thank you so much. Oh my gosh, we can't tell you how much we appreciate this. Thank you!"

I pumped my fist in the air. Victory!

❁

The next morning at school, I told my friends how my granddad was coming and that they could have the afternoon off. I was actually relieved, because it just didn't feel right for them to spend so much time on my project. Katie insisted she'd come by after she was done, but I asked her to save the trip until Thursday, when I'd really need her.

I walked quickly to math, knowing who would be there and on my team for the math rally practice too. I just wanted to get it over with, though. I hated Mr. Donnelly for a minute right then, for putting Olivia and me together. It was such a total downer. But the sooner it was finished, the better.

In the classroom, he'd already moved the chairs around into little clusters. But there wasn't anyone there yet. I sat in my seat, and guess who walked in next?

She and I looked at each other, caught and frozen, like deer in headlights. I opened my mouth to say something, but Mr. Donnelly came bustling in with a cheery hello. The moment had passed, and the room quickly filled.

Our group was good, and I hated to admit it, but Olivia was one of the best (along with yours truly, of course). She didn't say one mean thing to me for almost the entire class, either. Actually, she didn't say anything to me. She just acted like I wasn't there. She did say one meanish thing to George Martinez when he missed a question, but that was all. I started to wonder if my friends were right. Maybe I *had* won. It was a weird, new feeling—kind of powerful—and I'm embarrassed to admit to myself that I kind of like it.

But then I got a really hard question I knew the answer to, and in my excitement, I jumped up, and my chair knocked back and tipped over. Everyone laughed, including Mr. Donnelly and finally, me. It was funny, I realized. When I'd successfully answered the question and sat back down, Olivia leaned over, so everyone could hear, and said, "Very exciting. Kind of like a bake-off, right, Alexis?"

So I turned to look her right in the eye and said, "Meet me after class." Just like that!

OMG. After I said it, my whole body flooded with a cold feeling, then a hot feeling. My knees wobbled, and I didn't look around to see who'd heard me. I just willed myself not to blush. What the heck was I going to say to Olivia Allen after class? I did not know. All I knew was that this had gone on long enough and it was totally distract-ing me.

The remaining fifteen minutes of class flew by,

of course, and when the bell rang, I rose, packed my things, and waited for Olivia outside the door. It took her so long, I had to look back in to see if she slipped by without me seeing her (which really would have been impossible), but she was still there, slowly loading her bag.

Finally, finally, just when I thought I couldn't take it anymore, she came through the door and into the hall.

She stopped and then looked at me with a challenging tilt to her chin. "So?" she asked. "What do you want?"

I took a deep breath and just plunged in.

"To apologize. I may have said something rude about you, and I'm sure you heard about it. I wanted to apologize and to say that it wasn't nice and probably wasn't true."

Olivia just stared at me. A moment went by, and then she said, "It isn't true. I happen to be a really good skier. We used to go all the time."

So Maggie was right! Olivia *had* been holding this grudge all this time. Wow.

"Well, I am sorry for being mean. I regret hurting your feelings. And now I'd like you to apologize as well." I can't believe my nerve!

"For what?" Olivia asked, narrowing her eyes.

"For treating me terribly. For embarrassing me on purpose. For teasing me, mocking me, and humiliating me. What I said was wrong, but your punishment has been unbearable, and it needs to stop."

Olivia blinked.

"Well . . . ," she started. "Thanks. Thanks for apologizing. I didn't know why you said that, and I thought it was really mean."

"It was," I said. But I had to hold my ground. I wanted Olivia to apologize too. I took another deep breath. "But probably not mean enough that you had to torture me for the past few weeks. You were really mean back, and it's a terrible way to treat another person. Also, I'm not sure why you are so fascinated by me that you are always watching me. I guess I'm flattered."

Olivia looked around. None of her BFFs were around, and it was just Olivia and me. Was Olivia nervous? Embarrassed? I couldn't tell. "I don't watch you all the time," she finally said.

"Well, you seem to pay attention to a lot of things I do. I guess I'm just really interesting to watch."

Olivia tossed her hair. "It's not personal, Alexis."

"Oh, but it is," I said. "Especially when you

embarrass me. I mean, look how upset you got when I made fun of you for possibly not being a good skier. And that was only once!"

Olivia flinched. "I guess I'm sorry too, then."

We stared at each other for a moment longer, then I put out my hand. She looked down at it kind of scornfully, but then she took it, and we shook hands.

And then she walked away.

Meanwhile, I was about to faint. I fell back against a locker and just rested there to regain my strength before moving on. Could this be the end of it? It felt like a dream. I hoped it wasn't.

CHAPTER 10

The Finishing Touches

At lunch—I couldn't believe it—but I didn't run and find my friends to gloat. I grabbed a tray, loaded it up, and ate lunch alone in the math lab. I felt like a traitor and a chicken, but somehow, I couldn't face them and then not tell them what happened, but I also didn't want to sit at lunch and go through a huge I-said–she-said thing. Weirdly, it seemed disloyal to Olivia. What happened after math was private. I needed a little while to think of a way to sum it up to my friends that was truthful but vague.

After school I flew home on my bike to find my granddad's pickup in the driveway. He had some big thing under a tarp in the bed of the truck, and I hoped it wasn't a power tool we needed for the gingerbread house!

"Yahoo!" I yelled, and raced into the house.

"Hi, honey!" he called out upon seeing me.

I ran to him and gave him a huge squeeze, then I pulled away and beamed at him.

"Thank you!" I cried.

He hugged me again and said, "Glad to be of service, ma'am. Let's see what you've got."

So I walked him through the plans and showed him the gingerbread slabs, the outlines Matt had done, and explained what we needed to do. He seemed unruffled by all of it, but I guess when you've spent fifty years building big houses, a little gingerbread one doesn't seem so hard.

"Okay, so first, I'll lay out the board for the base, and then I'll make the royal icing," I said.

"Actually, first, I want you to help me to get your mom's present out of the truck," he said.

"Okay, what is it?"

"The dollhouse! Your dad called this morning and asked me to bring it."

I clapped my hands. "Yay! Do you think we need to hide it?"

"I think so."

I scurried to open the doors to the basement, and we carefully carried the dollhouse down there, setting it on my dad's workbench.

"He's going to make a stand for it and put it in the sunroom, from what I understand," said my granddad, winking at me. My dad's not that handy, but he always tries to make things, and Granddad always comes and fixes them. Kind of like me with the gingerbread house, I guess!

"We're really keeping you busy, Granddad!" I giggled.

When we finished with the dollhouse, we went back upstairs, brought in my granddad's overnight bag (he'd sleep over here tonight, because it would probably be late when we finished), and then we began.

I made the icing while he surveyed the pieces and got things lined up in the order in which we'd build them.

"We should build the three floors separately and then give them as long as possible to dry and set. Then we can construct the whole house," he said after a minute. "Because you won't have the time to let this dry in stages overnight. We might need to use some supports in the end—which is tricky— but we'll see how it goes."

Meanwhile, the icing was kind of runny. I lifted the spoon and poured some out. "This doesn't look right," I said with a frown.

He came over and looked into the bowl. "Add more sugar. Thicken it up," he suggested.

"You think?"

He laughed. "That's what you do with cement if it's too runny. Just add more powder!"

"Okay!" Now I was laughing too. But it worked!

The first thing we did was repair the broken wall. We could assemble that section last, to give it time to stabilize. My granddad said if it didn't work, we could add some stabilizers. He'd brought something called dowels, among other things, that we could set in with frosting to hold things in place. I hoped it didn't come to that.

Dylan came home after a while, then my mom, and finally my dad. My dad and granddad exchanged a nod and a wink when my mom wasn't looking, and my granddad gestured down, as if to say, *It's in the basement.* Meaning the dollhouse, of course.

The gingerbread house didn't look like much at that stage, and it was still pretty portable, so my mom had us move the assembly from the counter to the kitchen table; we'd eat in the dining room since my granddad was here.

As we picked up the various sections, a few walls began to wobble.

"Oh no!"

My mom jumped over to steady them, and we inched to the table.

"Phew!" I said, setting it down.

"You couldn't have made a costume?" my mom teased.

My granddad and I looked at each other, and smiled.

"Nah. Too easy," he said.

"Costumes are for wimps!" I added.

The timing worked out well. We ate dinner while the glued sections dried, then we went back to work. It was nearly nine o'clock when we set the sections on top of one another. However, things started to wobble almost immediately, and my granddad rushed to lift the second story off the first.

"Supports," he said grimly. "We're gonna need 'em after all."

I'm a little ashamed to tell you the next part of this story, but here's the truth of what happened: I went to bed, and my parents and my granddad stayed up till midnight finishing the gingerbread house. It's horrible but true. In business, it's called "outsourcing," which means having someone else do the work when you can't. Of course, you would usually pay those people, and I'm not about to pay my relatives, so the comparison ends there. The bottom line is, I bit off more than I could chew, and all to show off to an enemy. What a sorry reason for a project.

However, when I woke up the next morning, it felt like Christmas. I ran downstairs, and there it was, in the middle of the kitchen table: the finished gingerbread house, identical (in shape, anyway) to my mom's dollhouse.

"Oh!" I said, clapping my hands.

I heard someone behind me, and turned.

"Turned out pretty great, didn't it?" said my granddad, sipping his coffee.

"It's awesome. Thank you *so* much!" I gave him a big hug.

"Only one problem," he said.

"What?"

"How're you going to fit this thing in your car?"

It wasn't long before we realized that the only solution would be for my granddad to come back with his tarp and his truck and everything again tomorrow to transport the house to school. I don't know how I'll ever thank this man enough. All I know is, I'm glad I lined up Matt to help when we got there!

❁

That afternoon, my house was a festival of sugar. Katie, Mia, Emma, and I were like whirling dervishes getting this house finished. We had four little workstations, and we were like elves—busy, busy!

Katie trimmed and set the wrought-iron railings along the porch and roof with frosting and black licorice whips. That was the hardest part, if you ask me.

I shingled the roof with black candy wafers.

Mia piped white decorative trim around the windows as shutters and window frames. And Emma created the windows (the second hardest thing).

After about an hour, it was really looking good. After two hours, it was incredible. Katie wanted to keep going, but I had to put on my CEO hat and say enough was enough. We could work on this thing forever, but after a certain point it wasn't worth it. The result was already spectacular, and we didn't need to go on; it just wouldn't be an efficient use of our time.

Mia took out her phone and snapped dozens of photos for our website. We even e-mailed a couple to Matt, so he could see how well it turned out, and some to my grandparents, since they were in on it from the beginning. And, of course, we'd print out a photo for our time capsule.

We cleaned up, and then I sent my friends home with huge hugs and profuse thank-yous. We had a big day again tomorrow, so a break would do us all good. Plus, everyone had homework, and I had to put in the last finishing touches to my oral report.

After they left, I sat for a minute in the kitchen, admiring our work. It was really beautiful. It was funny how you felt like you could just keep working on something—adding this or that cute thing, improving what you'd already done, thinking up a clever new detail. It made me understand how my mom must've felt working on her real dollhouse. It could be an endless project if you wanted it to be.

When my family got home, they were totally wowed by the gingerbread house. Inside, I was bursting with pride, but I played it cool. The truth was, I still couldn't wait to see Olivia's face tomorrow when I brought it in. I knew I shouldn't care, but I did.

That night, I went up to my room and took one last look at my time capsule spreadsheet. I'd filled in pretty much everything, proudly inking in my mother's childhood hobbies (ballet dancing, doll-houses) and my own (math, business), as well as my goals for the future (the aforementioned marrying of Matt Taylor and running a large company). But the part I'd left blank, the part about enemies, I was finally ready to fill in.

I didn't want to name names, because things can change, and it just seemed so negative. Instead I gave a long answer.

Sometimes people will try your patience or do things that you think are pretty mean. But there's always a solution, even if it's not an easy one. You just need to remember all the good things you have going on in your life and let the not-so-good stuff roll off your back. Just act like a duck. Quack and let it roll off your back. My mom taught me that.

I lined up most of the items I'd be photograph-ing for the capsule: my business ledger; the pretty pink dress I wore to Dylan's sweet sixteen when Matt asked me to dance; a DVD of the first season of *Celebrity Ballroom*; a tag from my favorite store, Big Blue; and a photo of me in my homecoming parade costume, where I dressed up as a Greek goddess and went with Matt. I was pretty happy with the collection. At the last minute I added an eraser shaped like a cupcake, and a calculator, because why not?

Then I sat back, relaxed, and let myself daydream for a moment about being Mrs. Matt Taylor. I hoped our children would have his blond hair. Our babies would be smart *and* beautiful! It was the best daydream ever.

CHAPTER 11

Success!

$\mathcal{M}$y granddad arrived early Friday morning; he was there before I even got up. After a hasty breakfast, we carefully loaded the gingerbread house onto the bed of his truck, where he secured it with all sorts of padding and blankets and bungee cords and stuff. I couldn't look, but I trusted him. He'd also brought a little folding trolley that we could use to wheel the house into school.

We swung by the Taylors', and Matt came out to hop in for the ride. His parents and Emma and his little brother, Jake, came out too, to see the creation in the back of the truck. Everyone oohed and aahed over it, and I was really proud.

At school, Katie met us at the door. She had also come early. I am not that sentimental, but I had to say I was feeling a little teary and grateful for all these wonderful people who were helping me. I was pretty lucky I had them, or I would never have pulled it off. It reminded me of what my mom had said when we discussed Olivia. ("You are great the way you are. You have wonderful friends, a family who loves you, and one big, bad Olivia shouldn't get in the way of any of that. You need to act like a duck.") Quack!

I had made prearrangements to hide the gingerbread house in the teachers' lounge, so that it would be a surprise for our class, so that was where we wheeled it. The teachers who were there kind of freaked out at how cool it was, including Mr. Donnelly, which was nice since he's my favorite.

"Alexis! I had no idea you had this much artistic talent!" he said.

"Well, I had lots of help," I admitted, smiling at my granddad, Katie, and Matt.

We left the table, and Matt said he'd meet me back there during his study hall period to wheel the house in with me. I hugged my granddad good-bye and promised to call to let him know how it went. I hugged Katie too, and she left a little tub of frosting and a mini-spatula on the trolley, in case I needed it later.

I could barely sit still through homeroom, and I literally ran to the faculty lounge when it was time to pick up the trolley. Matt was already there, waiting for me. He must've run, too, which made me even more grateful.

"Ready?" he asked, with his adorable dimples and grin.

"Ready!" I said, and off we went through the halls.

Everyone we passed stopped in their tracks to look at the house. It was really spectacular. Plus, you don't usually see that much candy wheeling through school every day. I couldn't wait to see Olivia's face. Even though we'd made peace, this would be the icing on the cake!

Slowly, slowly we made our way down the hall. There was almost no one left by the time we reached our destination. Into Mrs. Carr's classroom we went, and everyone was already there, seated. For a moment, there was dead silence, then Sara Rex started to clap, and everyone joined in. Olivia (dressed as a fancy Victorian lady, in a high-waisted shirt and a long-sleeved, high-necked blouse) had a look of wonder on her face, shaking her head in disbelief, even as she clapped. I met her eye and smiled a small smile, and she smiled back. Pretty soon the whole class was cheering, and I was grinning, and finally, Mrs. Carr had to quiet everyone down.

Matt ducked out with a wave, and Mrs. Carr said, "Alexis, I think you should go first."

I put down my bag, got out my notecards, and began talking about home life in Victorian England. Halfway through, though, I waved my arm to gesture to a feature of the house, and I heard a sickening crack. I'd knocked the chimney off. For a second, everyone froze, and then, you will never believe this: *Olivia Allen* jumped up and quickly reattached it while I continued my presentation! Mrs. Carr smiled approvingly at Olivia as she worked. She was kind of pasting it with some extra frosting, and once it was back on, she took her seat until I finished. At the end I said, "And a special thanks to everyone who helped me on the house: my granddad, my friends at the Cupcake Club, Matt Taylor, and . . . Olivia Allen for saving the chimney, which was a huge part of Victorian life." She nodded in acknowledgment while everyone applauded and I bowed. It was a major triumph, in a lot of ways.

George Martinez called out, "Can we eat it now?" Everyone laughed while Mrs. Carr threatened them all with a trip to the principal's office if they so much as touched it, but I didn't care. I even considered saying yes, but I figured the feeding frenzy that would result would ruin everyone else's presentations.

That afternoon we all gathered at Katie's to do our weekend baking. I was feeling so relaxed, with everything resolved with Olivia, my project finished and turned in, and a handful of fun surprises lined up for my mom's birthday.

I did Mona's minis today, since Emma wanted to work on some of the new recipes—the strawberry shortcakes and the apple-cinnamon cupcakes in particular. Mia fried the bacon, and Katie colored the pink frosting for the ballerina cupcakes, and we were like an efficient, well-oiled machine.

"We've really got the assembly-line thing down!" I said later as we stood in a row frosting cupcakes at the counter. "Henry Ford would be proud!"

"Why? Who's he?" asked Katie.

"The car guy who invented the assembly line!" I said.

"Hey, I've been meaning to ask you. Whatever happened with Olivia?" asked Mia.

"Yeah!" agreed Katie. "We never heard another peep from you about it."

I hesitated, tempted to tell them the whole story, but then I decided to be a duck and let it roll off my back. "You know, I think we buried the hatchet," I said, shrugging casually.

"How?" asked Emma.

"We acted like ducks!" I said, and then I laughed maniacally.

Everyone started quacking, and that was the end of the discussion.

Early Saturday morning I went with Emma to deliver the mini cupcakes to Mona and then the apple-cinnamon ones to the baby shower for Jake's old teacher. Emma came home with me afterward to help set up the little birthday lunch my dad was organizing for my mom. The Taylors would be coming later (hopefully with Matt, but he might have a game), and two of Mom's other good friends and their families, and my grandparents, of course.

Dylan had bought a really cute pink table-cloth and napkins and party plates with a ballerina theme, and she was making her specialty: tea sand-wiches (four kinds: turkey, cucumber, egg salad, and tomato), and we'd have iced tea and coffee and chips, and then the cupcakes. It was going to be great!

My dad had just returned from the framer's when we walked in. "Oh good! I was just going to wrap these, but now you can see them first. Look!" He was really pleased, I could tell.

He pulled two large matching picture frames out of a shopping bag. The first one had my mom's yellow gingham dress with the pear on it, framed in a pretty yellow wooden shadowbox. It was cute and cheerful. In the lower right corner of the frame was the photo of my mom in the dress, all cute and scraggly and messy. The second frame was pink, of course, and had a pink tulle ballet skirt of my mom's that my grandma had also found, with the ballerina picture of my mom in the lower right corner. The two framed items made a pretty matched set. My dad planned to move some things around, so we could hang them in our den, above the sofa.

I hugged him. "Oh, Dad! They look amazing! She'll love them!"

"And the dollhouse!" he said.

"And the dollhouse!" I agreed.

"I also got her a little charm for her charm bracelet," he said with a mischievous grin.

"Cute! What is it?" I asked.

But he wagged his finger at me. "You'll have to wait and see!"

❁

At the party, my mom had a great time. She loved all the pink decorations and the food, and the doll-house was a huge hit with everyone! My dad had set it up in the living room for the party, and my mom was so surprised when she saw it. I personally couldn't wait to spend some time on it with her; one thing I wanted to find was a platter of tiny cupcakes for the little kitchen.

Speaking of cupcakes, when I explained to her the different kinds of cupcakes we'd made for the party and how they represented different parts of her life, she gave me a huge hug and got a little teary.

"Alexis, you are so special. Thank you for your thoughtfulness. I never knew you had such an interest in my past!"

"Neither did I!" I said. "Maybe it's just something you have to grow into."

When my dad presented her with the tiny jewelry box that I knew contained a charm, I held my breath. She unwrapped the tissue and opened the little velvet pouch, and in it was a gold . . . duck!

She and I laughed so hard, and we knew it was just the perfect thing. In fact, I couldn't believe she didn't already have one!

Dylan looked at us like we were cuckoo, but I didn't care since that was nothing new.

"Great job, Dad!" I said, and he beamed with pride.

Later that afternoon, Mia and Katie came over and, along with Emma, we worked on our time capsule and ate leftovers from the party.

We laid out everything to photograph, and I also went and photographed the framed items of my mom's.

It was fun to see what people had brought. Mia had some old costumes of her mom's from her wardrobe days, plus some crazy bell-bottomed pants she used to wear, and an exotic feather hat. Emma had an old book of her mom's that had stories she'd handwritten into it when she was a little girl, and Katie had a skateboard that had been her mom's! I couldn't even picture her mom riding it, but Katie said she was actually pretty decent at it. Katie also had the photo of her and Callie. I didn't say anything, because I didn't want to draw attention to it, but I was proud of her for including it.

Everyone passed around their biographies, and we read them. Then we loaded up the capsule, which was really a plastic Tupperware sandwich holder Mia had gotten from her mom. Then we put it into a giant Ziploc bag, and another and another and another! It seemed pretty watertight. I had received permission from my dad to bury it in a corner of the yard, under the magnolia tree, and that was where we headed now, armed with a big shovel.

We took turns digging, and when the hole was ready, Mia did the honors of placing the capsule into the hole.

"It feels like we're having a funeral!" remarked Emma.

"A funeral for our past," said Katie.

"Here's to the future!" I cried.

"Hooray!" we all said.

That night, my mom came to tuck me in.

"That was a great birthday, thanks to your thoughtfulness, sweetheart."

I snuggled happily under my covers. "It was fun."

"Your gingerbread house was wonderful too. You've had a very busy couple of days! But so many fun things!"

"I know."

"Now I hate to ask, but whatever happened

with Olivia at school? I kept waiting for you to mention it, so I didn't bring it up."

"Oh. Well . . . we've made peace," I said. "For now, anyway."

"Great! I'm so happy to hear that."

We smiled in the semidark for a minute, and then I said, "Mom, you know what? If you were a kid, we'd be best friends."

"Oh, Lexi! That's the best birthday present anyone could have ever given me! Thank you, sweetheart!" And she gave me a big squeeze.

I squeezed back and very softly, into her ear, I whispered, "Quack!"

Want another sweet cupcake?
Here's a sneak peek
of the thirteenth book in the

CUPCAKE  DIARIES

series:

Katie's
new
recipe

It's a Cupcake Code Red!

Make me a doggy! Make me a doggy!"

I started to sweat as the adorable five-year-old in front of me looked up with pleading eyes. I knelt down and waved a round helium balloon in front of his face.

"It's not the kind of balloon that you can make into animals," I said, using my sweetest voice. "It's just a regular, fun, yellow balloon, to match the cupcakes! See?"

I pointed to the cupcake table across the small yard, where my friends Alexis and Emma were busy placing dozens of yellow and green cupcakes on matching paper plates.

The little boy's lower lip quivered. "But . . . I . . . want . . . a . . . doggy!" Then he began to bawl.

Panicked, I turned to my best friend, Mia, who was filling balloons behind me.

"Mia! We've got a code red!" I cried.

"Katie, what's wrong?" Mia asked.

I pointed to the sobbing boy. "He wants a dog-shape balloon. I don't know what to do."

Mia quickly retrieved a black marker from her bag under a table and took the balloon from my hand. The marker squeaked as she drew a cute doggy face on the balloon, complete with droopy ears and a tongue sticking out. Thank goodness for a friend who can draw!

She handed it to the boy. "How's this?" she asked.

The boy stopped crying. "It's a doggy! Woof! Woof!" Happy again, he ran off.

I let out a sigh. "Mia to the rescue! Thank you. I knew this wasn't going to be easy. Running a party for a bunch of five-year-olds? It's much easier when we bake the cupcakes, serve the cupcakes, and then get out."

A while ago, my friends and I had started a Cupcake Club. We'd turned it into a pretty successful business, baking cupcakes for all kinds of parties and events.

"It's like Alexis said, it's healthy to branch out,"

Mia pointed out. "We're making a lot more money by running the games and activities."

I gazed around the yard. We had worked hard on this cupcake-themed party for a five-year-old girl named Madison. Last night we were up late baking cupcakes in Madison's favorite colors, yellow and green. This morning we got up early (which I never like to do on a Saturday) to set things up. We had a table where the kids could decorate their own cupcakes.

Later, we were going to set up the stuff for the games. We took regular party games and cupcaketized them. You know, instead of Hot Potato, we were going to play Pass the Cupcake. And instead of a donkey, kids could pin a cherry on top of a giant picture of a cupcake. It was going to be fun, but it was definitely a lot of work.

"Well, money isn't everything," I declared. "If Alexis wants us to do this stuff so bad, she can come over here and make balloons. I'm going to go work at the cupcake table. At least I know what I'm doing there."

"Aw, come on, Katie, balloons are fun!" Mia said, bopping me over the head with a green one.

I stuck my tongue out at her. "But crying kids are not! I'll see you later."

I walked across the room to the cupcake-decorating table.

"Alexis, you need to switch with me," I said. "I can't do the balloons. I just don't have it in me."

Alexis nodded, her wavy red hair bouncing on her shoulders. "No problem. There's not much more setting up to do. Mrs. Delfino said that the kids are having pizza in a minute, and then we're going to play some games before we do the cupcake thing."

Alexis walked away, and I took her place behind the table, next to Emma, who really loves dressing up for any event. She wore a light yellow shirt with a short green skirt that matched the cupcakes perfectly. A yellow headband with tiny green flowers held back her straight, blond hair. I had tried to get in the party spirit too, with a yellow T-shirt and green sneakers.

"Katie, you look miserable!" Emma said. "Come on, it's not so bad, is it?"

"I think it's because I'm an only child," I admitted. "I don't know how to deal with little kids."

"That's not true. You're so great with Jake," Emma said. Jake is her six-year-old brother. "He adores you!"

"That's different," I protested. "Jake is only one kid. This is, like, a hundred!"

Emma laughed. "It's only sixteen. But I know what you mean. When Jake's friends are over, it can be too much sometimes."

As we spoke, a woman with curly brown hair stepped into the yard.

"Okay, everybody! It's pizza time! Everyone inside!"

The kids cheered and raced inside, accompanied by the moms who had decided to stay for the party. Alexis approached the cupcake table.

"We should set up the games while everyone eats," she suggested. "Then we'll be ready when they come back out."

"Good idea," Emma agreed. We started to set things up for the games, and after only about ten minutes, the kids came racing back outside.

I shook my head. "Back already? What did they drink with their pizza? Rocket fuel?"

"Games! Games! Games!" the kids started chanting.

Mrs. Delfino smiled at us apologetically. "I hope you don't mind."

"Of course not," Alexis said crisply. When she's on a job, she's all business. "We're ready."

"Come on, kids!" Emma said loudly. "Who wants to play Pass the Cupcake?"

Sixteen hands flew into the air at once. "Meeeee!"

I kind of got into it when we played the games. We played Pass the Cupcake first. Mia had sewn a cute cupcake out of felt, and the kids sat in a circle and passed it around when the music played. When the music stopped, the kid holding the cupcake had to leave the circle.

It went pretty well until one little girl started crying when she got out. I almost panicked again. But then I had an idea. I grabbed the girl's hands.

"Everybody outside the circle gets to dance!" I cried, and then I started to dance and twirl around with her. It worked! She stopped crying, and soon all the kids outside the circle were laughing and dancing.

After that, we played Pin the Cherry on the Cupcake using a beautiful poster of a cupcake Mia had drawn, and big cherries cut out of paper. Then we did cupcake relay races, where the runners had to balance a cupcake on the end of a spatula while they were running (instead of the usual egg on a spoon). There was a lot of icing on the grass, but the kids seemed to really like it.

"Great job, everybody!" Alexis called out. "And now it's time to decorate cupcakes. Madison, since you're the birthday girl, you get to go first."

"Yay!" Madison's big brown eyes shone with excitement as she ran to the cupcake table. Her party guests were excited too, and they quickly crowded around her.

"One at a time! One at a time!" Alexis yelled, but the five-year-olds ignored her, swarming around the table and grabbing the cupcakes, sprinkles, and candy toppings.

"Hey! There are spoons for that!" Alexis scolded.

Mia, Emma, and I quickly jumped in to help. I picked up a spoon and tried to show one blond-haired boy how to gently sprinkle some edible green glitter on to his cupcake. He took the spoon from me, dipped it in the glitter . . . and then threw the glitter all over the little girl next to him!

The girl looked stunned. She brushed the green glitter off her face . . . and then started to cry.

"Oh no. Not again," I said, moaning. I didn't think dancing was going to help this one. "We've got another code red!"

But everyone was too busy to come to my rescue. Emma was wiping off frosting from Madison's face, Mia was patiently creating a smiley face made out of candies on another girl's cupcake, and Alexis was marching up and down the table, trying to regain order.

"Icing goes on the cupcake, not on your hands!" she shouted. "And, Leonard, do not put the sprinkle spoon in your mouth!"

Within minutes, the kids were more decorated than the cupcakes.

Mrs. Delfino approached the table, looking flustered. "Oh dear! This is quite a mess!"

We stopped and looked at one another. Our client did not look happy—and that was bad for business.

"It's, um, all part of the fun," I said cheerfully. "And don't worry, we'll clean it up. Who wants to play the Clean-Up Game?"

Sixteen sticky hands flew in the air. "Meeeeeeee!"

Luckily, Emma had thought to pack a big tub of wet wipes. I got out the box and gave one to each kid.

"Okay, now it's time to clean our hands, hands, hands," I instructed in a singsong voice, and luckily, the kids all played along. Next, I had them clean their faces, elbows, and even their knees (that's how messy everyone was!). In the end we had one big pile of messy wet wipes and one yard full of clean kids.

"It's time to sing the birthday song!" Mrs.

Delfino announced, and as the kids followed her inside, we collapsed on the grassy lawn, exhausted.

"Katie, you were so good with the kids!" Mia said.

"Yeah, I'll have to remember that clean-up game for Jake," Emma said.

I frowned. "Well, thanks, but that was still awful. Doesn't this prove we should stick to just cupcakes from now on?"

"Absolutely not," Alexis said. "It just means we need to perfect our plan. Until that big cupcake mess, everything was going really well."

"Yeah." Mia nodded in agreement. "It was kind of fun, too."

"Definitely," said Emma. "And let's not forget the extra money. It's worth it."

I sighed. "I guess you're right. You know me. I don't really like changing the way I do things. In fifth grade, I wore the same pair of purple sneakers every day for a year. My mother said she had to peel them off my feet, literally."

Everyone laughed.

"Don't worry, Katie," Alexis said. "Our new business plan is going to be great. You'll see."

"Fine," I said. "But next time, let's leave the icing *on* the cupcakes, okay?"

What's Up with Mom?

I was so tired from the party that I did not want to get out of bed the next morning.

"Katie, it's time to get up!" my mom urged.

I groaned and pulled my pillow over my face. Mom gently tugged the pillow out of my grasp. I opened my eyes to see her brown eyes staring at me through her eyeglasses.

"You know, for years you would wake up at five thirty every morning, no matter what, and come wake *me* up," Mom said. "And now I can't get you out of bed."

"So . . . tired . . . ," I said dramatically.

"Well, I made pancakes," Mom said. "So please come down and eat them before they get cold."

I quickly sat up. "Blueberry?"

Mom smiled. "Of course," she replied, and then she left my room. That got me up. Mom's pancakes are the best, even if she sometimes still makes them with little smiley faces with the blueberries. It's like she forgets that I'm in middle school now.

A few minutes later I was sitting at the kitchen table, eating pancakes with my mom.

"So I didn't get the details about the party yesterday," she said. "How did it go?"

"It was a mess!" I said, and then I told her everything that happened.

Mom laughed. "Well, it sounds like it worked out all right in the end."

"I guess," I said. "But I hope we don't do too many more parties like that. It's a lot of work!"

"A little hard work never hurt anyone," Mom said, and I shook my head.

"You sound like Grandpa Chuck," I said.

"Speaking of work, what's your homework situation?" Mom asked.

I had to think. "Um, one math worksheet and an essay for English," I reported. "I'll do it right after breakfast."

"Do you mind if I go for a run, then?" Mom asked. "I mean, unless you want me to wait for you."

"Go ahead," I said with a yawn. "I'm too tired to run today, anyway."

Mom smiled and then started to clean up the breakfast dishes. She started to sing a song while she worked.

"Mom, it's my turn to do those," I said. "I just want to sit here for a few minutes first."

"Oh, don't worry about it," Mom said cheerfully. "I don't mind."

Then she started singing again.

Wow, Mom's in a good mood today, I thought.

After breakfast I showered, put on a tie-dyed T-shirt, and jeans, and then settled down at the clean kitchen table to get my homework done. If I don't start it in the morning, then Mom starts asking what the "plan" is for the day. She gets kind of mad when I leave it all for Sunday night. I was halfway through my math worksheet when Mom came into the kitchen.

"I'll be back in about an hour," she said.

"I'm already doing my math worksheet," I said, holding up my paper. That's when I noticed Mom's outfit.

Normally, Mom wears her favorite sweatpants when we go running, the blue ones with the big white streak across the front from that time she accidentally got bleach on them. She pairs them with any old T-shirt and doesn't care if it matches. And she pulls her curly hair back into a ponytail. Sometimes, in the winter, she even runs in her pajamas.

But today she had on a pair of black running pants that looked brand new, and instead of an old T-shirt, she had on a pretty lavender top I hadn't seen before, with flowers stitched around the neckline. She wore a matching light purple headband in her hair, and she even had on lip gloss. And it wasn't clear—it was pink!

"Mom, why are you so dressed up to go running?" I asked. "You usually only ever wear lip gloss when we go out to a fancy restaurant or something."

Then I also noticed that she wasn't wearing her glasses, either! "And why do you have your contacts in? You always complain about your contact lenses and try to wear them as little as possible. You *never* run with your contacts."

Mom blushed. "It's no big deal," she said. "It's kind of a New Year's resolution to spruce myself up a little bit."

"But New Year's was months ago," I pointed out.

"Well, a belated one," Mom said. "Mia's mom is

such a fashion plate. I didn't want you to feel like you have the slacker mom."

"I've never felt that way!" I insisted. "Besides, I'm your slacker daughter. We match."

When I said it out loud, I realized that I like how Mom and I are alike in some ways, besides the fact we both have brown hair and brown eyes. My dad left my mom and me when I was just a baby, so it's just been the two of us for my whole life. We're like a team.

Mom laughed at my slacker comment. "Well, it makes me feel good to dress up a little," she said.

"Suit yourself," I told her. "But I am telling you I am *not* wearing lip gloss the next time we go running. You are on your own with that stuff."

"I don't expect you to," Mom said. She leaned over and kissed my forehead. "Be back soon."

I shook my head as she left. Parents can be so weird sometimes! But if it meant I got pancakes and Mom did the dishes, then whatever was going on was okay with me.

How about a

BONUS
CUPCAKE  DIARIES?

Mia
a matter
of taste

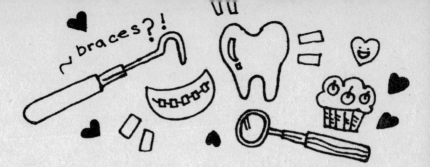

The Worst News Ever

"Okay, Mia, open wide."

"Open wide" might be two of the scariest words in the English language, don't you think? Because when you hear them, it usually means a dentist is about to look into your mouth.

Not that I have anything against dentists. My dentist is Dr. Brown, though I normally call her Mrs. Brown since she is my friend Katie's mom. She's supernice, and I'm sure most dentists are perfectly nice people. I just don't like the stuff they have to do.

Anyway, the person asking me to open wide wasn't even Mrs. Brown. It was her assistant Joanne, who is also really nice. She's tall, and she wears her blond hair up in a ponytail all the time, and under her blue scrubs I can always tell that her clothes are very fashionable.

Joanne must have noticed the nervous look on my face.

"It's cool, Mia. I'm just taking some X-rays. This doesn't hurt at all. You know that, right?" she asked.

I nodded. "Okay."

I opened wide, and Joanne stuck this white square thing into my mouth and told me to bite down. Then she straightened the heavy gray apron covering me and left the room. I heard a quick buzz, and then Joanne came back in and took out the square thing.

"You know, this really isn't that flattering," I joked, looking down at the apron.

She laughed. "Just a few more shots and you can take it off, and then you'll be ready for the runway again, okay?"

Joanne was right—the X-rays didn't hurt at all, but I was glad when they were over.

"Dr. Brown will be by in a minute to go over them with you," Joanne told me. "I'll send in your mom, okay?"

"Thanks," I said, and inside I felt a little bit relieved. Up until a couple of years ago, I lived in Manhattan. Mom and Dad worked during the day, and my babysitter always took me to the dentist. Now we live in the suburbs, and Mom mostly works from home and has her own company, so she has more time to do stuff like this. It's nice having her around, especially at the dentist's.

"How'd it go?" Mom asked as she came into the room.

"My teeth are superclean," I said, flashing her a smile. "And Joanne said it doesn't look like I have any cavities. So I'm thinking I deserve some kind of reward for being so awesome."

Mom raised an eyebrow. "You want a reward for not getting any cavities?"

"I was thinking a trip to the mall would be good," I said.

"Well, you don't have to twist my arm for that," Mom replied. I guess it's a good thing we both love shopping!

Then Mrs. Brown came in. She has the same friendly brown eyes as my friend Katie, but Mrs. Brown's light brown hair is cut short, with long bangs that are stylishly angled across her face.

"It looks like you're cavity free, Mia, but let me take a look in person, okay?"

I nodded and opened my mouth again until she was done.

"Very good," she said with a nod. Then she looked at me, and then at my mom. "But we should talk about your X-rays."

She pressed some keys on the computer on the table next to me, and the pictures of my mouth popped up. It was really weird to see how long the roots were underneath my gums, and I turned my head away. My teeth looked too creepy!

"Mia's got some crooked teeth on her bottom jaw, and her top jaw as well," Mrs. Brown said, pointing to the screen with the end of her pen. "Her bite is misaligned, which can cause problems down the road. I'm recommending you see an orthodontist. I'm not sure, but Mia may need braces."

A cold chill went right through me.

"Braces? Seriously?" I asked. It sounded more like I was squeaking, because I was so upset.

"Well, as I said, I'm not one hundred percent sure," Mrs. Brown said. "But it's very likely."

I looked up at my mom. I could already feel my eyes starting to well up with tears. I started shaking my head. "No way! I can*not* get braces. I will die!"

"Mia, it's okay," Mom assured, putting her hand on my shoulder.

Mrs. Brown gave me a sympathetic look. "I

understand. Nobody wants to hear news like this. But by correcting your teeth now, we can help make sure your mouth stays healthy for a long, long time. I have some brochures I'll give you, so you can find out what it's all about."

Then she turned to my mom. "I know a great orthodontist over in River Glen. I'll get you her card." She smiled at me. "She's the same doctor Katie used when she had her braces."

Mrs. Brown left, and I looked at Mom. "Please tell me this isn't happening!"

"There's no need to panic yet, Mia," Mom said. "Let's wait and see what the orthodontist says before we start worrying, okay? And anyway, braces aren't so bad. Katie had them! And your cousin Marcela had them, remember?"

Marcela is a junior in high school now, but she had braces when she was my age. I definitely remembered them. How could I forget a mouth full of metal and wires? I shuddered.

"She was always complaining that they hurt," I pointed out. "And when we all went to that farm she couldn't eat a candy apple, and she cried."

"That's just what you remember. I know that most of the time, she was fine," Mom said, and then she quickly changed the subject. "Hey, we should get out of here and get to the mall!"

Mom's strategy worked—at first. I never get tired of going to the mall. Since my dentist appointment was right after school, I was kind of hungry, so Mom got me a vanilla mango smoothie at Smoothie Paradise. I sipped the delicious tropical goodness through a straw as we slowly walked around, window-shopping.

"Well, if I get braces, at least I can still have smoothies," I remarked, and Mom smiled.

"That sounds more like my Mia. Stay positive!"

But I ruined my own mood by bringing up the braces, and it didn't even help when we went inside Icon, my favorite shop in the whole mall. They had all the new summer styles on the racks, in tons of bright, almost fluorescent colors.

I held up a neon-yellow sleeveless dress. "Wow, you could wear this in the dark and people could see you for miles," I said. I actually look good in yellow, so I brought the dress to the mirror and held it up to my face.

I posed and smiled, and then suddenly I got a vision of myself in the bright yellow dress with a mouth full of blinding silver metal.

"I can't wear this if I get braces!" I wailed. "It's too much! Aliens in space will be able to see me."

"Oh, Mia, that's not true," Mom said, trying to reassure me, but it was no use.

"If I get stupid braces, I won't be able to wear any of the new summer styles!" I complained. "I might as well go live under a rock somewhere!"

Mom sighed. "Come on, let's go to the candle shop. I think you need some calming scents."

I could feel tears stinging my eyes as I followed Mom out of Icon. And the scent of misty mountain sandalwood candles (my favorite) did not help one bit. I was convinced braces were going to ruin my life!

Want more

CUPCAKE DIARIES?

Visit **CupcakeDiariesBooks.com**
for the series trailer, excerpts, activities,
and everything you need for throwing
your own cupcake party!

Still Hungry?

There's always room for another Cupcake!

Coco Simon always dreamed of opening a cupcake bakery but was afraid she would eat all of the profits. When she's not daydreaming about cupcakes, Coco edits children's books and has written close to one hundred books for children, tweens, and young adults, which is a lot less than the number of cupcakes she's eaten. Cupcake Diaries is the first time Coco has mixed her love of cupcakes with writing.

How well do you know the Cupcake girls?

Take our quiz and find out!

(If you don't want to write in your book,
use a separate piece of paper.)

1. Emma has three brothers. What are their names?

   A. Joe, Mark, and Sam

   B. Matt, Sam, and John

   C. Jake, Matt, and Sam

   D. Tom, Dick, and Harry

2. Who *loves* to dance?

   A. Mia

   B. Alexis

   C. Emma

   D. Katie

3. What unusual ingredient do the girls use in one of their most popular cupcakes?

    A. Salami

    B. French fries

    C. Bacon

    D. Pizza

yum!

4. Where does Emma model?

    A. At the summer day camp

    B. At The Special Day wedding salon

    C. At the local swimming pool

    D. At school dances

5. Mia has a BFF in New York whose first name has three letters too. What is her friend's name?

    A. Amy

    B. Gia

    C. Ava

    D. Ivy

6. George teases Katie and calls her a funny nickname. (But it's okay though because Katie knows he likes her.) What is the nickname?

A. Chicken Legs

B. Silly Arms

C. Bigfoot

D. Man Hands

7. Which Cupcake girl has curly red hair?

A. Alexis

B. Mia

C. Katie

D. Emma

8. Who is the "mean girl" who loves to torture the Cupcake girls?

A. Sydney

B. Beth

C. Olivia

D. Both A and C

Did you get the right answers?

1. C   5. C
2. B   6. B
3. C   7. A
4. B   8. D

What your answers mean:

If you got all 8 answers right:
Wow! You know your Cupcake girls.
Four cupcakes for you!

If you got 6 to 7 answers right:
Pretty good! You just need to brush up a little bit on your four Cupcake friends. Two cupcakes for you!

If you got 4 to 5 answers right:
You need to reread your favorite Cupcake books, but you get one cupcake for your efforts!

If you got less than four answers right:
You're not paying attention. Reread this book (and all your favorite Cupcake books) right now! No cupcake for you—have a cookie!

If you're not an expert baker like the Cupcakers, that's okay—here is a quick and easy-to-follow recipe that's just as sweet! (Ask an adult for assistance before you start baking since you might need help with the oven or mixer.)

Pineapple "Upside-Down" Cupcakes

• Makes 18 •

BATTER:
1 box of yellow cake mix
1 cup sour cream
½ cup of pineapple juice (use juice from canned pineapples; see topping)
⅓ cup vegetable oil
4 large eggs, room temperature
1 teaspoon pure vanilla extract

TOPPING:
8 tablespoons unsalted butter, melted
¾ cup firmly packed light brown sugar
1 can (20 ounces) crushed pineapple, drained (set aside ½ cup of the pineapple juice for batter)
maraschino cherries (optional)

Center baking rack in oven and preheat to 350°F. Grease cupcake tins well with butter or cooking spray.

CUPCAKES: In a large mixing bowl combine all of the batter ingredients. With an electric mixer on medium speed, mix the ingredients together until there are no lumps in the batter. Spoon the batter into the cupcake tins so that each tin is about halfway full.

TOPPING: Mix the melted butter and brown sugar together with a spoon. Sprinkle about a teaspoon of the mixture on top of the cupcake batter in the tins. Now add a layer of about a tablespoon of pineapple. If you'd like, put one cherry on top, pressing it into the pineapple layer so it's level.

Bake the cupcakes about 18 to 20 minutes or until a toothpick inserted into the center of a cupcake comes out clean. Remove from oven and place on a wire rack to cool for about 5 minutes. Carefully run a dinner knife around the edges of the cupcakes and invert the cupcake pan onto the wire rack. Let the cupcakes cool for about 20 minutes.

yummy! :·

If you're not an expert baker like the Cupcakers, that's okay—here is a quick and easy-to-follow recipe that's just as sweet! (Ask an adult for assistance before you start baking since you might need help with the oven or mixer.)

Vanilla Cupcakes with Vanilla Buttercream Frosting

• Makes 12 •

BATTER:
½ cup unsalted butter, at room temperature
⅔ cup granulated sugar
3 large eggs, at room temperature
1 teaspoon pure vanilla extract
1 ½ cups all-purpose flour
1 ½ teaspoons baking powder
¼ teaspoon salt
¼ cup whole milk

FROSTING:
½ cup unsalted butter, at room temperature
4 cups sifted confectioners' sugar
⅓ cup of whole milk
1 teaspoon pure vanilla extract
food coloring (optional)

Center baking rack in oven and preheat to 350°F. Line cupcake tins with cupcake liners.

CUPCAKES: In a medium bowl, beat the butter and sugar with an electric mixer on medium speed until fluffy. Then add the eggs one at a time. Blend in the vanilla extract.

In a separate bowl whisk together the flour, baking powder, and salt. With the mixer on low speed, add the flour mixture to the butter-sugar mixture and alternate with the milk. Mix until there are no lumps in the batter.

Evenly fill the cupcake tins with the batter and bake for about 18 to 20 minutes or until a toothpick inserted into the center of a cupcake comes out clean. Remove from oven and place on a wire rack to cool completely before frosting.

FROSTING: In a medium bowl mix the butter with an electric mixer until it looks fluffy. Add in some of the sugar, alternating with the milk and vanilla until it is all blended. Add food coloring per package's directions and mix well to color the frosting. Then frost the cupcakes.

🌸 Cupcake Girls Haiku 🌸

A haiku is a type of poem. It only has three lines, but there is one important rule you must follow. The first line has five syllables, the second line has seven, and the third has five. Read the haiku poems below about the girls in the Cupcake Diaries books. Then you'll have a chance to write some of your own.

🧁 Katie

Smart, cute, and funny.
She started the Cupcake Club.
Her friend George likes her.

Mia 🧁

Fashion is her thing.
She turns heads in the hallway.
Always looks her best.

🧁 Alexis

Fiery red hair.
She loves to figure things out.
Has a crush on Matt!

Emma 🧁

She's a girly girl.
She's so pretty—a model!
Loves her Cupcake friends.

Your Turn!

Here's your chance to try writing your own haiku poems.
Write one about your favorite Cupcake girl here:
(If you don't want to write in your book, make a copy of this page.)

••
(NAME)

_____

_____

_____

Now write one about yourself or your best friend!

••
(NAME)

_____

_____

_____

Are you an
Emma, a *Mia*, a *Katie*, or an *Alexis*?
Take our quiz and find out!

Read each question and circle the letter
that best describes you.

(If you don't want to write in your book, use a separate piece of paper.)

1. You've been invited to a party. What do you wear?

> **A.** Jeans and a cute T-shirt. You want to look nice, but you also want to be comfortable.

> **B.** You beg your parents to lend you money for the cool boots you saw online. If you're going to a party, you have to wear the latest fashion!

> **C.** Something pretty, but practical. If you're going to spend money on a new outfit, it better be one you'll be able to wear a lot.

> **D.** Something feminine—lacy and floral. And definitely pink if not floral—a girl can never go wrong wearing *pink*!

2. Your idea of a perfect Saturday afternoon is:

   A. Seeing a movie with your BFFs and then going out for pizza afterward.

   B. THE MALL! Hopefully one of the stores will be having a big sale!

   C. Creating a perfect budget to buy clothes, go out with friends, and save money for college—all at the same time—and then meeting your friends for lunch.

   D. Going for a manicure and pedicure.

3. You have to study for a big test. What's your study style?

   A. In your bedroom, with your favorite music playing.

   B. At home, with help from your parents if necessary.

   C. At the library, where you can take out some new books after you've finished studying, or anyplace else that's absolutely quiet.

D. Anyplace away from home—away from your messy, loud siblings!

4. There's a new girl at school. What's your first reaction?

A. You're a little cautious. You've been hurt before, so it takes you a while to warm up to new friends.

B. You think it's great. You welcome her with open arms. (Maybe you can share each other's clothes!)

C. If she's nice and smart, maybe you'll consider being friends with her.

D. You'll gladly welcome another friend—as long as she really wants to be friends with you—and not just meet your cute older brothers!

5. When it comes to boys . . .

A. They make you a little nervous. You want to be friends first—for a long time—until you'd consider someone a boyfriend.

B. He has to be tall, trustworthy, sweet—and of course, superstylish!

C. He has to be cute, funny, and smart—and he gets extra points if he likes to dance!

D. He has to be loyal and true as well as good-looking. You look sweet, but you're tough when you have to be.

6. When it comes to your family . . .

A. You come from a single-parent home. It's hard for you to imagine your parent dating, but you will try to get used to it.

B. You come from a mixed family with stepsiblings and a stepparent. At first it was overwhelming, but you're starting to get used to having everyone in the mix!

C. You get along okay with your parents, but your older sister thinks she's queen of the world. Still sometimes you ask her for advice anyway.

D. You live in a house with many brothers—dirty, sticky, smelly boys! You love them all, but sometimes would give anything for a sister!

7. Your dream vacation would be:

A. Anyplace beachy. You love to swim and also just relax on a beach blanket.

B. Paris—to see the latest fashions.

C. Egypt—you'd love to see the pyramids and try to figure out how they were constructed without any modern machinery.

D. Holland—you'd love to see the tulips in bloom!

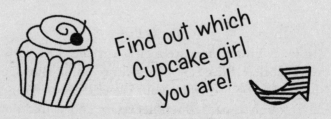

Find out which Cupcake girl you are!

Which Cupcake girl are you?
What your answers mean:

Mostly As:
You're a Katie! Your style is easy and comfortable.
You always look good, and you always feel good too.
You have a few very close friends (both girls and boys),
and you like it that way. You don't want to confide
in just anybody.

Mostly Bs:
You're a Mia! You're the girl everyone envies at school
because you can wear an old ratty sweatshirt and jeans
and somehow still look like a runway model. Your
sense of style is what everyone notices first, but you're
also a great friend.

Mostly Cs:
You're an Alexis! You are supersmart and not afraid to
show it! You get As in every subject, and like nothing
more than creating business plans and budgets. You love
your friends but have to remember sometimes that not
everyone in the world is as brilliant as you are.

Mostly Ds:
You're an Emma! You are a girly-girl and love to wear
pretty clothes. Pink is your signature color. But people
should not be fooled by your sweet exterior. You can
be as tough as nails when necessary and would never
let anyone push you around.

If you liked

CUPCAKE  DIARIES

be sure to check out these

other series from

Simon Spotlight

IT TAKES TWO

If you like reading about the adventures of Katie, Mia, Emma, and Alexis, you'll love Alex and Ava, stars of the It Takes Two series!

sew zoey

Zoey's clothing design blog puts her on the A-list in the fashion world . . . but when it comes to school, will she be teased, or will she be a trendsetter? Find out in the Sew Zoey series:

EVERY SECRET LEADS TO ANOTHER

SECRETS
of the MANOR

Hidden passages, mysterious
diaries, and centuries-old secrets
abound in this spellbinding series.
Join generations of girls from
the same family tree as they
uncover the secrets that lurk
within their sumptuous
family manor homes!

Beth's Story, 1914

Kate's Story, 1914

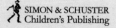